Angel Trumpet

ALSO BY ANN MCMILLAN

Dead March

ANN McMILLAN

Angel Trumpet

◆

A CIVIL WAR

MYSTERY

◆

VIKING

VIKING
Published by the Penguin Group
Penguin Putnam Inc., 375 Hudson Street,
New York, New York 10014, U.S.A.
Penguin Books Ltd, 27 Wrights Lane,
London W8 5TZ, England
Penguin Books Australia Ltd, Ringwood,
Victoria, Australia
Penguin Books Canada Ltd, 10 Alcorn Avenue,
Toronto, Ontario, Canada M4V 3B2
Penguin Books (N.Z.) Ltd, 182–190 Wairau Road,
Auckland 10, New Zealand

Penguin Books Ltd, Registered Offices:
Harmondsworth, Middlesex, England

First published in 1999 by Viking Penguin,
a member of Penguin Putnam Inc.

1 3 5 7 9 10 8 6 4 2

LIBRARY OF CONGRESS CATALOGING IN PUBLICATION DATA
McMillan, Ann, date.
Angel trumpet / Ann McMillan.
p.   cm.
ISBN 0–670–88148–1
1. Virginia—History—Civil War, 1861–1865 Fiction.   I. Title.
PS3563.C38657A83   1999
813'.54—dc21   99–34918

This book is printed on acid-free paper.
∞

Printed in the United States of America
Set in Minion
Designed by Betty Lew

#FIC 9-11-02
(myst)

For my mother, Ruth Robertson McMillan

Acknowledgments

I would like to thank:

Fenton L. Bland, Jr., and Calvin Walker of the A. D. Price Funeral Establishment, for showing me the Establishment's collection of historic hearses; Carolyn Carlson; J. T. Christmas, M.D.; Charles L. Cooke, M.D.; Charlotte Crystal and David Mattern; eagle-eyes Dick Conway and Rex Springston; Alfred W. Hahn, Argonaut Research, for a priceless bibliography of gaming; Jodi Koste, archivist at the Tompkins-McCaw Library, the Medical College of Virginia; Mary Ellen and Dick Mercer; Bekky Monroe and Tom Thorp, Henrico County Department of Recreation and Parks, for swamp lore; all the Obers; Sandra V. Parker, Ph.D.; Robin Reed of the Museum of the Confederacy; Teresa Roane of the Valentine Museum; staffs of the Library of Virginia and the Virginia Historical Society; Bob Wilcox, for lending me a book on animal magnetism; Nancy Yost; and of course Randy and Hunter, for teaching me every day.

Author's Note

One rebellion for the sake of liberty has often lit the fuse for another. The American Revolution inspired the French Revolution, and it also inspired Gabriel's Rebellion, the doomed slave uprising led by Prosser's Gabriel in Henrico County, Virginia, in 1800. The echoes of these and other rebellions have long reverberated through our country and will not soon fall silent.

In 1861, Southern slaveowners' demand for "liberty" from perceived Federal oppression helped fracture the Union. As they fought for their various definitions of liberty, slaveowners lived in constant fear that their slaves would do the same. Whenever a slave killed a white person, the act reawakened fears of spreading rebellion. Edmund Ruffin, the ardent secessionist from Hanover County, Virginia, who fired the first shot at Fort Sumter, admitted that the war had driven him to sleeping with a gun by his bed for protection against his slaves. In September 1861, Civil War diarist Mary Chesnut was shaken by the murder in South Carolina of her widowed cousin by "her own people"—her slaves. Chesnut noted the impassive faces of the servants standing behind the chairs at dinner and wondered what they were thinking.

Today, our feelings about slaves who murdered their masters or envisioned rebellion, as Gabriel did, for "death or liberty" are necessarily complex—as are, on the other hand, our feelings about slaves who remained loyal to white owners or betrayed the organizers of rebellion. Within white Southerners, too, a wide range of loyalties flourished, from those who defended slavery as God's will to those who, inspired by abolitionist sentiments, carried on throughout the war as spies for the Union.

The broadest imaginable spectrum of possibilities for loyalty, belief, and action exists within our common humanity. For the mystery writer, the pleasure lies in bringing imaginary human beings into violent conflict— and also in inventing, for at least some of them, a happy ending.

Angel Trumpet

Prologue

Colonel John Berton rode into the slanting sun. Powdered red-clay dust filmed his gray wool uniform and tanned face. He wore his slouch hat pulled low, shading his eyes. His horse knew the way and pursued it at a steady walk.

When he came to a narrow drive, lined with ancient cedars, that branched off the main road, he pulled up, wet his lips from his canteen, and looked down the drive into the deep, fragrant cedar shade.

Berton was thirty years old, brown-haired and bearded, of medium height and build. His colonel's insignia, as well as some things less tangible—the way he carried himself, the way he sat his horse—showed his aristocrat's blood. It was the invisible properties of blood, passed down from father to son, that made Berton heir to this plantation home, its thousand acres, its fifty slaves.

Berton's chestnut gelding pawed the dirt, scenting home. Berton tightened his thigh muscles, urging the horse onto the drive. They covered its mile length at an easy pace. Now and then, a break in the line of cedars afforded a glimpse of brown plowed earth and stubbled fields, then, farther, of dark green forests. The field hands would be plowing and ashing the acres from which the wheat had been cut, plowing and sowing winter wheat on acres where corn had been harvested, planting potatoes, felling oak, walnut, sycamore, and pine.

At last the drive met the brick walkway and curved away on either side. Berton held the reins in a gloved hand and stared at the two-story white frame house, classically symmetrical, with chimneys at each end and paired sets of windows spreading out from an unpretentious one-story portico. All was quiet inside the house and around it. Where was the servant who would meet a guest and see to his horse? He looked around, frowning. At length he dismounted and walked forward, holding the chestnut's reins.

Now he could see a figure that had been hidden in shadow: a brown-skinned girl sitting on an overturned box near the door. Her mouth hung open. She was grabbing at something in front of her face, and she took no notice of him.

Berton dropped the reins and walked up the steps, staring at the girl. She did not look up or pause in her repeated gesture: first one hand, then the other, clutched at the empty air in front of her eyes. The sound of his boots on the wooden porch seemed to rouse her. Her hands stopped their clutching motion, and she raised her eyes toward his looming form. Her eyes were deep black, their color swallowed up in darkness.

Berton took a step backward. As he continued to stare, he saw her gaze shift away from him, the clutching gesture resume.

Berton took off his hat, ran his fingers through his hair, and pushed open the door. He crossed the great hall to the river portico, swung open the heavy door, and walked halfway down the flight of low stone steps, held together with iron bands whose rust had left stains like old blood. He looked down the terraced slope to where the James ran reddish brown. He saw no one. Then he looked up at the house. Sunlight glanced off the tall, many-paned windows, repelling his gaze.

Berton trotted back up the steps into the hall and entered through the door on the right. Here, in the southeast corner of the house, was the room his family used most. A half-finished piece of embroidery in its hoop lay on a chair, the threaded needle stuck into the linen as a sign of its owner's intention to return. Berton frowned, opened his mouth to call out, then closed it again.

He crossed to the room opposite, glanced in. No one. This strange silence quickened his heartbeat; he was beginning to feel lightheaded. He shrugged it off and walked back across the grand hall into the north wing. This time he looked into the library—no one—then into the dining room. Here he paused. The long mahogany table that could seat ten was laid for four. The silver was polished, the stemware sparkling, the linen spotless white. A bowl of late roses sat in the center of the table. One fallen petal glowed red against the white cloth.

He walked over to the mahogany sideboard under the far window. He looked out to where sunlight struck sparks on the river, throwing long shadows on the lawn, then where it angled through the ancient panes, revealing names and dates—*Mary Anna Barbour, Col. Berton, March 20, 1780; Louisa Berton, J. Selden, 1854*—etched into the thick, wavy glass by the diamonds of newly engaged belles.

He turned away and walked the few paces to the south staircase. He put his booted foot on the bottom step, hesitated just a moment, and mounted the stairs.

Then he noticed the smell. Long before Manassas, he had known—as every countryman knows who has seen a hog butchered or carved up a deer—the smell of blood.

Chapter One

CHAMPS-ELYSÉES PLANTATION, NORTHERN VIRGINIA

"Oh, I don't believe in ghosts," Narcissa Powers said, then wondered why she'd made the statement. It wasn't that she wanted to stop the old woman from telling the tale she had offered up. A distraction from musing on this fool's errand, and on the high-handed doctor who had requested it, would be welcome. Anyway, saying *I don't believe in ghosts* was like saying, *You can't scare me.* The very need to make the assertion called its veracity into question. Narcissa smiled at her own naïveté.

Auntie Lora smiled in return, revealing soft gums where a few teeth leaned like ancient gravestones. Three women—the young white widow Narcissa, the old slave Auntie Lora, and the free black doctoress Judah Daniel—sat snapping the ends off beans and tossing the beans into one pot for the day's meal, the ends into another pot for the hogs. The clearing where they sat held a dozen slave cabins made of boards rough-hewn from the huge oaks and chestnuts that had grown there once. Now the forest was returning, sending out onto the bare dirt a tangle of waist-high trees and honeysuckle from which crickets sang their maddening one-note song.

"That is," Narcissa added, her expression growing thoughtful, "I do believe that the souls of the dead are interested in us. Even that they may linger on earth to right some wrong." She thought of her brother Charley, who had died in the spring, and of how, after his death, his spirit had seemed to guide her through the frightening events that followed. "But I believe they wish to help us, not to hurt us."

The old woman nodded. "Well, miss," she said at last, "supposing *they* hurt. Suppose their suffering in life was so bad that they died wanting nothing more than to hurt back." She stopped and looked at Narcissa with a humoring condescension. "Nice lady such as you be, I reckon you can't understand how people could be so hate-filled. But maybe you understand this better: supposing they love. They love a thing here on earth so much that they can't stand to leave it when they die, even to get to the heavenly kingdom."

Auntie Lora paused to let the thought settle, her gap-toothed smile widening. "But the dead and their feelings don't belong here amongst the living. Gets things all jangled up. Folks say that's what cause a place to be haunted. Like Champs-Elysées."

Auntie Lora's eyes shifted over Narcissa's head. Narcissa turned, following her gaze to the top of the hill, about a quarter-mile distant, where the magnificent plantation house called Champs-Elysées stood overlooking the Potomac. The house had been built more than a century before of brick brought over from England, built as the fashionable new dwelling for a son whose name was one of the most ancient in the colony. On this side was visible the shallow portico whose four columns rose almost the height of the house, surmounted by an elegant pediment. Sinuous vines of wisteria as old as the house softened the severity of its perfection.

Narcissa and Judah Daniel had come to Champs-Elysées at the request of Dr. Cameron Archer to meet his cousin Jordan Archer. She was expected this day, returning at last from the Maryland boarding school where illness had detained her through the summer. Narcissa and Judah Daniel were to bring her back to Richmond. It was an extension, to say the least, of both women's duties at the medical college hospital supervised by Dr. Archer. But the surgeon had a way of giving orders that made it easier to acquiesce than to refuse, however good the reason for refusal.

As the plantation was close to the Potomac, and to the armies camped on the river's northern and southern borders, its portable treasures had been removed to Richmond months before. But the Federal army that had been driven back at Manassas could march again at any moment and engulf Champs-Elysées. So the house remained deserted, guarded most nights by one or another of the soldiers from the Confederate encampment about ten miles away. Today—drawn no doubt by the news of Jordan Archer's expected arrival—the pickets were at their post earlier and in greater numbers than usual.

Narcissa turned back to find the old woman's eyes on her. Narcissa smiled inwardly. *The ladies of Champs-Elysées no doubt stay aloof from this kind of work. So what does she see when she looks at me?* She selected a bean from the pile in her apron. *I'm not quite a lady, but not a servant.* Snap! the stem was off. *A widow, by my clothes.* Snap! with the help of her thumb-nail, the blossom end was off. Drop the bean into the iron pot on the left, the ends into the pot on the right. Select another bean. *In straitened circumstances, perhaps, but young enough to marry again, pretty enough. Death, danger, loss of hope have come close to me, but they haven't marked me. Have they?*

"You, now, Judah Daniel." Auntie Lora's gaze shifted to the third woman. "You understand about them lost souls well enough, I'll be bound."

"I do that, Auntie Lora. I do that," was Judah Daniel's reply.

Narcissa watched the two exchange a look and felt oddly excluded. The talk about ghosts had taken her back to a time only a few months past—a time when buried evil and living madness had combined to threaten both Narcissa and Judah Daniel. She had come to think of Judah Daniel as an ally. Now she was reminded of the gap that remained between them. Judah Daniel and Auntie Lora, within moments of their meeting, seemed to read each other's thoughts. Yet apart from their brown skin, the two could hardly be more different. Judah Daniel was lean, sharp-eyed, with a per-ceptible power that ran through her even when she held herself quiet and still. Auntie Lora's eyes were clouded, and she slumped as if bone-weary. Her ankles, visible where she sat with her slippered feet propped up on a pile of feed sacks, were swollen to elephantine size—the result, Narcissa assumed, of some dropsical condition.

What would be best to treat it? Narcissa's nursing experience now in-cluded every conceivable injury of war, as well as those plagues endemic to the campgrounds—measles, mumps, dysentery, fevers—but not dropsy. Her brother Charley's medical books might have something about it. But no doubt Judah Daniel had already made her diagnosis and thought out whatever bark, roots, or berries she would need to help the old woman with the time-honored arts of the herb doctor. Narcissa resolved to ask her about it later.

The sun was getting high, and it was hot. Narcissa looked over at the foot-high pile of snap beans still waiting their preparation and sighed a lit-tle. "Tell us about the ghosts of Champs-Elysées," she said to Auntie Lora.

The old woman was drawing her breath to begin the story when a whoop rang out up at the house. The women's hands fell still as they

peered up toward the source of the commotion. Was the long-awaited battle at last engaged? Narcissa wondered for a moment, then dismissed the
thought. She had heard no shots, no alarums. She rose, shaking the beans
from her apron back onto the pile, and started running toward the house.
She glanced back to see Judah Daniel close behind her. Even Auntie Lora
was making surprisingly quick progress, walking in a fast, hitching stride.

At the top of the rise she could see four young soldiers fairly jumping
up and down with excitement, could see coming along the road a cloud of
dust that swirled around a figure bent low over the horse's mane, cloak
streaming in the wind. As Narcissa came up, one of the boys turned to her
and shouted, "It's her! It's Miss Archer!" Narcissa looked again. Yes, she
could see that the figure rode sidesaddle.

With a drumroll of hooves and an ever more frenzied outcry from the
soldiers—whose number had somehow swelled to a half-dozen—Jordan
Archer rode up to the wide verandah with which Champs-Elysées fronted
the river. The boys rushed forward, each offering his hand to her, but she
slipped from the saddle unaided and swept through them, acknowledg-
ing their clamorous welcome with an elated smile. Jordan's heavy blond
hair—which Narcissa had taken for a windblown cape—had come loose
from its netting and streamed down her back almost to the hem of her
emerald-hued riding jacket. Her triangular smile dimpled her cheeks and
spoke of mischief. As she tugged off her pearl-colored kid gloves finger by
finger, she looked around her, thin brows drawn down over her bright
blue eyes. Then the frown vanished and her smile burst wide. She rushed
past the others into the arms of Auntie Lora. Narcissa wondered what it
must feel like to the young soldiers, to wish for a moment to change places
with an old slave woman.

After a bit, Auntie Lora held Jordan away and frowned up into her
beaming face. "Don't you be telling me you done rode all this way with no
escort."

Jordan laughed. "No, Auntie, beat them here, is all. There's a slow old
wagon with all my trunks should be here in a half hour or so. Is there anything to drink? I'm parched!" Jordan pulled out the pins that anchored the
little straw hat, tore it off, and began to fan herself with it.

Arm in arm with Auntie Lora, Jordan mounted the wide stairs of
Champs-Elysées, Narcissa and Judah Daniel following behind. At the top
of the stairs, she looked back over her shoulder and called to the young
men gathered below, "I want you all to come for supper this evening, as

many of you as can. I'll send a letter to your commanding officer." Jordan turned to Auntie Lora but spoke loudly enough so the young men could hear. "I saw some chickens in the yard. Better we feed them to our boys than let the Yankees get them." The soldiers hollered approval. Jordan glanced at them over her shoulder and went on. "This will be the last gathering at Champs-Elysées, until we drive the Yankees out once and for all!"

For the next three hours, Narcissa worked alongside Judah Daniel and Auntie Lora to prepare a meal of plain country fare. They fried chicken, sliced sweet-cured Virginia ham, beat dough into biscuits and pie crusts, finished the snap beans, and put them on to simmer with chunks of red-streaked pork fat.

Jordan changed from her dusty riding habit into a girlish white dress and occupied herself pulling gowns, shoes, and swaths of lace from the trunks she had brought back from Washington. When Auntie Lora gave her a talking-to, she stuffed most of them back in, saving out a few from which to choose her ensemble for dinner. Apparently chastened, Jordan joined Narcissa in laying the table—boards placed on trestles brought up from the kitchen, covered with a mended linen cloth—with whatever odds and ends of cutlery had not already been shipped south to Jordan's relations in Richmond.

Narcissa saw Jordan eyeing her with interest, making no secret of surveying her black dress, and was not surprised when the girl came out with an abrupt question. "Who is it for—your mourning?"

Narcissa went on folding the napkin she held. "For my husband, almost three years ago now; and my brother, eight months ago."

"Oh," Jordan replied, "not a soldier then. You could be in half-mourning by now?"

She looked a question, but Narcissa only smiled in response. Jordan persevered. "It's too melancholic. Especially on this day, the day Champs-Elysées is to be left desolate for the first time in a hundred and thirty years. I have an idea!" Now she was staring frankly at Narcissa's face and figure. "I believe you can wear my dark red silk. The color's so dark it's practically half-mourning. Everyone says it's too old for me anyway, and I've lost so much weight with the scarlet fever, it would swallow me."

Narcissa had to laugh at the young girl's unself-conscious rudeness. At seventeen, would she herself have so patronized a woman of four-and-twenty?

"There!" Jordan exclaimed, holding up the napkin she had been folding so that it framed Narcissa's face. "You are so much prettier when you smile."

Torn between amusement and irritation, Narcissa nevertheless remembered the moment that morning when she had seen Jordan ride up, glowing like a jewel in brilliant green—when she had looked down at her own familiar black and felt herself wanting to shake it off, to fly free.

THE CONFEDERATE ENCAMPMENT NEAR LEESBURG, VIRGINIA

The sun was low, the air was cooling, the sky a spotless expanse of blue. The moon that would rise later was just off the full. Here in "Camp Havoc"—named for its "dogs of war," mongrels that kept up a continual reconnaissance for scraps—a comfortable monotony reigned.

Camp Havoc had commenced its daily preparations for dinner in the midafternoon. The men had become crack cooks, striving to outdo one another in inventing new dishes from the wealth of meats and produce provided by the store tent, or sold or traded to them by the country people.

Brit Wallace had copied out the day's bill of fare for a dispatch to his newspaper, the *Weekly Argus* of London. Soups: beef Virginia style and mutton *à la francais*. Roasts: beef à la mode, shoat stuffed with vegetables, *mouton* French style. Entrees: beans, potatoes, cauliflower, eggplant, peas. Wines and liquors: whiskey, brandy (a home-brewed variety called "red-eye"), and cider. Dessert: cakes, rice pudding, monkey pudding, apple dumplings, fruit, coffee.

The dinner had been a success, only the mutton soup having been ruled inedible and given to the eager dogs. The well-fed men had settled to games of cards and marbles. Those not made sedentary by the heavy meal tossed a football and scrambled for it on a patch of ground worn smooth by past games.

Brit threaded his way through the tents and came out onto a group of about a dozen soldiers dressed in dusty fatigues lounging in the clearing—some playing cards, some reading. Those who happened to glance his way hailed him with a laconic wave or nod. In the ten days he had spent at this encampment near the Potomac, the British journalist had ceased to be a cause for remark. At first the soldiers had sought him out to boast of exploits at Manassas or state in the strongest terms their desire to cross the river and invade the oppressor's land. Then they had settled back into what had been their pursuit for the last month and a half, since they had won the field at Manassas: waiting.

Brit had grown accustomed to them, as well. He had heard all their stories at least twice, and some of their tales he had written up and sent off to the *Argus*. He had separated in his mind the quietly courageous from the braggarts, the comradely men from the thieves and cheats. "In every ten, six true men," he had heard, and the proportion seemed about right to him.

Now he, too, was waiting.

He spotted the one he was looking for, a slender, fair-haired youth who seemed to be engaged in writing upon slips of paper. Brit smiled to himself. Archer Langdon was only seventeen, but already battle-tested, having acquitted himself well at Manassas. The young man had become Brit's personal guide through the intricacies of army routine and the even greater intricacies involved in escaping that routine. Langdon had just returned from picket duty, and Brit looked forward to hearing an account. The previous week Brit had sent off a dispatch to the *Argus* concerning the escape of Langdon and his friends (names omitted, of course) from camp to a party in Centreville. Disguised in rags, faces blackened with burned cork, the boy and three friends had got themselves an evening's freedom by raising such a ruckus with an old fiddle that their own captain had given the order, "Turn those darkies out of my camp!"

As Brit approached, Langdon looked up, motioned him over. "I know you are in funds," the boy said, "since you won most of my pay at poker. So here"—he held out his fist, in which were gathered perhaps a dozen slips of paper—"it's a lottery. A dollar a chance."

"What's the prize?" asked Brit, crouching on his haunches beside the boy.

"Supper at Champs-Elysées, with my cousin Jordan Archer as hostess. Jordan is a madcap, not one to tell tales on a fellow, and Champs-Elysées is quite worth seeing. One of the foremost plantations on the Potomac, fine example of the grand old style, etc., etc. But it can only be tonight. She has just come down from Maryland, where she was detained with an illness, and tomorrow she leaves for Richmond. Of course, it's quite good luck Colonel Berton is away—" Brit understood what he left unsaid: discipline would be looser in the colonel's absence.

"Champs-Elysées?" Brit asked with interest. "Is that the house that is supposed to be haunted?" He settled onto the ground next to Langdon, stretched out his legs, and began the business of lighting his pipe.

"Well," said Langdon, lowering his voice, "it's true no one wants to pull picket duty there. It's a lonely spot at night, and one does hear noises. It's all foolishness, of course," he added airily. "But the story . . . well, you should ask Cousin Jordan. She tells it with great conviction. She grew up there, lived there till she was fourteen, then got packed off to a female seminary in Maryland. She ran away twice," he added, smiling his approval for his cousin's spirited behavior. "Found she could crawl out her window, shinny down the drainpipe, then launch herself out over the rose hedge and land on the grass."

Brit smiled, thinking of his fearless sister, the youngest child in his family of boys. Yes, he might like to meet this hoyden. He hid his interest, concentrating on the tobacco he was tamping into his pipe. "How much are you asking for your chances?"

"There are ten slips here. I thought I might find ten fellows who'd be willing to spend a dollar on the chance of an evening's diversion."

A few of the regular poker players had already won the pay—and in some cases, several months' future pay—of the others. Brit himself had been one of the lucky ones. Archer Langdon had not.

"Um. Just a moment," Brit said. He rose and strolled over to the fire, stuck in a twig and held it there until it flamed, then applied it to his pipe. As he did so, his eyes scanned the scene before him. Free from the ennobling presence of mothers, wives, and sweethearts, the men had gradually sunk into a state in which any urge to slouch, spit, or scratch was indulged without restraint. Brit made his decision: a visit to Champs-Elysées was just the adventure the evening called for. And a haunted plantation house would surely yield a dispatch for the *Argus*.

He returned to Langdon's side, puffing busily to keep the pipe lit, then said, "Look: you'll get nothing but 'Order on Paymaster' from most of these fellows. Put away your slips, and I'll cancel your debt to me. Twelve dollars, that's more than a month's pay. More than fair," he added persuasively.

Langdon looked very serious. "Cancel my debt, *and* five dollars in cash."

"Five dollars! Is your cousin a siren?

"Four dollars. She *is* said to be quite a belle."

"Three!" Brit countered.

"Four. There is another lady there as well, for chaperone, but—" A slight smile and raise of the eyebrows completed the thought: the other lady was attractive, too.

"Very well," Brit said with a sigh. "Four."

Langdon grinned and stretched his hand out. Brit pulled his notebook from his coat pocket and fished out a roll of notes, still crisp from their recent printing. He fanned through notes issued for values ranging from fifty cents to fifty dollars; issued by the Confederate States of America, by the various states, even one issued by the city of Staunton. *Payable one year from date, Payable two years from date.* Some featured Liberty, an idealized female figure posed with a Phrygian cap, familiar emblem of the French Revolution; some depicted slaves at work in a field of cotton. Appropriate, that, since the notes were backed not by gold, which with the election of Lincoln had become a hoarded commodity in the South, but by cotton. He peeled off two two-dollar bills and handed them to Langdon.

His action caught the eye of the nearby poker players, who had just folded their cards. "Care for a game?" called one loser, ever hopeful. Brit shook his head and put his money back in his pocket.

The winner was raking in a pile that included banknotes, handwritten "Order on Paymaster" notes, a novel in a battered cover, and a pipe with a curved stem. He was an Irishman named O'Donnell, in civilian life a brick mason, now a private in the Confederate army. Langdon and O'Donnell were as unlike as two men could be, almost, Brit mused. O'Donnell, with his rough black beard and reddened blue eyes that disappeared into creases when he smiled, was a shaggy old mongrel; the slender and beardless Langdon a greyhound pup of the best blood. But both had drilled, and marched, and risked their lives at Manassas, and they now belonged to a brotherhood whose response to the beating of the long roll was as instinctive as the hound's to the hunter's horn.

O'Donnell rose, cradling his winnings in his arm, and came to stand by them. "Did you see the newspapers, then?" he asked, not waiting for a reply. "President Davis *regrets* no reinforcements can be furnished to chase the enemy across the Potomac and take Washington. His expectation of arms from abroad was *disappointed.*" O'Donnell's glare implied that Brit was somehow personally responsible for this disappointment—a flattering sort of accusation, however unfair.

Langdon spoke up. "And they won't come across to us. 'All quiet along the Potomac' has become a jeer in Washington."

O'Donnell could not be mollified. "We're as ready as we'll ever be. They all admit it, Johnston and Beauregard and Smith, even Davis himself. Meanwhile the Yankees been shamed into stiffening their backbones. And our president is *disappointed* that we let our chance to win it run through our fingers." He shook his head of graying black hair and walked on.

Langdon glanced over at Brit. "I hope you can do us some good with your dispatches," he said, his face solemn. "They must know our cause is just. And they need our cotton."

Brit couldn't answer. Day after day, the front pages of the Southern papers were given over to news from England and France, to reports and speculation concerning those countries' need for cotton, and to repetition of what Lord So-and-So or Minister So-and-So had said concerning slavery. Many in England regarded the institution as an absolute evil—he himself regarded it as such, come to that—even deplored their own country's dependence on cotton produced by slave labor. What good would it do to show his readers in England, many of whom had wept over *Uncle Tom's Cabin*, that his friends in the Confederate army, slave owners or not, were good fellows—not so different, after all, from the great British public? He was a journalist, with the limitations that entailed. And likely enough it would come down not to words, his or Mrs. Stowe's, but to cotton.

"Well," Langdon said with satisfaction, rising from the ground and dusting off his pants. "That's done, then. See you in a half hour." He smiled at Brit as if he hadn't a care in the world and strode off to his tent, hands in his pockets.

Brit chuckled, realizing that young Langdon, with his earnest eyes and unfurrowed brow, had pulled his nose in the matter of the supposed raffle. Then he stretched, squared his shoulders, and looked up at the indigo sky. He found he didn't care. He was tired of the doldrums of camp life. He was very much looking forward to the excursion to Champs-Elysées.

CHAMPS-ELYSÉES

The silver candelabra of Champs-Elysées had already gone south to Richmond for safekeeping. On the beautiful carved mantel and the rough trestle table burned smoky tallow candles in every conceivable manner of holder, gathered from around the house, from heavy iron bases topped with sharp spikes onto which the candle was speared to empty wine bottles to tin candleholders used by the house servants. Their flickering light played over not the usual brilliant display of silver and gilt but bent tin spoons and forks and old horn-handled knives that were made for rougher hands.

The thudding of hoofbeats in the road alerted them that the guests were arriving. Jordan caught up one of the candlesticks, grabbed Narcissa's hand, and pelted up the stairs, laughing, white lace petticoats foaming around her velvet-shod feet. In the big bedroom at the head of the stairs, the bed had proved too large and heavy to be moved, so on it Jordan had draped the gowns from which she would choose her dress for the evening. She set the candle on a low table, where it lit the silks to glowing in shades of strawberry, persimmon, sky blue, and deep wine. Using cold water from a bucket, the women freshened up as best they could.

"Put this on, Narcissa—don't argue." Jordan was holding out the wine-colored gown. "You've been wearing that dreary black all day, you'll be taken for my governess, and no one will speak to you! Please, for my last night at Champs-Elysées, wear something beautiful."

Narcissa took the gown that Jordan pressed upon her. Jordan's eyes were large and bright in a face that, lacking its earlier animation, looked thin and sad. Was it because of her illness, or was there some deeper cause? Then Jordan turned away to run her long white fingers through the silks and laces on the bed. In the few hours she had known Jordan, thought Narcissa, the girl had been by turns giddy, satirical, affectionate—everything, in short, but reflective. This lapse into quiet seemed to make the girl edgy and distressed.

When Narcissa came out of her reverie concerning the capricious Jordan, she was surprised to find herself smoothing the bodice of the wine-red dress into the waistband of the skirt. She knew the color would flatter her black hair and dark eyes and reflect a flush against her sometimes matte skin.

Jordan grinned her sharp-cornered grin and then turned back to the mirror. "Is your maid any good with hair?"

Narcissa replied, "I don't have a maid," before she realized Jordan was referring to Judah Daniel. The idea of the strong-willed doctoress as a lady's maid was so incongruous that it made her smile. "Come, I will do your hair. I am used to doing my own." She looked at Jordan, who had chosen the strawberry-colored silk. "Let's pull it up on this side—"

As she busied herself with Jordan's coiffure, Narcissa found herself remembering the exquisite parure Rives had given to her on the first an-
niversary of their marriage: garnets mounted in gold filigree, a necklace,
earrings, a bracelet. Their color might be perfect with this dress. Where
were they? She remembered the box of olive green velvet, the delight with
which she had opened it, which had no doubt shown on her face, for Rives
had whispered into her ear, "Rubies, next time." With the Powers family
wealth invested in railroads that were coming to span the growing, thriv-
ing nation, the promise seemed assured. Then he had grown sick, and
sicker still, and the garnets had disappeared into their box. After Rives's
death, the box was put away and forgotten.

In another twenty minutes the two were ready to join the guests. In the
parlor, the young men had discovered the old, out-of-tune spinet that
had been judged not worthy of refugeeing and were banging out "The Girl
I Left Behind Me." Then a posted lookout called above the boisterous
singing that the ladies were descending the stairs. The playing ceased and
the soldiers rushed into the hall, jostling each other for the favored posi-
tions. Narcissa felt herself blushing, though most of the soldiers looked by
their slight forms and smooth cheeks to be closer to Jordan's age than
her own.

"Mrs. Powers! As I live and breathe."

Narcissa stopped in confusion, then smiled as her friend the British war
correspondent Brit Wallace stepped into view. She had met him in the
spring, just after her own arrival in Richmond from the Hanover countryside. He had been new to the city as well, just in from the home country
that had supplied his nickname. Brit Wallace, together with Judah Daniel
and Narcissa's sister-in-law, Mirrie Powers, had become involved with her
in investigating deadly events involving the medical college. In the course
of finding the truth, Wallace had become an ally. His regard for her held
an unspoken element of personal admiration that she found flattering
even as she ignored it.

"You have shed your raven's feathers to become a bird of paradise," Brit
said, taking her hand at the last step and pulling it through his arm. Jordan, meanwhile, was greeting with presses of the hand and pecks on the
cheek an assortment of friends and relations among the eight or nine
young men in uniform gathered there.

Brit explained that he had spent the past ten days touring the Confederate encampments on the Potomac for a series of dispatches concerning

how the young men were spending their time while awaiting the next engagement. "I made the acquaintance of Private Langdon—*Archer* Langdon; the first families of Virginia don't give up their family names easily with marriage—and he invited me along this evening. Actually, I got the invitation in payment of his poker debt! If only I had filled my pockets with playing cards when I came back south," Brit said with a wry smile, "I would be a rich man today."

Narcissa smiled back, admiring his resilient good humor. Just a few weeks before, Brit had been a prisoner of war. At Manassas in his capacity as a reporter, he had been caught up in the rout of Federals, captured by the Confederates, herded into a railroad car, and sent to Richmond, to be imprisoned in a tobacco warehouse less than half a mile from his lodgings at the fashionable Exchange Hotel. Surely, judging by his elegant dress and his rather indulgent manner of living, Brit had means beyond whatever salary or payment he might obtain by his dispatches. Not for the first time, she wondered about his family and his home in England.

"And how do you come to be here?" Brit inquired in turn. "I assume our mutual *acquaintance*—not to say *friend,* at least for my own part—Dr. Cameron Archer deserves my thanks?"

"Yes," Narcissa replied with an exhalation of breath not quite a sigh. "He asked me, and Judah Daniel, to come to meet Miss Archer, who had been preparing to return home from school in Baltimore when she fell ill with brain fever. Dr. Archer was concerned about her health," she added unnecessarily, wondering if Wallace had heard of Jordan's cavalry-raid dash over the dozen or so miles from the ferry to Champs-Elysées. The slight smile that came to his lips suggested he had.

"Then does this mean," Brit asked, "that the sick and wounded soldiers in Richmond have taken up their beds and walked? That would indeed be a miracle."

Narcissa shook her head. A thousand soldiers languished in hospitals throughout the city, many more suffering from disease than from wounds. Two hundred crowded the medical college hospital where she served as a nurse, with others filling public buildings and private homes turned into hospitals to meet the need. A new hospital being prepared on Chimborazo Heights would house more than three thousand. Again she fought down her irritation at being diverted from her duties, being consigned to the role of Jordan's duenna.

Jordan turned to see the two of them. "You are acquainted, I perceive?" she remarked with enough sharpness to make Narcissa aware of the intimacy of their conversation. It was not an unpleasant feeling: Mr. Wallace was a handsome man, with his blue eyes and black, curling hair, and the company of these very young soldiers lent a mature cast to his usual boyishness.

"Miss Archer, allow me to present Mr. William Wallace, war correspondent for the *Weekly Argus* of London. Mr. Wallace, Miss Archer. Miss Archer is the cousin of our mutual . . . acquaintance, Dr. Cameron Archer."

"Miss Archer," Brit said formally, bowing over her hand. "And I owe my invitation tonight to another of your cousins, young Langdon. I think most highly of both your cousins, more so than ever now that I have met the flowering branch of the family tree." Narcissa noted the look Jordan gave him, filled with all that a seventeen-year-old charmer could muster of beckoning warmth. When Brit looked back at Narcissa, his freshly shaven cheeks were pinker than they had been before.

A sandy-haired soldier with the ambitious startings of a mustache was looking intently at Narcissa. He stepped forward. "Mrs. Powers?" he asked doubtfully. At her answering smile he said, "It is! Fellows, this is the lady who saved my life in the Richmond hospital after . . . well, a terrible illness. She's a regular Florence Nightingale!" The young men gathered around to be introduced. It seemed that many remembered—or had heard tell of— Porter Andrews's bout with measles, and of the dark-haired lady who had been a ministering angel. Andrews retold the story with zest.

Brit smiled and said in an aside to Narcissa, "See the interest you inspire? And yet you always resist my attempts to write about you in my dispatches! Readers of the *Argus* would be most taken with an accounting of Richmond's 'lady of the lamp.' "

Narcissa, self-conscious in the glowing, low-cut silk so different from her familiar nursing garb, looked over at Jordan to see her chewing on her bottom lip, frowning. Then the frown disappeared, and the impish, three-cornered smile returned.

"How fascinating!" Jordan exclaimed. "You must show me around the hospital when I am in Richmond." She paused and looked mischievously around at her audience. "And now, would anyone like to take a candle and help me venture down into the cellars? I believe there is some very old French wine down there, which my father dare not have moved." The crowd around Narcissa dispersed, and Jordan was borne off as the fairy queen Titania among her taper-bearing subjects.

At Narcissa's urging, Brit went with the others—casting a flatteringly regretful glance over his shoulder—and Narcissa had time to examine her surroundings more closely. The interior of Champs-Elysées was built on lines as majestic as its exterior; but, stripped of superficial decoration, the rooms had a forlorn look. Darker rectangles where pictures had been removed showed up the fading of its paint. The elaborate plaster molding that ornamented the ceiling had crumbled in places, and more than one mouse hole was visible along the baseboard. One would not expect a place like Champs-Elysées to be slicked up in the latest fashion, but the state of the house bordered on neglect.

A staccato beat of footfalls on some unseen staircase, and then a voice—"Mrs. Powers!"—joined by others calling her name. Narcissa felt her heart jump at the urgency in the voices. In a moment the young soldiers were crowded around her, all talking at once. "She's gone!" "Disappeared!" "Miss Archer—she was with us one minute, then—"

Narcissa looked over their heads to meet Brit's eyes. He nodded, his mouth twisted strangely. The boys fell silent, waiting for him to speak. "Miss Archer was with us in the wine cellar. A sudden rush of air blew the candles out, all except for the one Langdon had out in the hall. We thought she was hiding in the shadows, but when we got our candles lit again, she was nowhere to be found."

A rush of air, Narcissa thought. A door had been opened somewhere, to the outside of the house, or perhaps to a passageway within the house.

"Did you call out?" she asked.

"Yes!" "Of course we did!" They were all speaking again, frowning and gesturing. Then she noticed the wine bottles they were clasping. Surely, had their alarm been serious, they would have set aside the bottles? She looked again at Brit. Was his mouth twisted that strange way so as to hold in a laugh?

"Shame on all of you for making such a jest!" Narcissa said, frowning and smiling at the same time. The laughter Brit had been holding in burst out.

Then, as if by a conjuring trick, Jordan stepped through the wall into the room. A section of paneling under the stairs had rotated on some hidden pivot to make the narrow opening through which she appeared, pressing down her wide skirts with one hand and holding a bottle of wine in the other. She pushed the panel back into place and stood laughing.

Brit came over to Narcissa, an expression of contrition on his face. "Langdon mentioned the hidden passage—it's always been a favorite game of the young people at this house—and Miss Archer wanted to demonstrate."

A favorite trick to play on a new governess, no doubt, Narcissa thought, and was glad she had not been truly alarmed.

The candles had guttered, and a dozen excellent bottles of wine had been liberated in advance from the Yankee invaders, when Jordan turned to the subject of her sudden reappearance.

"The secret passageway has always been very useful in times of trouble. It was originally made as an escape route in case of Indian attack. But soon there will be no one here to be troubled. No one . . . but the ghosts." Jordan rested her cheek on her hand and stared dreamily into the glow of the candles.

The soldier boys knew the part they were being called on to play and played it with relish. "The *ghosts?* Tell us!"

"Almost a half-century ago now, a young woman was living in this house. She met a young man, and fell in love."

The young men whistled, rolled their eyes, or otherwise demonstrated appreciation.

"But not with a friend of the family, or even a Virginian."

Groans and hisses arose from the family friends and Virginians gathered.

"No one ever knew his name, but it was said her lover was descended from a French aristocrat who had fought alongside the marquis de Lafayette for America's independence. He returned to his native land but was executed in the Terror. His son escaped death and later returned to the New World. While a visitor here, he won the love of this young woman, whose name was Eulalie. Of course her parents disapproved, but she persuaded one of her sisters—my great-aunt Caroline—to take her side. Eulalie made plans to run away with her lover and be married. She borrowed my great-aunt's wedding gown, satin and lace, with a net veil, and satin slippers embroidered with seed pearls. On the night of the elopement, her lover was to come up from the river through a tunnel into the wine cellar—the cellar we were in tonight—and into the hall through the secret panel. Eulalie stood just there, waiting for him, at the top of the stairs." Jordan gestured through the wide archway to where the staircase flowed into the marble-floored grand hall. "She waited and waited. All at once, there was a rumbling sound from somewhere under the house. It was the tunnel caving in! She started to run down the stairs, and she tripped! She fell all the way to the bottom of the stairs, and there she died. Her neck was broken. And her lover was crushed in the tunnel."

The young men were enjoying the story; Brit Wallace had taken out his little notebook and pencil and was making notes under the table. But Narcissa felt herself uneasy at Jordan's wide-eyed earnestness, the tremor in her voice. It was as if the accident had happened only a few days before, to her sister or her close friend. The lively Jordan Archer was moved almost to tears by this story of her relative, whose youthful recklessness so many years ago had had fatal consequences.

Jordan went on, her voice hushed with portent. "Eulalie was buried here at Champs-Elysées. Sometimes at night you can see her there on the stairs. I can see her, so clearly it's as if I remember it, as if I were there. The gown, ivory satin, gathered high in the Empire style . . . the band of tiny pearls that attached the veil to her blond hair. . . . You look again, and she is gone, but at the bottom of the stairs . . . something . . . a sound . . . like weeping. And then, from beneath the house, a scratching sound, like someone digging, clawing at the dirt with his hands—"

"You've seen the ghost?" an eager voice called out.

Jordan sat very still, frowning, her eyes fixed on nothing. Then she shrugged her shoulders as if giving up the effort. "Sometimes I think that's what it was. I try and try, but I don't remember seeing the ghost. And yet I've had the memory of her in my mind for as far back as my memory goes—a real person, not floating or transparent like a ghost. Her dress, her veil, her hair . . . and there is a treasure, pearls, diamonds, gold, heaped up and glinting. The brightness hurts my eyes sometimes when I see it."

Some of the young soldiers looked taken aback, as if they were having second thoughts about leading this particular belle to the altar.

This house may or may not be haunted, Narcissa thought, but its daughter certainly is.

Out back, in the little brick building that served as the plantation's kitchen, Judah Daniel and Auntie Lora sat drinking coffee. The cooking fires had died, and the night breeze cooled the room, making welcome the warmth of the coffee. Judah Daniel felt the old woman wanted to talk but was unsure how to begin, so she bided her time.

At last the old woman spoke, looking down at the dark liquid in her mug. "I don't hardly know how to speak my feelings, Judah Daniel. About leaving this place. Champs-Elysées been my home since my mammy give me birth. I figured to die here." She took a drink of the coffee, put the mug down, and rubbed her swollen fingers. "I ain't afraid to go when my time come, but to die so far from home. . . . At the last trump, I don't want to be raised up from the grave in some strange place, in amongst a bunch of souls I don't know, and don't know me."

Judah Daniel tilted her head back and shot an appraising look at Auntie Lora. "Now I know a man in Richmond, a man of God, can talk with you about that. Seem like he always got a word to salve the soul. But I expect God's got some work for you yet in this life, and you got to keep strong for it."

"Don't you be telling me my *work* is to run after that nuisancy child Jordan Archer," Auntie Lora shot back. Then she sighed. "I love her like she was my own. And she wears me out like she was, too. Seem that child can't stand to be alone, to be quiet. If it's just the two of us, seem like she always calling for me, 'Auntie Lora!' "

Not much different from Jordan's cousin, Dr. Cameron Archer, Judah Daniel thought wryly. She didn't know that she'd expected a reward, exactly, for having saved his life. But the reward she'd gotten was to be called on whenever the surgeon needed help with an especially difficult patient, and now when he needed help with his spoiled young cousin. The hospital paid her pretty well, she had to admit that. She was better off in that regard than Narcissa Powers, who also had to jump when Archer called but was an unpaid volunteer.

"How long her mother been dead?" Judah Daniel asked.

"Ever since she was three. I raised her, not that I'm bragging about that. That father of hers she dote on, he always turning up, making a pet out of her, then going off again, not seeing her for months at a time. He can't settle to nothing. How come he ain't come back down to Virginia? How come he sold so much away, sold his slaves, let his house run down?" The old woman held Judah Daniel's gaze and nodded slowly as if the answer was obvious. "It'd about kill the child if he turn traitor. That girl loyal, I give her that."

Judah Daniel was silent. If Jordan's father had turned his back on his home, his state, even his daughter, he sure wasn't likely to consider the wishes of an aged slave to remain in the only home she'd ever known. Yet the old servant, sharp-tongued though she was on the subject of her young mistress, seemed to worry more about Jordan Archer than she did about her own self.

"Any doctor been to see you about that swelling in your ankles?" Judah Daniel asked after a moment.

"Oh, a doctor a few years back told me something. I don't recollect what it was. You get to be eighty years old, you expect some troubles."

Judah Daniel leaned forward. "Holly-leaf tea good for that. Help you piss out some of that water collecting in your ankles. You could do with a good tonic too. You get to Richmond, I'll see you get some. Blue-flag root boiled down into a syrup, maybe mixed with spirits."

"I don't take *no* spirits," Auntie Lora responded, dismissing the temptation to sin with a wave of her hand.

"Well," Judah Daniel answered back with a quick grin, "you being eighty years old, I reckon there ain't much chance of you becoming a drunk."

Auntie Lora laughed heartily at that, rocking back and forth on the plank bench.

"And talking of spirits," Judah Daniel went on, "tell me about the ghost that's supposed to haunt Champs-Elysées."

"Oh, that was a tale," the old woman said, still now and wiping away the tears of her laughter. "A great disgrace, though the white folks don't tell it that way. There was two daughters in the house then. The son, Miss Jordan's grandpa, was off at school. The older daughter, Miss Caroline, was married to a Mr. Jennings, but she come back to her Champs-Elysées whenever she could in those days. It's her house we going to in Richmond. Anyway, the younger, Miss Eulalie, was a beautiful girl, but headstrong, just like Miss Jordan. She fell in love with a man and wanted to marry him, but her folks wouldn't have none of it. So she got it into her head to run off with him. On the night they was to meet, she was coming down the stairs in the dark. She fell and tumbled all the way down them long stairs and laid there moaning at the bottom. The servants called my momma, she was the midwife then. She saw Miss Eulalie been in the family way, just a few months along, and the fall made it come before term. Miss Caroline sent my momma away. Next thing we know, Miss Eulalie dead, not laid out or nothing, just shut up in her coffin and buried in the family plot. The way Miss Jordan tell it, the tunnel fell in and buried the man. But didn't nobody go digging for him. All I knows is, no lover ever did show hisself. The family blocked up the tunnel so wouldn't no other young ladies get the notion to run off."

"And the ghost?"

Auntie Lora nodded. "I ain't never seen it myself, but I knows some who has. A woman, all misty-white, at the top of the stairs. Then a sound of something falling, and a moaning. Well, I ain't seen it, but I done heard the moaning plenty times. Once it get the hounds started up, it's an eerie thing." She paused, sipped her coffee, and went on.

"With this war, and Mr. Archer gone so long, the hounds all been sent away. Wonder will the ghost be lonesome, with nobody here to haunt? Maybe it'll cheer her up to see the boys in their uniforms. Seems to me I heard tell her lover was a soldier? I reckon he wasn't so much of a brave man, though; reckon he ran away."

Chapter Two

MANAKIN

OCTOBER 6

Cameron Archer, wearing his surgeon's oversleeves and leather apron, mounted the stairs to the second floor of Manakin House. He had told John Berton to wait below. Whatever Berton had found must have driven him out of his senses; why else would he have waited all night to send to Richmond, when—if what he'd said was true—his ancestral home had been turned into a slaughterhouse?

Archer stopped in the doorway of the first room he came to. Though he was used to scenes of carnage, he had to gather himself before he could step forward. He had known Dorothea Berton, John's wife; had danced with her before she was married. Now she was lying on her chaise longue, her head turned away, her throat slashed in a thin red line just under her jaw. Blood had soaked the front of her dress, run down her arm, pooled onto the delicate rose-patterned carpet.

His second look took in the slave woman lying on the carpet near her mistress—it was the wife's maid. Berton had told him her name, Zemora. She was on her side, facedown, near the bloody pool. He took a few steps and took hold of her shoulder. None of the blood appeared to have come from her. Her eyes were closed, and her breathing was ragged. Near her right hand was a bloody knife, Dorothea's silver-chased penknife, looking absurdly small to have done this work. He looked at Dorothea's white, long-fingered hands. She had not fought back.

Archer looked for a long moment, then passed down the hall to the next room. Old Mrs. Berton, John's mother, lay on her bed, wearing her clothes and shoes. Her hands were placed on her chest as if she had been positioned for viewing. The blood had run from her severed throat onto the white counterpane. On the floor, propped up against the bed, sat her maid, Dorcas, an old woman herself. The servant was kneading her gray homespun skirt, stiff with her mistress's blood. Her eyes were open but vacant.

Archer turned on his heel and went to the next room. The shutters were closed and the room in near darkness. He had to stand over the high bed to see that old Mr. Berton, the colonel's father, had not escaped the fate of the two women. His throat had been hacked so brutally that his head was almost severed.

Lying on the floor near his body was an ornate sword, a bloody patch midway along its blade. The sword with its engraved blade was made not to arm a soldier but to reward a victor. This was not a frenzied attack, Archer thought: more like an execution. It appeared that Hiram, the old man's butler, patriarch among the blacks as Berton's father had been among the whites, had used the sword to cut his master's throat. John Berton had locked Hiram in the old man's dressing room before summoning help. Now he was confined in one of the outbuildings. Hiram, alone of the house servants, did not show symptoms of physical and mental disorder.

Archer stepped out into the hall and took a deep breath of the fresher air. Then he climbed the stairs to the nursery.

The room was stiflingly hot and malodorous. John Berton had described finding his son, blessedly alive, in the arms of his slave nurse, a young girl called Hetty, who had taken the child and hidden in the wainscoted cupboard under the eaves. Hetty, now laid out like a corpse on the bed she had shared with little Johnny, had neither moved of her own volition nor spoken since being found there, huddled, holding the child. Archer found the cupboard standing open and looked inside. Just big enough for a slender young woman to hide in if she drew her knees up close. Had she been supposed to kill the boy?

Two more servants, the cook and kitchen maid, had been found—the cook in the kitchen, an outbuilding connected to the dining room by a narrow brick wall, and the little maid wandering in the yard. Had they taken part in this murderous madness?

No point in speculating. It was time to begin the examinations.

Archer rinsed his bloodied hands in a basin held by a boy whose hands trembled so violently that the water sloshed onto the floor. "Put it down, soldier," the doctor snapped, and the youth rested the basin on the floor. The doctor pulled off bloodstained oversleeves and dropped them into the water. He frowned at the boy, who seemed to be trying to make himself invisible, then squared his shoulders and walked down the stairs and into the library.

The two privates who stood near the door shifted their weight away from their rifles to stand at attention. One had his left eye bandaged; the other showed the fading marks of chicken pox. "Get the servants out of here, someplace clean and ventilated," Archer ordered. "And get the bodies on ice, if you can find any."

Archer turned and scanned the room. Colonel Berton was sitting in a wing chair pulled up before a brightly burning fire. He was looking into the fire and seemed not to notice Archer's entrance.

Two other men were in the room, both middle-aged and prosperous-looking, one in a major's uniform and one dressed in civilian clothes. Major Wynn Harris represented the military authority in Richmond. Archer was relieved Harris had been sent in response to his summons. Harris was bullheaded, but he was at least a Richmonder, sensitive to the unspoken rules and unwritten laws of his city and state—not one of the Baltimore plug-uglies General Winder had brought down to police the city, who were sensitive to nothing but their own importance.

The civilian was James Cantrell, a cousin of Berton's and his closest neighbor. What was it about Cantrell, Archer wondered, that marked him as inferior to his cousin, John Berton—and had done for all the years he had known both men? Cantrell was only a few years older than Berton, but Cantrell had obscured the family resemblance with the marks of self-indulgence. He had Berton's small, delicate ears, but they sat at angles to his bloated, drink-reddened face—the face of a man who keeps up the habits of a misspent youth until taken by heart failure or apoplexy in middle age. No apparent disability in Cantrell disqualified him from service—or from high rank, given his stature as the owner of a minor plantation and the designated heir, after John Berton and his young son, to Manakin itself. But Cantrell would not make a good officer. He would be autocratic in small things, unsure and vacillating when lives depended on a quick and correct decision. To sense that about him required no medical training. The most ignorant hill-country private would know it instantly, and would follow him grudgingly.

Archer waited as Cantrell walked toward him. For Cantrell to approach first, rather than defer to Harris, was itself a mute statement of Cantrell's self-importance. Cantrell was mopping beads of sweat from his forehead with a handkerchief. He seemed genuinely distressed, Archer thought; but then, the room was hot.

"Ah, Archer. Good of you to come. Though it's a little late for a doctor. I haven't seen the . . . bodies, but I understand . . ." Cantrell faltered, looked down at the sweat-stained handkerchief in his hand as if surprised to see it there. He was silent for a moment, then started again. "In any case, it was clever of you to bring these convalescents from Richmond. I thought to bring some of my servants to keep order—my wife insisted on bringing her maid—but I thought, in view of the circumstances—"

Archer smiled grimly. The *circumstances* appeared to be that every white person in the house, with the exception of Berton's infant son, had been murdered by those servants to whom they had entrusted their lives. Now those servants were confined under guard. The field hands, who numbered about four dozen, were sitting or lying in small groups around the open yard, where soldiers watched them. They had been commanded not to talk to one another, and if they knew what had happened at the big house, their weary demeanor gave no sign of it.

Harris, emboldened by his major's star to rebuke a social superior, broke in, pointing a stubby finger at Cantrell. "You realize that no word of what happened here must escape this room. You and your wife must give your solemn word not to speak to a soul about it. These men"—he jerked his chin toward the sickly young men with their rifles—"will be returning to their units, and their oath will be sworn on pain of court-martial. The field hands will be questioned, of course. If no evidence is found they were involved, still we can never be satisfied they did not know about it. They will have to be dispersed, put to work on the fortifications, or sold away south."

"And what of a trial?" Archer asked. "Unlike the Federal government, the *Confederate* government has not declared martial law."

The question seemed to irritate Harris, who glowered, wrinkling a broad expanse of forehead from which the gray hair had receded. "This incident seems simple enough in itself: disgruntled slaves rise up to strike their masters and then are overcome, driven mad, by the horror of what they've done. We need no trial, Archer, for a trial means talk. And if the rumor spreads, inspires other slaves, then . . . unless I am very much mistaken, the worst will be to come."

Archer shot a glance toward where Berton sat hunched near the fire. "I doubt he would see it that way," he said dryly.

Harris frowned. "Even with the quick apprehension of the guilty parties, the arrests I have made, just the rumor of what has happened could spell disaster for our army. If our soldiers' attention was deflected to the specter of slaves cutting their families' throats, raping, pillaging—"

Archer broke in. "I have seen no evidence of rape. Is there anything missing from the house?"

Harris's frown grew more pronounced. "Colonel Berton noticed nothing missing, no. The slaves' own madness, their bloodlust, overpowered them before they had time to— Well, as I was saying, the whole of Virginia and the South has sent its men to repel the invading Federals. All that are left at home to keep the slaves in check are women, children, and old men."

Archer could not resist a glance at Cantrell. The civilian was staring at Harris, and his teacup-handle ears glowed red. "Damn good thing some of us are around to keep the slaves under control, prevent just the kind of thing you're talking about. I have always been firm with my slaves, and they respect me. My man Ike, for example—trust him with my life." Cantrell glanced over at Berton and lowered his voice so that his cousin would not hear. "John's always been too easy with his coloreds. Why, he took his body servant to war with him, and when the boy got up there to the camp, just across the river from freedom, he ran away! John won't take a servant with him again, he says. Too soft with them, if you ask me."

Archer inclined his head. "If you will excuse me, I must attend to my patient."

Archer crossed the room and drew up a chair next to Berton. The two men looked at each other. Once they had been acquaintances, almost friends. Tragedy had made them strangers. Archer had seen it before in men he had known whose wounds would prove to be fatal. For a time, at least—until healing came, if it ever did—Berton was alone, in a world far different from the one he had known.

Berton smiled slightly as if apologizing for not being a better host. But the smile did not reach his eyes, which wandered, red-rimmed and unfocused, as if he had stared too long into the sun and seen horrors there.

Archer spoke gently. "Before dawn my men—I call them that, since they were recently my patients, and as an army surgeon I bear the rank of major—will take the prisoners into Richmond and lock them up. Major Harris, there, is General Winder's second in command in charge of internal security in Richmond. He has spoken of the necessity of keeping events here from general knowledge. I concur."

Berton nodded.

"Some will clamor for the summary execution of the prisoners. I do not concur. If we act precipitously, we may never know the truth of what happened. The slave women are unconscious, or deranged. They cannot answer my questions—or they will not. I wish to bring in a woman, someone they might trust, to question them."

Berton's gaze slid back to the fire.

"But you need not concern yourself with that," Archer said quickly. "Just tell me, as clearly as you can, what you found when you arrived here."

Berton turned back to face Archer. "I rode down from our encampment near Leesburg. I came alone. My body servant, Quintus, took off from the camp a month ago. The proximity to the North, and freedom, was too great for him, I suppose. Anyway, I rode up alone to the house, wondering why it seemed to be deserted. I could see the field hands at work, but far off. I doubt if they saw me.

"When I came onto the porch, I saw one of the servants, a girl about ten years old. I didn't recognize her at first as the kitchen maid. She seemed not to see or hear me. She was grabbing at something in front of her face"—Berton made clutching motions with his hands just in front of his eyes—"though I could see nothing there. It gave me a start, that Hiram—" He paused and looked away, shuddering, then went on. "That he should have posted a demented child to give me welcome!"

"You were expected then," Archer remarked.

"I had written, yes, and I believe my message was received, because the table was laid for four." He looked at Archer, anguish in his face. "I know they had not been dead many hours. If only I had arrived a little earlier, I might have saved them."

Archer frowned. "If you had arrived earlier, you might have been killed as well."

Both men stared into the fire for a moment. Then Archer said, "So tell me, once you got past the child, what did you see and hear in the house?"

Berton spoke haltingly. "Everything was so still. As you know, we are a small family since my sisters married and moved away, but always there was activity, people going back and forth, servants, visitors. . . . I don't know that I was ever before in the house, in the daytime, that I could not see or hear another person. So it was strange things that struck me, things I never noticed before. Dust motes in the light. A buzzing like insects, but so faint it almost seemed to be inside my head. It was like . . . I was coming back from the dead, into a place from which every living creature had died long ago."

Berton pressed his hand over his eyes. The three-stranded gold braid on his uniform sleeve reflected the fire's light. Archer nodded toward the brandy, saying, "It's the best thing for shock."

Berton drank, then went on. "It sounds mad, I know. But it was like a waking dream. Ideas came into my head. Any minute I expected some enemy to leap out. Yankees. Even Indians, my old mammy used to scare me with stories about them. When I got up the stairs, I found my wife, just as you saw her, with her maidservant Zemora lying on the floor next to her. In the next room, my mother, and her maid, Dorcas. In the next, my father, and Hiram."

John Berton swallowed hard, fighting down an emotion that could have been grief, or anger.

"The nurse, Hetty, was hiding with my son. Thank God I found him quickly, or I think I would have gone mad. When I had made certain he was all right, I went back through the rooms one by one. Hiram seemed to be asleep. When I pulled him up, he came docilely enough, as if he'd just been waiting to be caught. I tied his hands and locked him in my father's dressing room, which has no windows.

"The maidservants, I couldn't wake up. I left them lying where I found them. They were overcome by what they had done; it sickened them. But Hiram—" Berton's hands dug into the arms of the chair. "He didn't say anything. But something about the way he looked enraged me. He knew what he had done, and he was glad of it. I wanted to kill him."

Archer considered. "All this took place yesterday evening. Your summons reached me this morning, carried by one of your field hands, I believe. Why did you not send right away?"

Berton frowned as if trying to remember. "I . . . I'm not sure."

"Did you touch the bodies at all?"

"I . . . no," Berton replied, frowning a little. "I knew they were dead. I dared not give way to my feelings. The enemy was somewhere close by—"

"Was not the *enemy* those servants you found with the signs of their guilt on them?"

Berton was looking into the fire. His strong-jawed, rather fleshy face sagged. He had chewed his bottom lip until a drop of blood appeared. Then he looked at Archer. "Yes. Of course."

RICHMOND
THE FOLLOWING DAY

Since the spring, Narcissa had made her home with her late husband's father and sister in their comfortable house just west of Richmond. The old man, retired as a professor of ancient languages, treasured Narcissa as the widow of his son, Rives. But Mirrie, Rives's sister, had become Narcissa's good friend. After the day-and-a-half journey from northern Virginia, Narcissa had brushed the soot from her hair and clothes and joined Mirrie and Professor Powers in their comfortable, book-lined back parlor. The professor, his gold-rimmed spectacles on his nose, was reading the latest issue of the *Southern Literary Messenger*. The professor suffered from the infirmities of age and spent most of his time in his wheeled invalid's chair. But his mind was still strong, and his eyes, fortunately, could still make out the words on a page, whether they were written in English, French, German, Latin, Greek, or any of a half-dozen other languages.

Professor Powers had passed on his keen intellect to Mirrie; but now that Narcissa had spent several months in their home, she felt acutely the differences between father and daughter. The professor was content to know the world without wanting to change it. But for Mirrie, it seemed, knowledge fed discontent. Mirrie read and studied subjects from the British involvement in China to, of course, the abolitionist movement, of which she was a devoted follower much out of place in secessionist Virginia. She worked out what she believed were the appropriate answers to knotty political questions. But having no power to effect these solutions—having simply to watch as the rest of mankind erred—made her tyrannical when posing solutions to problems closer to home.

"I can't say Dr. Archer thinks very much of you, Narcissa, to make you the nursemaid of his troublesome cousin." Mirrie's pretty, pink-and-white face was drawn into a frown, as it was too much of the time these days. She was beginning to look the old maid that, unmarried and in her late thirties, she might be styled by those who did not know her passionate heart. Just now, she was sounding like an old maid as well.

Narcissa forced herself to make a mild reply, smothering her own dissatisfaction with the errand on which Dr. Archer had sent her. Any admission of her feelings would be met with Mirrie's demands that something be done: Talk to Archer, tell him you're a nurse and not a nursemaid, insist that he . . .

All Narcissa wanted to do was go back to being a nurse. But she had not been sought out to work at the hospital, she was not being paid, and after many months she had to admit she was still there on sufferance. The lack of pay was not so important, since her late husband had left her well provided for. But being a nurse meant obeying—whenever possible, anticipating—the orders of doctors, especially of Archer, who was now the surgeon in charge at the medical college hospital. Narcissa could forget about a few wasted days. And she could forget about the spoiled child-woman Jordan Archer—after tonight, that is, since she felt obligated to attend the reception being held in Jordan's honor.

Mirrie was staring, as if aware that Narcissa's attention had wandered from their conversation. "He treats you like his servant. Or his wife," Mirrie said at last, turning away. Narcissa was thankful the rebuke, though fiery, had been brief. These days, it seemed that Mirrie—who had been so against the war of secession—was herself only too eager to do battle. The war had disrupted Mirrie's life far more than it had her own, Narcissa thought. Infuriated at the South's secession from the Union, Mirrie felt the wartime constraint on her outspoken abolitionism as a constant affront. War had dispersed Mirrie's circle of like-minded intellectuals and shattered her comfortable platonic friendship with Nat Cohen, who, in donning a Confederate uniform and asking for her hand in marriage, had become a stranger. Mirrie would not even read the letters Nat sent to her father—though it seemed to Narcissa that she listened closely when the professor recounted their contents.

Narcissa sometimes wondered how her own life would have been different had her late husband lived to see the outbreak of war. Though quieter by nature than his sister, Rives had believed wholeheartedly in the abolition of slavery, as Mirrie did. Narcissa herself was more hesitant, more doubtful about a simple solution.

But would Rives have refused to serve in the Confederate army, maybe even fought for the Union? The Powerses had kin in the North, including a United States senator. If Rives had gone north, as some in Richmond had, would she have gone with him? It was hard to imagine Rives betraying his loyalty to Virginia. It was harder still to imagine herself being disloyal to Rives.

In any case, Rives had died before the question had come to crisis. With his death Narcissa had become a widow, a nonentity—until the Confederate army had given her a purpose in living. She had become a nurse in the hospital run by the Medical College of Virginia. Her work was to heal the bodies and spirits of Confederate soldiers, like the thousands who had been brought to Richmond after the battle at Manassas. Since the Confederates had not followed up that victory by taking Washington, there would have to be another battle—perhaps many more battles—before the seceding states would be allowed to depart in peace. Now the soldiers along the Potomac marked time in their camps. But death did not wait for trumpet calls and artillery blasts. There were fevers, epidemics, the omnipresent dysentery. Her work, unpaid though it was, would leave her neither energy nor inclination to argue about her dignity with Cameron Archer, or to fret about Jordan.

There was a bustling in the hall, an opening and closing of doors, and the Powerses' maidservant, a free black woman named Beulah, entered carrying a bulky package wrapped in silvery tissue paper. "It's for you," said Beulah, "from a Miss Archer."

Narcissa took the bundle and untied the gray satin bow that held it together. There lay the claret-colored dress she had worn at Champs-Elysées. She held up the tiny card engraved *Jordan Archer* and read aloud, "Now I have seen this on you, I would not feel right wearing it again. Please accept it with my compliments and wear it tonight."

Eyebrows raised, Narcissa looked at Mirrie, whose laughter was for once free of bitterness and all but a touch of irony. "Why, the girl is a wit! Who would have thought it? Are you going to wear the gown, Narcissa, so dubiously blessed by its owner's refusal to be seen in it?"

"I don't know; what do you think?" Narcissa replied, shaking the dress free of its wrapping and holding it up in front of her. She was surprised by the pleasure she felt at its silky feel and glowing color.

"Oh, do wear it!" Mirrie said at once, warmth replacing the sarcasm in her voice. "Rives would have loved to see you in it," she added quietly.

"Thank you," Narcissa said, giving Mirrie a hug that concealed her sudden tears. Narcissa thought of the garnet parure, felt the guilt of having wished to wear it even before the wish itself had formed itself in her head.

"Anyway," Mirrie said in a moment, shrugging off the emotion, "I have determined to attend this evening after all. The touch of vinegar in this young lady has piqued my curiosity. Even though I can't abide that old lady, her great-aunt Caroline. She thinks so highly of herself because she was born an Archer. She insists on being called 'Mrs. *Archer* Jennings.' In a moment of weakness she married a Mr. Jennings—a man of no family connections who survived just long enough to have his portrait painted, and she has worn mourning the half-century since."

"Does not that show her great love?" Narcissa asked, suddenly doubtful about putting off her own widow's weeds.

"Ha!" was Mirrie's response. "Wait till you see her. Eyebrows climbing up to her false front of blond hair and mouth pursed as if she'd just bitten a lemon. She may be in mourning for her lost girlhood, or for these degenerate times, but for poor old Jennings? I hardly think!"

How would old Mrs. Archer Jennings and her great-niece get on together? The prognosis was not good. Brushing the back of her hand over the soft silk of Jordan's gift, Narcissa felt a pang of sympathy for the girl. The gift of the dress was a generous one, perhaps inspired by real gratitude on Jordan's part. Really, Mirrie was too satirical.

———

Something was wrong. Judah Daniel could sense it. The easygoing feeling she'd always had at the Chapman family's bake shop on Main Street, and at their house a half mile or so northwest, where she'd lived the past few months, had been replaced with tension. Rooms fell silent when she entered. The men's brows were furrowed. Elda fussed over the baby and darted nervous glances at the men. Seemed Elda, too, was being excluded from discussions of whatever it was: so whatever was causing the trouble, Judah Daniel reasoned, was something the men considered their business.

Maybe business was the trouble. Already the pinch of wartime was being felt by Richmonders. Many free blacks were employed—it was said they'd be paid, but that remained to be seen—in digging fortifications around the city. But hotels were crowded to overflowing, and John Chapman and his family were staying busy meeting their demands for baked goods.

Judah Daniel wondered if the trouble was between John and his son Tyler, Elda's husband. Tyler had been known to talk about taking up arms for Lincoln's army. But he was a responsible young man. She couldn't see him walking away from Elda and their son, or from the business that would be his someday, God willing. The Chapmans' house gave regular welcome to at least a dozen more family members of all ages and both sexes, but Judah Daniel hadn't spotted any one of them as the source of the trouble.

She didn't have to wonder long. When the trouble reached out to draw her in, she was boiling down some sweet-flag root to make the medicine for Aunt Lora's dropsy. The wooden spoon scraped against a sticky place at the bottom of the pot where the liquid had overheated. Judah Daniel's nose wrinkled at the smell.

"Darcy!" she turned toward the door and called. "You best come here and spell me before I ruin this batch of tonic!"

Only a few moments passed before Darcy, Judah Daniel's ward and a promising apprentice, slipped soundlessly in, almost without opening the door, it seemed, she was so skinny and so light-footed. She looked up at Judah Daniel, eager yet serious, grown up for her eight years. Judah Daniel was handing her the spoon just as John Chapman walked into the room. A glance at his face told her that a summons for her healing arts had come.

Chapman put his hand on her arm and drew her to the far corner of the room from Darcy. "It's a dog bite. A bad one."

"Dear Jesus," Judah Daniel whispered. "If it's a mad dog, ain't nothing I can do." Death from the bite of a mad dog was the most horrible she had seen, filling its victims with a wild-eyed bloodlust before killing them.

"I don't know about that," Chapman replied, "But the skin's been torn, and it's festering. It's a boy about seven years old. Thing is"—his eyes darted to where Darcy stood, then back—"it's about a half-hour's ride from here. Tyler will take you in the bake-shop wagon. He knows the way."

A stony set to his jaw told her not to ask questions. She ignored it.

"I got a right to know."

John Chapman sighed. "It's a group of folks calling theirselves the Loyal Brethren, helping runaway slaves on their way up north. Don't know much about it myself. Don't *want* to know." He paused, sighing again, as if it cost him an effort to say the words. "Tyler's a grown man. If he make up his mind to something, I can't stop him."

So that was it. No wonder tension cracked in the air at the Chapman house. John Chapman ruled among his family and the larger free black community like a tribal chieftain—ruled with his smile, which warmed like the sun, and his frown, which stung like a January wind. His weakness was his love for Tyler, his only son, father of the only grandson to bear the Chapman name. And Tyler must have used that love at last to get himself a little freedom from his father's rule. She hoped he wasn't using it to take risks that would harm his family. Not that the Loyal Brethren weren't worthy of support for their work in helping slaves flee along the Underground Railroad. But dangers pursued them at the best of times, and with this war . . .

Before she thought to wonder about the risk to herself, she was sitting next to Tyler in the wagon. To pass the time, she told him the ghost story from Champs-Elysées that Auntie Lora had told her: the woman, dead from her fall down the stairs, moaning; the man, buried in the collapsed tunnel, or run off to save himself from the family's wrath. Tyler, maybe relieved not to be questioned about their errand, asked a lot of questions about Champs-Elysées and its families, black and white.

At last Judah Daniel began on the subject that was uppermost in her mind, asking Tyler, "How you get mixed up with the Loyal Brethren?"

Tyler grinned at her. "Can you keep a secret?"

"Ha!" A rare laugh rumbled up from Judah Daniel's throat. "I hope you ain't forgotten I'm a healer and a midwife. Someone like me brought you bare-bottomed into this world, same as I done your own son. You better hope I can keep a secret."

"Well, so can I!" Tyler laughed at his own witticism, then grew serious. "I mean no disrespect, Judah Daniel. Nobody knows much about the Brethren, and those that do ain't supposed to pass it on. But I can tell you this. A message come two nights ago when you was away, from the Reverend Truesdale."

Tyler watched to see the effect of the name on Judah Daniel. Zed Truesdale, in his eighties and blind now, had earned the respect of slaves and free blacks for a lifetime of preaching the Word in defiance of the law. Judah Daniel wasn't surprised that Truesdale was involved with the Brethren, but she was interested to see how much the old man's name meant to young Tyler, who used it like a talisman.

Tyler went on. "The message was about a family on the run from South Carolina. The ma and pa, two half-grown children, and a boy about seven years old." Tyler paused, and Judah Daniel, seeing the solemn expression on his face, knew he was thinking about his own son. "They needed a way up around Richmond to the Brethren at Fredericksburg. Turned out they couldn't make it that far. The boy had a gash in the meat of his leg"—Tyler bent down and rubbed his calf muscle—"where one of the hounds got him. He been on it for days. Now it seem like he's feverish and too sick to travel."

Judah Daniel felt the tightness in her chest ease. The dog was a slaver's hound, not mad, probably, but taught meanness. There was a chance she could cure the boy.

Tyler glanced over at her and added, "They's holed up in the Chicka-hominy Swamp. Holed up with King."

Judah Daniel's husky voice rose in a note of doubt. "King an old story, told to scare children. You telling me he still alive, hiding out in the Chickahominy Swamp?"

Tyler laughed, pleased at her surprise. "He still alive, must be upwards of fifty years old now. He like to have folks scared of him, but I ain't never heard he killed more than those two men, and that was kill or be killed. I don't reckon we'll see him today. But if you ever want to talk to him," he went on, "here's what you do: go to the dead sycamore there at the edge of the swamp, it's white as a bone and more than a hundred feet high. Wait close by the tree. By and by, King come to you, if that what he want to do."

"So," Judah Daniel said, shaking her head wonderingly. "That's your news for me. Well, I got some news for you. Young John's going to be get-ting him a little brother or sister."

Tyler's head whipped around, and he looked at her, openmouthed. Then a grin spread across his face. "Elda hadn't told me yet," he said at last.

"Elda don't know yet," Judah Daniel responded, smiling back at him.

* * *

The Archer house on Church Hill—no one could remember it having been called the Jennings house in honor of that man's brief tenancy—was decorated in the clean-lined neoclassical style that had been popular ear-lier in the century. But to Narcissa, gazing around her as she followed Mir-rie through the grand, high-ceilinged rooms, the house had a look of being overadorned, with silver bowls and candlesticks, china figurines, gilded and painted ewers, and serving dishes covering every available sur-face, and family portraits crowded together on the walls. Narcissa sud-denly realized she was seeing the treasures refugeed from Champs-Elysées, added to the already lavish appointments of the newer city house. Narcissa wondered how Caroline Archer Jennings felt, knowing the home in which she'd grown up—in which these treasures belonged—could at any mo-ment become a casualty of war.

At the far end of the long room, close to the fireplace adorned with marble caryatids, sat Mrs. Archer Jennings in a tall, heavy chair carved of wood almost black with age. One gnarled hand, weighed down with rings, rested on the silver top of a slender cane. Beside the chair a manservant stood at attention, white-haired but vigorous looking, dressed in black and white with gleaming white gloves.

Narcissa and Mirrie made their way through the room to pay their respects. Perhaps twenty young officers, and a few older ones, stood around the spacious room and talked with a dozen young ladies. Narcissa recognized the Stedmans' daughters among them and exchanged smiles and nods. Dancing would begin soon: an old Negro with his fiddle under his arm was settling onto a high three-legged stool. Meanwhile, the crowd was thick around the punch bowl. Narcissa saw Beaumain Newton, the made-up old dandy, in former days a consul to many countries whose medals adorned his antique tail coat. He was deep in conversation with the Prussian major, Von Wulfen, who had come over to join the Confederate cause. As they walked past, a third man came up and addressed the two in what sounded to Narcissa like French. She looked in his direction, curious as to who this sophisticated individual could be—some member of the Richmond Howitzers, perhaps, the company famous for its highly educated soldiers. She saw a handsome, dark-haired man, a civilian whose black frock coat and erect posture were both *à la militaire*. The stranger had noticed her interest and was responding to it, meeting her eyes, smiling and nodding, then looking away so as not to give offense. She wondered if he would seek out an introduction, and found herself hoping that he would.

At last they reached Caroline Archer Jennings. Narcissa found the widow so like Mirrie's description that she had to restrain her smile from becoming a grin. And to think this crone was the sister of Eulalie, Jordan's ghost, whom early death had kept forever young and beautiful. It was impossible to imagine Mrs. Archer Jennings ever having been young, or beautiful, though the man whose portrait hung over the marble fireplace was dashing—in the prime of life, with thick dark hair and beard. The subject's features and pose were stiff; but the artist had captured the man's pride in the details of his dress, especially his green velvet coat adorned with gold buttons.

"Is that Mr. Jennings?" Narcissa whispered.

"Yes," Mirrie whispered back. "He does not look as if he would bear henpecking, does he?"

Narcissa looked at the painting for a long moment, wondering what it would be like for a proud man of no family connections to find himself connected by marriage to one of the foremost families in the country. Most people would consider it an advantage, a chance to rise in the world. Mr. Jennings had not been so fortunate.

At last it was Narcissa's turn. Mrs. Archer sat through the introductions with a pursed-lipped look of disapproval that would have made Narcissa uneasy had she not been warned it was the lady's habitual expression.

The widow's eyes searched the room. "I can't think what can be taking that girl such a time. It is very rude not to be here to welcome her guests. Girls did not do so in my day."

Narcissa tut-tutted and backed away a half step to test the dowager's interest in keeping her as an audience. Seeing no reaction, she took Mirrie's arm, and they withdrew.

"Is our Miss Archer playing the belle?" Mirrie asked.

"Oh, I believe so. She took the first guests' arrival as the signal to begin her toilette."

"Oh, look, isn't that Mr. Wallace?" Mirrie had screwed up her near-sighted eyes and was peering at the black-haired, clean-shaven young man. Brit crossed the room to them.

"Miss Powers! Mrs. Powers! *Vastly* pleased to see you!" He paused, a grin dimpling his cheeks. "You see, I am studying to speak like a Southerner."

"Not a Richmonder, though, Mr. Wallace," Mirrie responded tartly. "You must put pebbles in your mouth to achieve that distinction."

Brit laughed. "Well, I shall never achieve that distinction, not being born to it. But, thank heavens, our hostess values a foreign accent"—he gestured with a nod toward the Prussian Von Wulfen—"almost as highly. An ocean between being the minimum requirement. It is all very well to march into battle side by side with 'crackers.' But to pair off with them in the Virginia reel or the Lancers!" Brit pantomimed an expression of horror. "*Old Richmond* will fight against the leveling of wartime until every last drop of their blue blood has been spilled—or dilutes itself with intermarriage," he concluded with a laugh.

"Oh, Mr. Wallace, you exaggerate," Mirrie protested. "Richmond's best families have generously opened their parlor doors to the South's fighting men—so long as they have commissions, of course."

"Miss Archer must have been taken with you," Narcissa teased gently.

Wallace blushed in response. When he spoke, it seemed a non sequitur: "Do you know, Mrs. Powers, that gown is enormously becoming."

Narcissa smiled her thanks.

"Enormous?" Mirrie asked, eyes wide with mock seriousness. "Do you think the skirts are too wide?"

Brit gave it up and laughed with them at his own expense. "You will drive me back to the army camps, where manners are gentler. You know, I could almost wish I had been twiddling my thumbs to the western rather than the northern part of the state. I could have been at Cheat Mountain, to watch 'Granny' Lee lead the Confederate retreat."

"Ssh!" Mirrie warned. "Mrs. Archer Jennings might not find that joke amusing, since the Archers and the Lees are related in some degree."

Brit looked around to see who might be listening and then said more quietly, "It was an insignificant engagement, really. But I plan to be on hand for the next battle along the Potomac, if only McClellan will ever order his men to cross the river into Virginia and engage the enemy."

Suddenly everyone's attention was drawn to the door. Jordan Archer was framed in the wide archway, dressed all in black, her light hair bound with a black chenille snood.

The old lady's snorted exhalation of breath was audible. "What are you got up as, my miss?"

Jordan held the pose, and her tongue, for a moment. Then she swept through the room to confront the old lady.

"I have resolved to make myself useful to the Cause. I intend to begin at once my service as a nurse to the wounded on the field of battle."

A smothered laugh broke the room's silence. Then it seemed everyone spoke at once. Mirrie spoke behind her gloved hand to Narcissa. "She has given you her dress, and she has taken yours. How it must have piqued her to see you admired! But it is not enough for her to help in a hospital. Too many young ladies are already doing so."

Brit Wallace turned to them. "What a noble resolve! Do you not applaud her, Mrs. Powers?"

"Assist the wounded on the field?" Narcissa asked. "Surely she would be more of a distraction than a help, since the men would feel they had to protect her."

Brit's eyebrows rose. "Are you making the old argument of 'ladyship'? The very argument you rode down when Dr. Stedman opposed *your* work in the hospital?"

Narcissa was silent. She felt herself doubting Jordan's sincerity, but how much of her suspicion was based on her own rivalry with Jordan—a feeling she now realized had arisen the moment she had seen Jordan riding like a Tartar to the steps of Champs-Elysées?

Again there was a stir at the door. Cameron Archer, unshaven and wearing the rumpled uniform of a field surgeon, did not pause to be framed in the entranceway but strode grim-faced across the room. The revelers fell silent, heads turning, watching him. Narcissa, heart pounding, knew the questions that were in their minds. Could there have been an action? No, others here would have known. Was he bringing news of a death?

Not a word was spoken until the surgeon reached Mrs. Archer Jennings and stooped to say a few words to the old lady in her chair. Narcissa made out the waspish tone of her reply but not the words. No cry of grief and loss: a sigh went through the crowd, and conversation resumed. Narcissa saw Archer kiss Jordan on the cheek in greeting, then turn away, leaving her frowning at his retreating back. Then he crossed the room to where she was standing. Nodding a perfunctory greeting to Mirrie and Brit, "Mrs. Powers," he said formally, "a word if you please."

Mirrie, giving Narcissa a look that said *Stand up to him,* allowed Brit to take her arm and lead her away.

Archer's usual drawl was clipped. "I regret I must call you away to assist with a medical emergency. We feel a woman's involvement is essential. Judah Daniel is waiting in the carriage." He paused and surveyed her. "Your . . . dress could not be more unfortunate."

Narcissa felt the blood warm her face as she stared back into his frowning eyes. "An emergency, you say? Then my *dress* is of no importance."

Damn the man, she thought. Just because she had chosen to be a nurse, was she no longer allowed to be a woman? But it was no good. Her cheeks continued to burn as she apologized to Mirrie, collected her wrap, and followed Cameron Archer out into the night.

Chapter Three

RICHMOND

Judah Daniel waited in Cameron Archer's carriage, looking up at the elegant mansion of Mrs. Archer Jennings. So this was what Auntie Lora had come to, along with her impetuous young mistress, Jordan Archer. How would the old woman be taking this upheaval? she wondered. It would be good to stop by, visit with her awhile in the welcoming kitchen ruled over by the widow's cook, Tildie. A visit would give Auntie Lora a chance to talk about the old times. Do as much good or more than the medicine she and Darcy had been preparing for her when the summons came from the Loyal Brethren.

Had Darcy been able to finish making it up, the blue-flag-root tonic? There hadn't been time to ask. She'd not been back at the Chapmans' long enough to finish brushing the mud from her skirt when a soldier had come to the door with another summons, this one from Dr. Archer. She was not in a position to go against Archer. A white man of good family, with an important job and now high military rank, he was one of those who could lay their hand on her anytime, like a housewife choosing a chicken for the pot, and put an end to her hard-won freedom. Besides, she had to admit, this summons had her curious.

So here she was. But her mind was elsewhere, in the treacherous swamp that ran along the Chickahominy River north and east of town, where Tyler Chapman had brought her to find the family of slaves who were running to the North, running for their freedom. It wasn't just a matter of crossing the line from South to North. Once they got to the other side, there were plenty that would send them back for the reward, or sell them to some other master. The father was free, but not his wife, nor his children. The child follows the condition of the mother; that was the law that so conveniently protected the white man's property. And now that the freedman father was a thief in the law's sight, he too would be sold if they were caught.

She'd doctored the boy's dog bite, cut away some of the proud flesh, swollen and bad-smelling, and bound the place with cleansing herbs. He would live, but would he be able to run, as soon as he would have to do? How long could they stay in the swamp, in that strange mix of elements— land and water and something that was both, and neither—with the nights already cold? Was it true that King—the one word served as both name and title—had lived there more than twenty years now as head of a raging bunch of runaways? The wounded boy's mother, whose life had been no easy thing, had told of making their way through the swamp in the tones of one who'd passed through hell.

Judah Daniel squeezed her eyes shut and sent a thought, almost a demand, to God to keep the fleeing family safe.

Brit handed Mirrie one of Mrs. Archer Jennings's crystal punch cups, filled with a straw-colored liquid. Then the two stood in preoccupied silence, watching the dancers. Brit raised his cup to his lips. The little bubbles clustering along the sides of the cup were a good sign. Ah . . . yes. The punch was delicious, the kind served everywhere before the blockade. Now it was growing increasingly difficult to get all the ingredients, which included, if he remembered correctly, tea, lemon, rum, cognac, and champagne. When they could be obtained, liquors, coffee, and tea, as well as other luxuries, were most often sent to the hospitals and the camps, where they could stimulate the bodies and the spirits of Southern soldiers. Brit felt thankful that Mrs. Archer Jennings's patriotism stopped short of self-sacrifice. He especially needed the punch now that Narcissa Powers's departure had made his own mood a little flat. Once again Cameron Archer had demonstrated his ascendancy over Mrs. Powers by charging into the midst of the party and summoning her, as if she were his servant—or his wife.

Brit sipped the punch slowly, enjoying the warmth it kindled in him, a warmth that made a man feel he was capable of anything. He was thinking about death, the kind of death he had seen at Manassas, that stripped a man of everything he had thought was his own before it let him die. His experience at Manassas had sobered him, made him question the importance of stringing words together to illuminate a particular time and place. But what he felt now, in this room, surrounded by young men in somber yet dashing uniforms and girls in bright, swirling silks, rushing together and apart in the steps of the Virginia reel, was not sobering but intoxicating. Such was the thrill of war: that it made life something to be run into headlong. Marriages had been celebrated all during that summer. After Manassas, he had thought perhaps Narcissa Powers . . . but he knew he could not make a declaration that she would take seriously, not until he had set his course and declared his purpose in life. He did not think she would laugh at him, but he could imagine a distant, disappointed look in her dark, expressive eyes, a cool restraint descending on their easy friendship.

The music stopped. "Abolitionists!" Mrs. Archer Jennings shrieked into the sudden hush. Brit turned in her direction and saw Mirrie's head turn as well. The dowager was frowning up at some abashed-looking lady. "Don't say that word in my house! They are a serpent in my bosom! A serpent!"

Brit smiled as a humorous sketch took shape in his mind. It was the kind of thing his editor at the *Weekly Argus* was ever eager for. A serpent in my bosom . . . he could quote that remark, together with some witticism concerning the uncomfortable nature of the bosom in question. No, better not, if he ever wanted to taste Mrs. Archer Jennings's punch again.

"I will not allow abolitionists in my house. They're traitors, all of them." The voice of Mrs. Archer Jennings reached him again. Then the old woman's gaze shifted from the guest she was hectoring to where he and Mirrie stood. After a moment's self-consciousness, Brit realized it was Mirrie at whom the old woman's stare was aimed. And Mirrie was staring back. It was a duel of basilisks, to see whose look could poison the other.

What was all this about? Well, Mirrie Powers had long been outspoken in her support for Unionism and abolitionism. It was Mirrie's good fortune to have the protection of impeccable Virginia ancestry, a manner that, though acerbic, could be charming, and the tolerant friendship of many important people in the community.

"Mr. Wallace," Mirrie said abruptly, "pray excuse me."

Before Brit could respond, Mirrie swept through the room to where Mrs. Archer Jennings sat. "Thank you for a most entertaining evening," she said in a penetrating voice. "I must excuse myself to call upon the family of a dear friend in the neighborhood."

An unbecoming flush rose in Mrs. Archer Jennings's face, engulfing her rouge. Brit knew Mirrie's missile had reached its mark, but who—? Oh, the "dear friend" had to be Mirrie's erstwhile suitor, Nat Cohen. Colonel Cohen was a Jew—a fact he would expect Mrs. Archer Jennings to view with vigorous disapproval, though she doubtless shopped for her fancy goods at Cohen and Sons.

Mrs. Archer Jennings held out a beringed hand. Mirrie gave it the merest touch with her fingertips, then turned away with a swish of hoops and headed for the door.

Brit downed his punch in a gulp and rushed to intercept her. "Allow me to escort you, Miss Powers."

Mirrie stopped, smiled. "You are a gentleman, Mr. Wallace. But there is no need. I only said what I did to annoy *that woman*. I shall have a quiet evening at home. I do not belong here in any case." She glared back in the direction of Mrs. Archer Jennings, then smiled again at Brit, who grinned back and made a sweeping bow.

Brit poured himself another cup of punch and again stationed himself where he could pick up snippets of several conversations as well as watch the dancers. His eyes fell on Jordan Archer in her black dress. She was a lovely girl. Perhaps she would "sit for her portrait" as the Confederate Florence Nightingale. Narcissa Powers had steadfastly refused his entreaties for an interview. Jordan Archer would not be so modest, he guessed.

Brit strolled over to the group gathered around the old dandy Beaumain Newton. At their first meeting Brit had found it difficult not to laugh at the man's powdered, rouged face, his dyed, overblack hair with its greenish tinge. But Newton knew everyone, told wonderful stories, and seemed to enjoy the prospect of having them repeated in the British newspapers.

Newton's greeting was extravagant. "Ah, 'tis our young laird, William Wallace of that ilk! You've met the major, I believe?" Von Wulfen made a smart bow, which Brit returned.

Standing between Brit and the Prussian major was another man, not in uniform. The man, in his thirties, had slightly curling brown hair, a darker beard, neatly trimmed, and green-flecked dark eyes.

"M. Lucien," Newton addressed the stranger, "allow me to present Mr. Brit Wallace. Mr. Wallace, M. Lucien."

The stranger bowed. Brit returned the greeting.

"M. Lucien is attached to the French court, to Prince Napoleon, in particular," Newton said breathlessly.

"Loosely attached," the stranger corrected with a smile and a shrug. "I follow my own inclination."

Newton's voice dropped to a whisper, and he touched the side of his nose with his index finger. "You know the prince made a secret visit here during his tour of America. Cotton diplomacy, don't you know. They're feeling the pinch, however much they may deny it."

Then he turned to the Frenchman and said, "Mr. Wallace is a journalist for one of the London papers."

Lucien smiled, extending his hand. "I am so very pleased to make your acquaintance. For which of the papers do you write?"

Lucien's eyes were fixed on Brit as if the answer to that question were of the utmost interest. A charming trick; Brit had used it himself. The man's speech reminded Brit of foreign students at Oxford, whose English was just slightly too perfect, too melodious, to be native. There might be something in the *r* and *th* sounds that marked him as French. He wore a black tunic-coat, buttoned and with the collar up, as close to a uniform as one could get. Brit had a similar one. In these crowds of soldiers, a light or patterned fabric or a too-loose sack style looked clownish. Clearly Lucien was a clever man, not least in allowing others to boast of his supposed connections while he himself downplayed them. Should his hand ever be called, he could pass off his pretensions as rumors not of his making.

Brit realized Lucien was still waiting for a reply. "The *Argus*," he said briefly. Accustomed to blank looks, he was not surprised when the Frenchman smiled politely and changed the subject.

Lucien spoke in a lowered voice, distancing the two of them from the other men's conversation. "Forgive me, but I was wondering . . . that officer who just came in and vanished again, so rudely taking with him that charming woman with whom you had been talking. His wife, I suppose? Did he not approve of her being here, a married woman? I understand that is the case with many husbands in this country."

"Oh—no." Brit corrected him with a laugh. "That was Dr. Cameron Archer. The lady you mention serves as a nurse. I assume he summoned her for some purpose related to the care of patients." Brit did not elaborate, feeling that this conversation with a man who did not know Mrs. Powers verged on the indelicate.

I'll talk to him about what he's doing here, Brit thought. *Sure to be a story in it.* Then he saw Jordan Archer turn her head slightly his way. He saw her smile begin, then vanish, her eyes widening for an instant. Then she turned away to give great attention to her opposite in the figure. Something, someone, had made her shy. Brit turned back to see Lucien, his light-flecked eyes still on Jordan Archer.

As Brit returned to the general conversation, he felt a twinge of envy for Lucien's ability to stir a belle into uneasiness with no more than a glance in her direction.

For more than an hour, the carriage jogged along the River Road west from Richmond. The three of them—Judah Daniel, Narcissa Powers, Cameron Archer—made awkward company, and the time was passed in silence. At last torches lit up the road in front of them and revealed a small band of soldiers who were stationed, rifles at the ready, to block a turnoff in the road. A voice called out, "It's Major Archer!" At once the soldiers parted to admit the carriage. They snapped to attention and gave the salute. Narcissa, looking out, was surprised to recognize one of the faces as a soldier whose leg wound she'd dressed only the day before. She had assumed this summons was to help some woman through a difficult confinement. But if so, why a guard of soldiers?

They turned into a tunnel of deeper darkness made by the bows of over-arching cedars. The carriage's lanterns threw weird shadows that made the rough, ropy trunks of the trees seem to writhe like snakes. It was another ten minutes before they came out from the tree-tunnel into the yard of a house she recognized.

"Manakin?" she said aloud, turning to catch Archer's eye. He hesitated as if he would deny it, then nodded.

Narcissa looked back out the window and spoke her thoughts aloud. "I was here once . . . for a wedding party. It must have been four years ago."

She was surprised when Archer answered, "Yes. I was here that day as well."

She turned back to see him looking at her. Her memory of Manakin seemed to come from a century ago, another life. It was soon after their own marriage that she and Rives had attended the grand party celebrating the marriage of John and Dorothea Berton. Caught up in her own romance, she had seen the newlywed couple, the gaily dressed guests, as bright blurs. With the passage of time, her world had darkened. She had become a widow. Now something had cast a shadow over Manakin too.

The carriage pulled up at the end of the drive. Uniformed men with rifles and torches were running back and forth between the house and the outbuildings. Even those soldiers who were still had something in the very stillness, the tension, of their poses that cracked with alarm. This was strange enough, but there was something stranger. It took a moment before Narcissa realized what it was. Nowhere among any of these people— running, standing, watching—were there any black faces.

As he handed Narcissa down from the carriage, Archer spoke in a rapid whisper. "The women slaves must be questioned, three of them. Thought they might open up to one of their own, so I got Judah Daniel. You are to be witness to everything they tell her. And think of how we might induce her to keep quiet about it."

Judah Daniel and Narcissa Powers followed Cameron Archer down a lane past several outbuildings—a kitchen, two cabins for the house servants—to a pair of little windowless buildings no more than ten feet square. The nearer appeared to be guarded by one soldier, the farther by no less than three.

Archer stopped at the first and spoke to the soldier closest to the door. As he did so, a man with officer's insignia hurried down the path from the house, holding up his hand palm-out as if to stop them. Archer looked up. "Bloody hell!" Judah Daniel heard him say under his breath. He stepped quickly to intercept the man.

Judah Daniel saw the other man's shoulders bunch up and his face redden as if he'd been slapped. She couldn't hear his words, but his glances in the women's direction and his fighting stance showed he wasn't yielding easily to Archer's demand that they be admitted. The women were left on the path for a long moment while the two men argued. Archer had his slouch hat off and was thwacking it against his thigh as if he wanted to hit the other man but couldn't let himself do it.

At last the other man stalked off, and Archer came back down the steps. His words were polite, but his voice was rough with anger. "I apologize for keeping you waiting."

He collected himself and went on more calmly. "Mrs. Powers, Judah Daniel, I know this will seem strange to you. I am not going to explain anything about the women you will see. I think it's important to get your impressions first, before you learn anything of the background of these individuals or why they are locked up. I want you to examine these women. If they are able to respond, get them to tell you what happened here today." He hesitated a moment, then went on. "A couple of them were wild at first, tearing their clothes and dashing themselves against the walls. I had their hands tied lest they do an injury to themselves, so of course they cannot hurt you. There will be a guard stationed outside the door in any case—all you need to do is call out."

The soldier swung open the door to a little storehouse. The only light came from the lantern held by the soldier waiting outside the door. Archer remained outside; Judah Daniel could hear him berating the guard about the filthy conditions in which the *prisoners* were being kept. *Prisoners . . .* On the bare wooden floor lay four women and a child, house servants by the color of their skin and their dress. The women's hands were tied together at the wrists with strips of cloth. Judging by the smell, and the filth on the floor, the women had lain there for hours.

The child, about ten years old, was lying in the corner. Judah Daniel went over to her first and found her fast asleep. She let her lie.

The first woman she came to looked to be about sixty. Her gray homespun dress was torn and marked with slimy, foul-smelling stains. Judah Daniel knelt beside her and put her hand on the woman's forehead, then on her throat, where the pulse beat fast under her hand. The touch held all the tenderness and reassurance Judah Daniel could put into it, and the woman responded by opening her eyes. She moved cracked, whitened lips and whispered the word "Thirsty."

Judah Daniel looked into her face, then turned to Narcissa, who was standing a few paces behind her. "Ask for some water, and a candle." As soon as the words were out, she stopped to wonder how the white woman would take what might seem to her an order, but even as she wondered, Narcissa went to the door and relayed the request to the guard who stood outside.

Judah Daniel sat stroking the woman's forehead. She could feel the tense muscles relax, and then a warm wetness on her hand. Silent tears were running down the woman's face.

The water came, in a brown mug smelling of earth. The soldier handed it in, and after it a candle in a tin holder with a looped handle. Narcissa offered them to Judah Daniel. She took the water first, put her left arm under the woman's shoulders, and held her head so she could drink. When the woman stopped drinking, Narcissa took the cup and placed the candle in Judah Daniel's hand.

"Can you see me?" Judah Daniel asked the woman softly. The woman opened her eyes wide and looked into her face. Judah Daniel moved the candle into the woman's line of sight. She squinted and turned away. Judah Daniel handed the candle back to Narcissa. The woman's eyes sought Judah Daniel's face again as if reassured by it.

"How you feeling?" Judah Daniel asked.

"You the angel?" The question was asked with curiosity, maybe a little hope, not much fear that Judah Daniel could see.

"What happened?" Judah Daniel asked, as gently as before.

"It was"—the whisper was so faint Judah Daniel had to put her ear almost to the woman's mouth—"the trumpet of the Angel Gabriel. I seen the light over their heads. I see it now, over yours. Little devils . . . play in the light. Don't you see them?" Now the woman's eyes were searching the air between her own face and Judah Daniel's. "They get inside my head, inside my clothes. I can't get my hands up to brush them away, so I close my eyes."

"Huh?" Just a murmured breath with a question in it: too much curiosity would alarm her, drive her back into silence.

"The trumpet blow on the Day of Judgment. *We will not all die, but we will all be changed.*" The woman's eyes were wide on Judah Daniel's. "Are they . . . all dead?"

In the windowless, stinking room, Judah Daniel felt cold. Those words—*all dead.* Something terrible had happened, worse than she'd imagined. This woman was one of its victims. Something, fear maybe, had driven her out of her wits. Archer had said the women were tearing their clothes off, dashing themselves against the walls. Like the Bible story of the man who had devils in him and lived among the tombs, crying and cutting himself with stones. Jesus asked his name. *My name is Legion,* the devils had spoken through the man, *for we are many.*

The woman's eyes were shut now, so tight her whole face strained with the effort. Was she blotting out what was before her now or something she recalled? Judah Daniel gave her a last caressing stroke across the forehead and said, "It ain't your fault. Ain't nothing you could have done."

She moved the candle to illuminate another woman lying in her own filth, this one much younger than the first. Her eyes were closed, and her heartbeat fluttered fast and uncertain. Judah Daniel held her up and let the water trickle between her lips, then gently lowered her back onto the floor.

The third woman slept as soundly as the child. A light sifting of flour was still visible on her dress. The cook, Judah Daniel thought.

The fourth woman lay as straight and quiet as a corpse laid out for burial, her pleasant, unlined face relaxed in complete repose. Judah Daniel touched her forehead, her hands, her throat. She's died, Judah Daniel thought, feeling no pulse beating under the cool, dry skin. At last she felt it, a sluggish, almost imperceptible throb. She spoke to her in a low, friendly voice, then took her by the shoulder and shook her gently: no response.

The door opened to admit Cameron Archer, who crossed the filthy floor in two strides to stand over the corpselike woman. "She's been like that since they found her. Look at this." Archer bent over the woman. Narcissa came up to stand behind him. He took hold of the woman's left wrist, which was not manacled, extended her arm to its length, and raised it over her head. Then he took his hand away. The arm stayed suspended in the air.

Archer looked around at them, so engrossed in the woman's symptoms he seemed to forget he was not addressing medical students. "I tried this earlier today. It'll take fifteen minutes, maybe half an hour, for the arm to descend. Meanwhile, she will show no signs of strain. She is not frozen by a deliberate act of will. It's catalepsy. I've only seen one other case like it, and that in a man who'd been insane for years. Yet a day ago, this woman was apparently perfectly normal and had never shown signs of lunacy."

Catalepsy. Judah Daniel remembered when Darcy, her ward, now eight years old, had first come to her. Darcy, a toddler then, had been badly burned on the face by a kitchen fire. The tiny child had been like a rag doll, like a body that the spirit had gone out of, for weeks had barely moved, didn't speak for nearly a year after. So Judah Daniel had seen something a little like this. Whatever it was made the woman this way, it had to be something terrible.

Archer turned toward the door, motioning Judah Daniel and Narcissa to follow him. They went back up the path and into the comfortably furnished outbuilding that apparently served as the plantation's office. There was a fire going, and an oil lamp on the desk. The light and warmth felt good on Judah Daniel's skin, and she wished it could sink down into her bones. Archer took his position behind one of the slatted wooden chairs, hands gripping its back, foot resting on the rung below the seat.

"I have brought you both here to help unlock the secrets of the crime these persons—and one other—are accused of committing. Before I go any further, I must have your assurance, Judah Daniel, that you will not try to hide or distort the truth, whatever the consequences should be. Can you give me that assurance?"

Judah Daniel returned his gaze for a moment. "You mean, if I hear or see something means they're guilty, I tell it and not stand in the way of their punishment." Archer nodded. "I make that pledge," Judah Daniel answered. Long as I get to decide for myself what's guilty, she added to herself. These women need somebody's help, don't look like anyone else is offering. "But if I can prove to you they ain't done nothing, you got so see to it they ain't punished."

Archer looked away. Judah Daniel saw the questioning go across his face. It showed he knew how hard it would be to keep his side of the bargain. Like as not, he'd brought her here to get the women's confidence, disarm them into saying something to her that would be heard—and reported to Archer—by Narcissa Powers. But it was to his credit that he looked uneasy.

At last Archer met her eyes. "Agreed," he said.

Judah Daniel nodded slowly.

'Well, then," Archer said, apparently satisfied, "what are your impressions of the women you have just seen?"

"What are their names?" she asked Archer.

"Of those you came across first, the older is named Dorcas, and the youngest is her daughter, Zemora. The cataleptic is called Hetty. She has no relations on the place. The fourth woman is the cook, Clara. The child is the kitchen maid, Litabet. Clara is her grandmother."

Narcissa spoke up. "They must have been through a terrible ordeal of some sort, something that sickened them and drove them out of their senses. With rest, though, and the assurance that they are safe . . . But the way they were tied up, locked in . . . Did they do something—wrong—while they were out of their heads like that?"

Judah Daniel nodded. "If it wasn't for the crazy talk, I'd just think they ate some spoiled food. Except for Hetty. But this was something, had a strong force over them." Or someone, whose power over them was so great that their effort to resist drove them mad. A conjurer? What was it they had been made to do?

She asked the question. "What was it they done?"

Archer's face took on the don't-tread-on-me look of a surgeon whose patient has just died. "Three members of the Berton family were butchered, throats slashed, by their house servants, apparently. Except for the butler, the servants are all women. The women you have seen."

Narcissa gasped. Judah Daniel felt her jaw tighten, keeping in the anger. It wasn't that she was surprised at his words—she'd been prepared for strong accusations. Still, it was hard to believe that the women she had seen could even be suspected of something like that, done in such a bloody way. She had heard of slave women who had murdered their masters or mistresses by poisoning, or smothering with a pillow. She suspected it happened more than people knew. But this didn't look like killing to escape punishment, or to strike back after unbearable pain. For all these slaves to go mad at one time, to use knives—it was as if they were writing a message in blood.

Archer recounted the scene described by Colonel Berton on his return home: the house at first giving no sign of occupancy; the apparently imbecile slave child grabbing at invisible insects in front of her eyes; the table laid for four; the entrance into rooms in which his wife, mother, and father lay slaughtered, their servants lying nearby, weapons to hand; the nurse hiding with the baby, her own consciousness gone into hiding within her body.

"Do you really think those women did murder? Can't they at least be cleaned up, made more comfortable?" Narcissa asked, and saw Archer's mouth twist with anger.

"I've already spoken to Harris about the filthy state they're in. They'll be taken to Richmond soon. I'll see to it they are treated more humanely. Now: do I think they did murder?" Archer gripped the back of the chair so tightly that his knuckles showed white. "The old master was found with his throat cut. His wounds differed from those of the women. Both women were killed with a smooth stroke across, moving the knife from left to right. Knives were found in or near their maids' hands, but they weren't the knives used to do the killing. They were too dull. One was a penknife." A humorless smile lifted the corners of Archer's mouth.

"The old man had two wounds. One, I suspect, was done with the same weapon as the injuries to the women. But another cut had been made over the first, and it nearly took off his head. It was made by a hundred-year-old sword that hung over the fireplace in the library. There is clear evidence that the second cut was made by the servant Hiram.

"But I believe that all is not what it appears. I believe Hiram did the killings but tried to put the blame on the women for all but the one which he surely did. I suspect the women are innocent. But I fear that, despite the precautions that have been taken to prevent it, the story will get out. There will be a clamor to put all of them to death, and I'm not sure I can prevent it. And if what happened here inspires more killings, which God forbid—that would surely lead to widespread reprisals taken against slaves and free blacks."

Judah Daniel said nothing but sighed inwardly. The doctor hadn't said anything she hadn't already thought of. But coming from him, it was a threat, a warning to her to keep silent about what she had seen and heard, and it chafed her like the manacles they had put on her at McDaniel's Negro Jail when, a few months back, she had been falsely accused of doctoring whites. Violence against us, slave and free, is everywhere, every day, she thought. If we try to fight violence with violence, we're just tightening our own chains. The bitter despair this threat called up in her made her feel once again how satisfying it would be to strike out.

She was a root doctor, a conjure woman, she could kill as well as cure. She'd come close before to taking justice into her own hands against a cruel master. She'd even planned how she would kill him and never be found out. Then she felt what it was doing to her own soul. The feeling of power, of purpose, centered in her. It had an aftertaste of sin. She'd known it wasn't God putting the thought in her mind.

The call to kill another human being could come from God, she supposed. No one doubted that was true. Moses had been living a comfortable life as an Egyptian when he had killed a man for striking a Hebrew slave, and God turned that crime into deliverance for the people of Israel. But the call could be a false one: now, half the whites in the country were seeking to kill the other half in causes they believed came from God. But what had happened here, and the wreckage of bodies and minds it had left, must have come from Lucifer, son of the morning, the bright and fallen angel.

Archer explained briefly about the presence of Mr. and Mrs. Cantrell, who, as neighbors and kin, had been called to help John Berton. Judah Daniel was sent to wait in the kitchen with the maidservant that had accompanied Mrs. Cantrell, while Narcissa was taken to sit with the lady herself in the green-painted family parlor of Manakin.

There in the near corner of the room Narcissa saw the baby's cradle. She made a little apologetic smile at the woman, then went to look at the fair-haired child, who slept with his fist burrowed into his plump cheek and his mouth slightly open. He was more than a baby—a year or even eighteen months old. Narcissa watched him sleep for a long moment, fighting the impulse to pick him up and comfort him for a loss he was too young to comprehend. It was she who would be comforted, she realized, by the weight of his small body in her arms, reminding her of her own baby she had held for so short a time. Sighing, she turned to take a seat near Mrs. Cantrell.

"The child is so precious," Narcissa said to her.

The woman seemed to become aware of Narcissa for the first time, her gaze traveling up Narcissa's skirts and bodice to her face. Mrs. Cantrell's own face—thin, middle-aged, pinched into lines of discontent—was disapproving. Narcissa looked down, saw the stains on the red silk gown— that gown that she now knew she would never wear again—and wondered if she stank from the bodily effluvia that had fouled the storehouse. She felt shame for an instant, then wondered how a woman who'd just had relatives brutally murdered could be troubled by a smell. Maybe hospital work has coarsened me, she thought, with interest more than regret.

"I am so sorry about your loss," Narcissa said gently. The woman nodded acknowledgment, her cold expression unchanging.

"I am sorry," Narcissa said again, apologizing this time rather than offering sympathy, which was so clearly unwelcome. "They did not tell me how you are related. . . ."

The woman frowned. "I am Mrs. Cantrell," she said in a clipped accent. "My husband is Colonel John Berton's cousin. Of Cantrell Hall, of course. *I* am from New York," she added, as if Cantrell Hall were a secondary distinction.

"What a terrible tragedy this was," Narcissa said to fill the silence.

"Yes," Mrs. Cantrell said, glancing off into the fire. "Everyone will say so. Of course, I always knew she would come to a bad end. Though to be murdered by one's own slaves . . ." Mrs. Cantrell shuddered and pulled her shawl tighter around her shoulders. "Slavery must be abolished."

Narcissa was surprised. Even if Mrs. Cantrell was faithful to the abolitionist principles of her native state, this was hardly the time and place to voice that opinion.

Mrs. Cantrell continued. "It would be far better if they were all returned to Africa. There is a degenerate strain in the race. White Southerners think they are immune to it. *Ha!* He that toucheth pitch shall be defiled. My

husband"—her lips curled away from the word as if it had a bad taste—
"thinks his slaves are loyal. He boasts about that body servant of his, Ike,
how loyal he is. *I* know Ike would as soon stab him in the back as brush his
coat. Look what John Berton's man, Quintus, did: saw his opportunity and
slipped across to the North. And what do we want with them there, I ask
you, with no cotton to be picked? The women are just as bad: dirty, deceit-
ful, no morals. My maid, Kezia, is cleaner than most, but I watch her, I
don't let her get familiar. I control her. John Berton could not control his
slaves."

This pronouncement sounded final, but the woman went on in an
undertone, "Or his wife, either."

Narcissa fixed startled eyes on the woman's face and was surprised to
see her teeth bared in a mirthless grin that did not reach her pale blue eyes.
"They will say, 'What a tragedy—so young and beautiful, a wife and a
mother.' " Mrs. Cantrell paused, seemingly in the grip of some emotion
that was forcing its way out of her in her speech. "A whore of a wife, and a
bitch of a mother! And what an irony. The baby calls for his slave nurse,
not for his mother!"

Narcissa stared, horrified at the words and the hatred they expressed.
Mrs. Cantrell's face went white; her smile vanished. Then she gathered her
skirts in her hands and turned herself away from Narcissa, toward the fire.
The woman's back was ramrod straight, but her shoulders shook a little, as
if she were sobbing—or, Narcissa thought with revulsion, laughing.

After a few seconds, Narcissa rose. "I am very sorry to have disturbed
you," she said in a low voice, then went out of the room into the grand
hall. There she perched on an armless chair and waited, relieved to be out
of the company of a woman who seemed so much more evil than the ones
accused of murder.

Manakin's kitchen was a one-room building, a little larger than the storehouse, made of whitewashed brick. The fire had gone out in the spacious
fireplace, and a candle in a simple tin sconce hung on the wall was the only
source of light. There Judah Daniel had found Mrs. Cantrell's servant, a
pretty, thirtyish woman named Kezia.

"What do you think happened here?" Judah Daniel asked.

"Think?" the servant repeated, laughter in her voice. "What call would I
have to be thinking? Deaf and blind, that's me—when it comes to goings-
on of white folks."

"And dumb, most of all." Judah Daniel joined in the joke.

The servant barked a short laugh in response. "I know one thing, though. I expect what happened here work on my mistress better than her tonic."

"*How* you say?" Judah Daniel responded in disbelief.

Kezia nodded, face twisted in an ironic smile. "She hated that young Mrs. Berton, Mr. John's wife. Hated the interest her own husband took in his cousin's wife. Oh, yes, Mrs. John Berton was mad for anything in pants, except maybe her own husband. She been going to Richmond a lot, I hear, since her husband left for the army. And Mr. Cantrell, he spend more time in the city than he do at the plantation these days. That's a relief to the young girls on the place. But when Mr. John went off to war, my master was rubbing his hands and licking his lips." She pantomimed the motions. "I reckon if the war lasts, Mr. Cantrell have to go sometime, but meanwhile he was going to have him a feast. I heard the mistress screaming at him, begging him to get him up a regiment and go fight. That surprised me, being as she come from up North, and I know for a fact she want to go back. He say no, if he join up there be nobody to look after Cantrell Hall . . . and Manakin. When the mistress heard him say Manakin, she broke down sobbing. She called for a double dose of her tonic and took to her bed."

"The young girls?" Judah Daniel asked. "Does Cantrell bother the womenfolk on the place?"

"Oh, Lord, yes. But I tell them, scared as they is of him, he scareder of his wife. He ain't never bothered me since the day I told him if he laid a hand on me again, she'd know about it." Kezia made her strong, capable hands into fists and rested them on her hips. She didn't look like a woman to be trifled with.

"What about John Berton, and the old man, his father? Did they mess with their women in the quarters?"

"No," Kezia said, shaking her head, "I ain't never heard that they did." Kezia dropped her voice. "Is it true the old folks got took off, them and Mrs. John, just like that? The house servants too?"

Judah Daniel gave Kezia a look that said she could not confirm the rumor but would not deny it.

Kezia's eyes widened. Then she teased Judah Daniel. "I know: you don't say nothing, you *dumb* just like me."

Kezia excused herself to see to her mistress. Judah Daniel walked over to the wall and lifted the candle sconce down from the nail on which it hung.

She walked around the room, directing the candle's light onto the table, lifting lids and peering into pots. All were scrubbed clean. She ended with the fireplace, where she looked into the copper kettle, so big around her arms could not have encircled it, that hung on the pothook. It too was empty. Below it the ashes were piled high in the grate. Picking up the poker that rested nearby, she poked in the ashes. She dug at a sticky residue she found at the bottom, then brought the end of the poker close to her nose and sniffed. Something other than wood had been burned there, she thought, something with juice or sap in it, but it had burned so thoroughly that she could not tell what it had been. Nor could she tell why the discovery seemed to nudge her mind like it wanted her attention.

Archer walked up to the guard at the door of the smokehouse and spoke a few words in a low tone. The boy opened the door just wide enough to let him pass through, then closed it again. Archer heard the key turning, locking the door behind him. He was alone now with a slave who had killed three whites. What kind of monster could do such things?

The lantern Archer carried cast the only light. Except for the hanging carcasses of hogs, and the reeking can in the corner where the prisoner had relieved himself, there was nothing in the room, not even straw to form a pallet. Hiram was sitting on the floor, back against the wall, knees drawn up to his chest. Archer stood just inside the door and studied the man. His hair was thick and white, cut close to his head. He had medium brown skin, a wide, intelligent forehead, a broad nose, and smallish eyes—now very red—that turned down slightly at the corners. The bloody clothes in which he'd been found had been replaced with a homespun shirt made to pull over the head and shapeless pants held around his waist by a rope.

Archer crossed the room in three strides and stood over the slave, who looked up at him. There was neither hope nor fear on Hiram's face. Archer bent down and held the lantern in front of him. His pupils contracted, and he squinted a little, but he did not flinch. Archer bent his knees and lowered himself to sit on his haunches, placing the lantern to the side. He took hold of Hiram's hands and drew them outward so as to see the palms. Hiram's only movement was to shift more of his weight to his back where it was braced against the wall.

Archer flexed Hiram's fingers outward to open his hands. Hiram winced. Archer examined both hands, front and back. There were deep cuts across the insides of the fingers and palms of Hiram's left hand.

"Did you feel it?"

Hiram looked at him, waiting as if to see what the doctor had guessed.

"You took the sword and held it like this in both hands." Archer held out Hiram's two hands in front of him, palms down, wrapped the fingers into fists. "You grasped the hilt in your right hand. Your left hand took hold of the blade. It must have hurt like hell. Did you feel it?" Archer asked again, more insistently. Hiram nodded.

Archer rose to his feet, pulling Hiram up with him. He held the slave by his wrists.

"Why did you kill him?"

Hiram exhaled a deep breath. "Because, fifty-seven years ago, he sold my brother."

Archer tightened his grip on the old man's wrist. His voice was cold, disbelieving. "You killed your master for something he did more than half a century ago?"

The slave nodded, eyes still fixed on a point over Archer's shoulder.

"What about the others?" Archer's voice was low now, menacing. "Two women. Had they spoken to you sharply about the folding of a napkin?"

Hiram shook his head. His eyes, veiled by their drooping lids, looked weary.

Archer paused a moment. Then: "Why did you wait so long to kill your master?"

Hiram's eyes shifted, met Archer's. There was pride in his voice. "I been told to kill when the trumpet give the signal."

He went on, as if suddenly eager to explain, to be understood. "The women . . . I ain't glad they dead, and I ain't sorry. But the old man . . . I been waiting since I was ten years old for the chance to kill him."

Archer dropped the black man's wrists and stepped back. "So, Hiram," he said almost conversationally, "you're sixty-seven years old. You won't see sixty-eight. You might as well be out with it. You killed those women."

Silence.

"You put bloody knives next to their bodies so the blame would fall on the maidservants."

Hiram's mouth twitched in a grimace. He looked as if he would speak. But he pressed his lips together and said nothing.

Archer drew back his right arm and slapped the old man across the cheek.

Hiram's head was still turned aside from the force of the slap when he said, "The angel blowed the trumpet."

"What?" Archer growled.

Hiram spoke softly, slowly. " 'At the last trump . . . we shall not die . . . but we shall all be changed.' "

"Don't quote the Bible to me! You're not crazy." Archer drew back his hand to strike again. Then he let his hand fall at his side and stood staring at the slave. At last he spoke. "Think about it, Hiram. Those who question you next won't be so gentle with you."

Returning to Richmond at last in the carriage, Narcissa pondered the strange case of the maddened, murderous slaves. What was this disease that affected the mind? "Can'st thou not minister to a mind diseased?" Was that *Hamlet* or *Macbeth*? Lady Macbeth, seeing again in sleep the blood she could not clean from her hands, and washing, washing . . .

How could servants, women, as plain and peaceable as these seemed to be, ever have become entangled in this horror? Was it possible that the madness that had gripped them could spread to other plantations, drive others to murder?

Or was there another explanation, a more familiar madness?

Narcissa opened her eyes. "Judah Daniel?" she whispered. The woman next to her shifted. In the faint, erratic light from the carriage lantern, Narcissa could see her face, masklike, with its sharp chiseled lines.

Narcissa spoke in a low voice. "I met someone tonight who seemed to me capable of killing. But it wasn't those women, the servants. It was Mrs. Cantrell. She hated the younger Mrs. Berton, the colonel's wife."

Judah Daniel looked at Narcissa for a moment. Then she said, "Her maid told me the same thing, there in that kitchen. Mr. Cantrell been chasing after young Mrs. Berton, and she been leading him on." For just a moment emotion was visible on her face. It was anger. "No white man ever going to do it, but I reckon there's a couple people ought to get some hard questions asked them."

"Yes." Narcissa spoke slowly, gathering her thoughts. "Mrs. Cantrell may have so hated her rival that she induced Hiram to kill her, and the older Bertons as well. Or perhaps Mr. Cantrell was maddened with jealousy, since Colonel Berton was returning home. And the Cantrells seem to be the closest relatives. Perhaps . . . what if Colonel Berton was supposed to be killed as well? He was expected that day. What if Cantrell's plan was to kill them all, so that he could inherit Manakin—only John Berton came too late?" Narcissa reached over and put her hand on Judah Daniel's arm. "I truly believe that Dr. Archer wants justice done. If we find out something of importance, even if it goes against Mr. or Mrs. Cantrell, he will listen."

Then she took her hand away and sat back, wondering if what she had asserted about Archer was true. She wondered, too, about her own ability to ask questions of everyone whose answers could be important. How could she scrape an acquaintance with Mr. Cantrell, without him taking her for an adventuress? She breathed out a sigh that seemed to carry her bold resolution with it. Then she thought of Brit Wallace. He could go where she and Judah Daniel could not. She had trusted him before. Maybe she should do so again.

Chapter Four

MANAKIN

EARLY THE NEXT MORNING

Zemora, maid and perhaps murderer of Dorothea Berton, died just after midnight. The other slaves implicated in the crimes—by proximity to the bodies and by symptoms of madness—would be taken to Richmond. They were Hiram; Dorcas, the elder Mrs. Berton's maid; Clara, the cook; Hetty, young Johnny's nurse; and the kitchen maid Litabet. They would be confined at the city jail on Twenty-second Street, a dilapidated building whose stout brick walls and stone floors nevertheless served their purpose.

Cameron Archer had not opposed Major Harris in this decision. Archer was saving for a different battle any ammunition he might have through his connections with the army, the medical school, and the city.

"I am taking the bodies of Mr. and Mrs. Berton and Mrs. Dorothea Berton to Richmond for autopsy. I assure you that I will perform the anatomies myself, and that the utmost secrecy will be preserved." Archer phrased the statement so as not to seem to be asking permission, but no nicety of phrasing was able to deflect Harris's reaction.

"Autopsy! Certainly not!" Harris's face went an unhealthy red. "It's iniquitous to put Colonel Berton through more suffering. And for what? The cause of death could scarcely be more obvious. In each case, the murderer was still in the room, with the murder weapon close by. Hiram has confessed, and likely the others will do so as well as soon as they find out their humbug of pretended insanity is not fooling anyone."

Harris's sneer made Archer's hands ball up into fists, but he kept them at his side and replied coolly, "It's obvious their throats were cut, certainly.

But consider: a maid attacks her mistress, a healthy woman not past her twenty-third year, with a penknife. Her mistress remains reclining on her chaise longue, not making any attempt to defend herself sufficient to break a fingernail or dislodge a hairpin. And the old master and mistress are equally obliging to *their* servants. There's nothing to indicate they so much as raised a hand in self-defense."

"They must have been asleep," Harris protested.

Archer persisted, speaking with exaggerated patience. "To cut someone's throat with a penknife—even a very sharp one, which this one was not—you'd have to hack through it. She slept through that? And to do it with a sword, like the one found by James Berton's body—even a very sharp sword, which this one was not"—he repeated the phrase—"you'd have to stand over the person and drag the blade across. In fact, the sword cut was made by the middle part of the blade, with a sawing motion; made, I believe, after the old man was already dead." He was speaking faster now. "The cut that killed him was made with a very sharp, thin-bladed knife, the same knife that was used to cut the two women's throats, and this knife we haven't found yet. What does that suggest to you?"

"It suggests," Harris said coldly, "that if I came to you to have a corn removed, I would be in very grave danger of having my leg amputated. When I explain the facts to the provost marshal, I am sure he will agree with me. You are manufacturing complexities where none exist. These concerns of yours are just a diversion from the business we should be about: bringing the accused slaves to Richmond, and to execution."

"Very well. I shall get the necessary permission from John Berton." With that, Archer turned on his heel and walked away. How Harris—who'd made a good deal of money as a tobacco broker but whose family had come from who knows where—had inflated himself in his association with Provost Marshal Winder! If men like these could pretend to lead the new government, then the Confederacy had best be dissolved at once, for the Yankees had already won.

Composing himself, Archer went out to talk with Berton, who despite the chill in the night air was sitting on a stone bench in the terraced orchard behind the house, looking down to where the river ran invisible in the dark.

Archer sat next to him. "John, you know how much I feel for your loss. Please do not be offended if I am direct. I want to perform an autopsy."

John Berton turned toward him. "Autopsy?"

"On your mother and father. And . . . Dorothea." This was harder than he'd thought it would be, Archer realized, conscious of the shudder that ran through John Berton's body. "I am not satisfied that the facts are as they appear to be."

"But Harris . . . he seems satisfied?"

"He is," Archer admitted, "but I am not. As a doctor, there are things . . . I believe the attacks may have been committed by a single hand."

"Oh, by whom?" Berton responded in a voice dulled by pain. "Do you think Hiram alone was responsible?"

"I think so." Archer answered carefully. "But I need to get a better look at the wounds."

"All right, then," John said resignedly. "If you must." He looked out toward the river, his fists resting on his thighs, pressing down hard. "She had the most beautiful skin. Like a baby's, white and perfect. She was most particular about it. The sun never touched it."

He is thinking about the dissector's knife piercing that skin, Archer thought with a pang. *But there is nothing I can say.*

Berton went on. "She was so young. She never should have married me." Berton put his face in his hands. Archer patted him on the back and walked quietly away so as not to humiliate him by witnessing his tears.

RICHMOND

When Narcissa arrived back at the Powerses' house just west of Richmond, it was quite late. She was surprised to see that Mirrie was still awake, sitting up in bed with a book open on her knees.

"Narcissa!" Mirrie exclaimed, looking up over her reading glasses. "Whatever was the emergency?"

Narcissa stood in the doorway, reluctant to enter the room. An interrogation by Mirrie concerning the events of the night was the last thing she wanted. "Just one of those cases where they prefer to have a woman in attendance," she said vaguely, putting a cheerful face over her weary and anxious thoughts. She wanted to tell Mirrie, to gain her sympathy for the accused women, and her help—for Mirrie would be fierce in their defense, she knew.

But that very ferocity kept Narcissa silent. Cameron Archer had stressed the need for secrecy so strongly that Narcissa had realized that the doctor's own reputation was on the line. In order to get her and Judah Daniel into Manakin, Archer had argued down Major Harris. If word of the murders got out, Harris would find it convenient to blame two women with no official standing—and, through them, to blame Archer.

"Well, after you left the party, I did something rather silly, I'm afraid," said Mirrie, sitting up and patting the bed next to her. Narcissa went in then and sat beside her. There were lines of weariness around Mirrie's blue-green eyes, but there was a sparkle in them that Narcissa had not seen for some time. "I announced—or, at least, implied—to Mrs. Archer Jennings that I intended to call on the Cohens. Now the news of my engagement to Mr. Cohen will be meeting me on every side, however much I deny it."

"You intended to call? But you did not?" Narcissa asked.

Mirrie shrugged. "No. Frankly, I find all the Cohen ladies—his mother, his brother's wife, his widowed sister—a little overwhelming. But when I arrived here, there was an unexpected caller in *our* parlor: Colonel Cohen himself. He was visiting my father, of course, but waiting for me. Poor Father had fallen asleep in his chair!"

Despite Mirrie's studied nonchalance, the news that Nat Cohen had called delighted Narcissa. "How is he?" she asked eagerly. Mr. Cohen was a good man, and she often found herself wishing that Mirrie would allow him to propose marriage—and that she would accept, though it seemed unlikely, given her heated rejection of his suit.

"He is well," Mirrie responded offhandedly. "We got into the most ferocious argument." Mirrie ran a hand through her red curls, faded now with streaks of white, and lifted them away from her face. "I simply remarked that Lincoln's claim to moral authority was undermined by his rejection of Fremont's insistence that the slaves in Missouri be emancipated. Mr. Cohen turned beet-red and lost no time in taking his leave. I was disappointed, I admit," Mirrie went on. "I was so hoping for a friendly wrangle, such as we used to have, before—"

"Before Mr. Cohen took on the uniform and pledged his life to a government you berate at every turn! Really, Mirrie, how do you expect Mr. Cohen to converse when you imply that the cause he is fighting for is immoral?"

Mirrie snapped back, "It *is* immoral."

"No! I will not let you say it! Slavery may be immoral, as you believe, but we are fighting now for *our country*. If we are not for our own country, we are traitors. If we lose this war, crowded hospitals will give place to crowded prisons—and scaffolds!"

Mirrie shifted her weight, looked away. Narcissa expected an angry retort, but Mirrie's words were mild. "Ah, so you *can* stand up for yourself, my dear. Remember, when next Dr. Archer gives you an order contrary to all reason: I have shown you what you are capable of!" She smiled a rueful half-smile. "God help us, Narcissa, we are all of us in a sad fix."

Mirrie held out her hand. Narcissa clasped it for a moment, then wished her friend good night.

As Narcissa headed wearily for her own room, she pondered the secret she was keeping from Mirrie. Had Mirrie been less preoccupied, had she pressed Narcissa about where she had been, the story might have come tumbling out. It would be a relief to tell what she had seen and heard: the helpless women accused of murder; the little child left to the care of his coldhearted cousin; the knife strokes that not only destroyed one plantation family but struck at a whole way of life. But what she had to say would only give Mirrie an opportunity to comment once more on the depravity of that way of life. *It is the world we are in,* Narcissa thought, tears of exhaustion welling in her eyes. *It is the life we have.*

Giving in to her lack of sleep, Narcissa stayed home from church that morning but arrived at the medical college hospital at her usual time. Observance of the Sabbath as a day of rest did not apply to nurses. Judah Daniel was there when she arrived, helping turn patients in the beds and change their linen, but the two women talked only of that day's work, not of their experience the night before. This was her first visit to the medical college hospital in almost a week, since she had left to bring Jordan Archer back from Champs-Elysées. She always found it difficult to come back after an absence, to learn that some of "her" patients—men whose wounds she had dressed, whose hopes and fears she had heard and felt in her own heart and written down to send to their loved ones—had died. But the demands of the living soon pushed grief away, a luxury to be indulged in at some other time.

Late in the evening, Cameron Archer came in to check on some difficult cases and asked Narcissa to come see the bodies of the three murdered Bertons. It was not an unpremeditated impulse, she realized; he had chosen a time when no medical students would be in the building. When she suggested bringing along Judah Daniel, he hesitated, but acquiesced, and the three of them crossed over to the Egyptian building together.

Entering between the two stout pillars, under the Egyptian priest-signs of sun disk, curving cobras, and buzzard's wings, always seemed to Narcissa like passing into the realm of the dead. The building's thick walls kept the rooms cool through all but the hottest months. But the building's chill no longer affected her spirits. The sights and smells of death had become familiar. The wounded brought down from Manassas to the medical college hospital, place of last resort, had borne every type of mutilation. She had seen rottenness creep along a limb, delayed but not defeated by the work of the surgeon, until there was nothing left to cut off and gangrene was the victor. She had seen a man brought in ten days after the battle, his head split open, maggots feasting on his living brain. If she had had a pistol, she would have ended his agony herself, but the doctors had sworn an oath: First, do no harm.

In silence they passed down the stairs and into the dissecting room. Bright light from gasoliers flooded the room, which held a half-dozen tables. On three of them, draped sheets outlined grisly burdens. A long counter running the length of the room held basins, bottles, and equipment for chemical testing. The stench of decay was strong: Archer would not have long to complete his work.

Archer scanned the room, and Narcissa followed his gaze. He walked over to the table on the left, pulled the sheet away from the face, and beckoned to the women.

The face was that of an old woman. The withered skin was just a little grayer than the sheet. The wound that had drained away her life was a vivid purple-red slash. Narcissa could see that it was a clean cut: the edges were smooth, puckered a little now but not torn by repeated attempts to saw through the flesh and sinews, the muscular windpipe. The knife had been sharp, the stroke assured, severing veins and arteries. Death had come in the few moments it would take the heart to pump out its life's blood.

She sensed Archer watching for her reaction. She stopped to examine what she was feeling. Not horror. Certainly not the fear that had risen in her for a moment when the specter of slave rebellion had been raised. For the moment, at least, this slashed throat represented a problem to be solved, engaging her intellect but not her emotions. What did Judah Daniel make of it? she wondered, but she could not read the black woman's face.

Archer came around the table and crossed to the middle of the three bodies. He rearranged the sheet as before. Narcissa saw a young woman whose mottled face may once have been beautiful. Her luxuriant brown hair had been pulled back from her face and throat, and it poured over the end of the table almost to the floor. The cut on her neck looked identical to the first.

He stepped to the third table. "This is the most interesting of the three." He pulled down the sheet. The old man's head lolled back. "You can see the openings of the trachea and esophagus." Archer gestured as he spoke. "The bone was sawed almost through. I say *sawed,* not *cut.* There are nicks in the bone that show several attempts to get a purchase with the blade."

Narcissa looked down to where the right arm and hand dangled over the side of the table. "Do his hands show any wounds?" she asked Archer.

"No."

Archer led the two women back the way they had come, switching each sheet back into place over the exposed faces.

"You noticed there was no resistance," said Archer. "That is why I insisted on the postmortem examination. When I open the bodies tonight, I expect to find evidence of poison. I suspect the victims were poisoned before their throats were slashed. The poison rendered them unconscious, or at least helpless."

Narcissa suppressed a shudder. There was something so coldhearted about it. Yet if the victims hadn't even known what was happening, wasn't that more merciful than to try to fight off a slashing knife, only to be overpowered at last?

Judah Daniel was nodding, as if she had expected to hear Archer's words. At last she spoke. "The women's clothes was stained with vomit. And Dorcas, her eyes was sensitive to the light. It was something tugging at me, something I knowed deep down but couldn't bring it to mind. Dorcas even said it. *Angel trumpet.*"

Archer motioned with his head for her to continue.

"That's a name for jimsonweed, the white flower fans out like a trumpet. Could be they was poisoned with jimsonweed, both the slaves and the masters."

Jimsonweed. Narcissa knew the plant: it grew to a bush about waist high in neglected fields. Despite the "angelic" appearance of its prominently borne white flower, nature had stamped it with emblems of its malevolence. First, the rank odor of it, a warning to cattle, which would not eat it.

Then the trumpet-shaped blossoms, attractive from a distance, made up of conjoined petals that ended in cruel-looking hooks; and the brown seedpods, roughly the size and shape of a hen's egg but barbed with thorns. She and Charley had played with the black seeds, pretending they were doctors' boluses, but they had known better than to swallow them. That was what would be on the plant at this time of year, the seedpods.

Archer's tired face had regained its energy in response to what Judah Daniel had said. He looked over at Narcissa. "*Datura stramonium*," he said, giving its scientific name. "Called Jamestown weed, hence jimsonweed, from the first Virginia colony. There is a famous account from the early 1700s of its effect on some soldiers who ate it as a boiled salad and suffered temporary insanity for some days afterward."

"Insanity?" Narcissa asked, wondering. "Enough to make someone kill?"

"A murderous rage is not among the known symptoms of datura poisoning." Again, it was as if they were his students. "Dilated pupils—clever of you to notice that, Judah Daniel. Hallucinations, especially of spots or insects before the eyes; rapid heartbeat; nausea and vomiting; fever; great thirst. In cases where a great deal of poison is ingested, coma and death. One of the servants, Zemora, has died, and Dorcas is comatose. But Clara and the child are returning to themselves, though I doubt they will have any memory of what happened. The condition of the cataleptic has not changed."

"Cataleptic?" Narcissa pursued eagerly. "Were the strange symptoms shown by the child's nurse—Hetty?—also caused by jimsonweed?"

Archer shook his head. "Not likely. I've not seen catalepsy listed among the recorded symptoms. And Hetty was not feverish; her pupils were not dilated." He went on, thinking aloud. "But the other servants—the lady's maids, the cook, the little girl—could have been poisoned with jimsonweed. Why? My guess is, to render them helpless. Too sick to interfere with what was happening, or to give a clear report of it afterward. This supports my view that Hiram did all the killings. It would have been too much for one man to kill three people who were conscious and resisting. Hetty . . . perhaps he meant to poison her as well, but somehow she escaped it."

They went out into the hall. As Archer was locking the door to the dissecting room, Narcissa heard quick footsteps on the stairs. Benjy, the young slave boy who performed odd jobs at the hospital, appeared in the hall, handed a folded piece of paper to Archer, and slipped out again. Archer turned away, unfolded the paper, and read. Narcissa saw him stiffen, heard him swear under his breath. Then he wadded up the paper and threw it hard to the floor. He looked around at them. His jaw was tight with anger when he said the words, "Hiram is dead." He turned away to compose himself for a moment, then went on.

"He was in solitary confinement in the 'black hole' at the city jail. Good God, he'd only been there a few hours! That"—he gestured contemptuously at the paper that lay crumpled on the floor—"said they found him hanged by a rope tied to the grille that covers the spy hole in the door.

"Well, yes"—Archer was staring at the opposite wall, speaking as if in response to an imagined questioner—"he *could* have taken the rope from around his waist, tied one end to the grille, made a noose of the other, put his neck through it, and hanged himself. It would take great self-control for a man to keep his knees bent double for the time it took him to choke to death. But it is not impossible. I long ago ceased to be surprised by what a human being is capable of."

Suddenly he turned and faced the women. "Judah Daniel. You may think that I have already violated our agreement. But I had it by his own admission that Hiram gave his master his death stroke. Even though he had not confessed to the other murders, Hiram got the punishment that was deserved—that was inevitable, whether by his own hand—"

Narcissa watched Judah Daniel's jaw grow tight, holding back words she could not allow herself to say. In the next instant Narcissa was saying them herself.

"The women. What punishment do they deserve, and what will they receive? Will they also be found dead in their cells?" Archer looked startled at her vehemence, but she pressed on, calmer but no less determined. "We have to see them again, question them if they are able to speak: especially Hetty. I've been doing some reading about catalepsy, in my brother's medical books. The condition may be brought by strong and sudden emotion—shock, grief, anger, fear. Hetty must have been terrified, and she fled with the child, hid in the cupboard under the eaves. But when that did not seem safe enough, her mind fled further. If she can be brought back somehow, she may be able to tell what she saw. The suggested treatment is a change in life and surroundings, and"—she paused to remember the exact phrase—" 'removal of the exciting cause.' " She looked up at Archer, her voice low but roughened with anger. "Hetty has been taken, in the dark, in chains, from one confined and stinking prison to another. She has no idea

that the danger she feared is over, is gone." If only to be replaced by another, she added to herself. "We must find out what caused her great emotion, and assure her that it is past."

"How exactly do you propose to do that?" Archer asked with exaggerated patience.

"Let us see the other women again. You say they are returning to themselves. Let Judah Daniel question them. We may find out something from
them that will guide us in our approach to Hetty."

Archer's jaw worked impatiently. "It may take several weeks for them
to recover fully. Even at that, I don't expect them to remember much of
what occurred after the datura was administered. Still, I will consider what
you ask."

Narcissa found her thoughts spiraling out of control. What is essential
here? she asked herself. The women . . . their guilt or innocence. If they
were guilty, had they followed the lead of Hiram? Or of someone else, as
yet unknown? If they were innocent . . . Surely they were innocent. That
was enough to start with.

Judah Daniel left the Egyptian building on foot. Narcissa stood waiting for
the Powers carriage, and Cameron Archer waited with her, arms folded
across his chest, looking up. She followed his gaze to where the stars shone
bright in the clear fall sky.

Archer's voice when it came was as different from his usual commanding tone as night from day. "Strange to think they are up there—Orion,
Ursa Major and Minor, Cassiopeia's Chair—minding the steps in their in-
tricate dance. Our human travails affect them not a whit. Since first we
raised our eyes to look at them, we humans have believed the stars governed what happened here below. Governed even our own puny bodies,
making us sick, making us well. How reassuring it must have been, to
think that they were connected to us."

Archer spoke again, hesitant. "It's been preying on my mind. When Judah Daniel mentioned 'angel trumpet,' I remembered, but I didn't like to
speak of it in front of her. When I questioned him, Hiram said something
like this: 'I was told to kill when the trumpet give the signal,' and 'the angel
blowed the trumpet.' Could there have been someone else there, someone
with a measure of power over Hiram, who instigated the killings somehow, who provided the poison, or at least gave him the notion for it, if not

the 'signal'? I fear Harris may be right in seeing these murders as part of a larger slave rebellion."

Cameron Archer, cold and sharp as a surgical blade. Narcissa had seen Archer the surgeon stand ten hours at a time, up to the elbows in blood, sawing gangrenous limbs from the bodies of men he labored to save. She had seen Archer the scion of old Richmond drawl a compliment that wounded more than any insult. She had even seen him off his guard, forced to laugh at his own pretensions. But to see him unsure of himself was something new.

"Dr. Archer—" Vexed at the shaky sound of her voice, Narcissa stopped and started again. "It is possible that Hiram could have had another accomplice in the murders, one we have not thought of, who stood to gain from the deaths in a different way."

Archer seemed to be waiting to hear her thoughts. Narcissa took a deep breath and went on. "Colonel Berton's arrival was expected. If he had been killed as well as his family members, James Cantrell would have inherited Manakin, or at least been its master until Johnny Berton comes of age."

Archer broke in, his words cutting like a whip. "To accuse a gentleman, and in the absence of any evidence! Had I thought you capable of such dangerous fantasies, Mrs. Powers, I would not have involved you in this."

Narcissa winced but stiffened her backbone. "But you did involve me, however much you may regret it. Never mind; I will do the job you have set me to. One of the slave women may have seen something, and until they are questioned, we are both playing guessing games."

As Archer's frown bore down on her, Narcissa feared that his next words would dismiss her from the investigation entirely. She was less necessary to him, she knew, than Judah Daniel, whom the slave women would trust and whom Archer himself was inclined to trust, based on the fact that she had once taken a risk to save his life. But the frown at last relaxed, and a tight smile lifted the corners of Archer's mouth.

"Touché, Mrs. Powers."

The Powers carriage, with Will Whatley driving, turned the corner and pulled up. Archer offered his arm, but Narcissa shook her head and strode off alone. Archer had not shaken her resolve to investigate the Cantrells; he had simply relieved her of the obligation to tell him about it.

Cameron Archer watched with regret as the carriage made off toward Broad Street. He shook his head. Why was it, he wondered, that he so often felt regret regarding this young woman? She had exercised logic as he would have expected of a man. And he knew her conclusion was worthy of consideration. Why had he refused to acknowledge that? He sighed, then walked slowly back into the Egyptian building, empty now save for the dead. He would welcome a task in which he felt sure of his powers.

Archer returned to the table where Dorothea Berton lay, pulled back the sheet. Even now, it was easy to see what a handsome woman she had been. He put the blade to her breastbone and began.

Once the body was opened, Archer was once again able to put aside kinship and fondness and contemplations of who would or would not grieve. The body that lay before him was reduced to flesh, sinew, bone, organs. His hands moved among them as they would turn the pages of a textbook. But before he could even begin to look for what he expected— evidence of datura poisoning—he found what he did not expect.

Dorothea Berton's uterus was enlarged, the size of both his fists, when it should have been no larger than a plum. Archer shook his head, too sure of what he would find but wishing not to find it. He picked up a scalpel and sliced the uterus open. There it was, a fetus. For a moment, Archer ceased to think in terms of medical texts. John Berton's child would never be born. He would have to be told, and his grief would be multiplied. Archer cut away the umbilical cord, then put down the blade and took the miniature body in his right palm. Not three inches long from head to butt.

"No more than twelve weeks," Archer found himself saying aloud. Then suspicion came like a cold hand on the back of his neck. He made the calculation. John Berton had told him he had not seen his wife for a full four months. This child was not Berton's. Dorothea Berton had been unfaithful to her husband. And now she lay murdered. Was her unfaithfulness the reason she was dead?

Archer settled the fetus back in the womb, stood looking at it for a moment. He pushed his tangled emotions aside, picked up the scalpel again, and laid the blade to the dead woman's stomach.

❦

THE NEXT MORNING

Cameron Archer rode out early, spurring his horse to a gallop along the grass-covered slopes of Shockoe Hill below the residence of President Jefferson Davis. The clean, cold air filled his lungs but could not reach down to the center of him, where the fear lodged. He must go to Harris, tell him about the poison, and request—demand, if necessary—that Judah Daniel and Mrs. Powers be allowed to see the accused slaves. But first he must decide whether to tell Harris about the fetus. Something in him rebelled against betraying Berton's shame to the contemptible Harris. But was it not his duty to inform the provost marshal's man? No: Harris would use the knowledge clumsily. But if he told Berton himself, Archer reasoned, he could read his reaction, discover whether Berton knew of his wife's pregnancy or, if not that, her infidelity. Archer resolved to call upon the bereaved man, who was staying at the Spotswood Hotel for a day or two longer before leaving to rejoin his regiment. John Berton's reaction to the news would tell him what he had to know.

Cameron Archer had arranged for Judah Daniel, in the company of Narcissa Powers, to speak with Clara, the cook at Manakin, who was the first to recover from the bizarre symptoms of jimsonweed poisoning. An office at the city jail was vacated for the purpose, and Clara entered on the arm of a young black girl whose manner was gentle despite the fact she was employed by the jail.

Clara looked to be about sixty years old. She had a strong, stout frame, though weak still, and there was an energy about her, in her movements and the way she held herself, that Judah Daniel hadn't often seen in prisoners. Clara made her purpose plain with her first words. "Litabet. She my granddaughter. She going to be all right?"

"When I saw her at Manakin, she was sleeping peaceful. Is she with you now?"

Clara nodded, and Judah Daniel thanked God for this mercy, more likely the result of overcrowding in the jail than of any concern on the part of the jailers.

"You tell me: how does she seem?"

"She sleep all right, and she eat what they feed us." Clara answered. "But she real quiet . . . confused . . . sad," she added, her own face sagging with pain for the child.

"Well," Judah Daniel responded carefully, "that ain't nothing but to be expected, with what's happened to her. When y'all was sick, we know now that was from poison, jimsonweed. You and Litabet both had it, and you both come out of it." She wondered if she should say anything about the others, decided she had better not. "You all the family she got?"

Clara nodded. "Her mother passed years ago. And her father—my son—he gone." As she mentioned her son, Clara's eyes shifted away from Judah Daniel's. There was something she didn't want to say in front of the white woman. Judah Daniel resolved to try to find a chance to speak to Clara in private.

"Poisoned," Clara said then. "It don't seem right to me they gone. I been told the Bertons was killed, but it just don't seem *right* to me." The "not right" she was talking about, Judah Daniel realized, was the fact of what had happened, not its moral import. Clara couldn't believe old Mr. and Mrs. Berton and their son's wife were dead. "*Is* that right?" Clara was looking intently at Judah Daniel.

"Yes," Judah Daniel said quietly. "They was murdered."

Clara shuddered. "Poison. I expect when it's poison, the blame fall on the cook. But they don't believe *I* killed them. Master John don't believe *that.*"

"No, he don't believe that," Judah Daniel assured her. She didn't know what Berton believed, really, but she hoped he wasn't so much of a fool as to think this woman had done murder.

"It ain't like I never dreamed what it would be like not to belong to them . . . to be free . . . to be where there wasn't nobody telling me what to do, just me and mine, in my own place." The woman's eyes clouded for a minute, and she swallowed hard. "But just look around you. Can't say them dying done me one bit of good, can you?"

Judah Daniel shook her head in silent agreement. Then she said, "Don't you remember nothing from that day?"

"I made breakfast same as usual. The old mistress was excited about young Mr. John coming home from the war for a while. She kept asking me had I remembered this or that, his favorite things to eat. The master didn't say much. Young Mrs. John, she was acting excited, not in a good way. I reckon she been saving up bones to pick with her husband. I heard her cussing out Litabet, about how the table was set, which showed a mite more care than I'd expect.

"But then, pretty soon after breakfast, I was making biscuits, and I started to feel sick. I ain't never felt nothing like it before. I thought I was dying—sick to my stomach, dizzy, and I couldn't see good. I wanted to go back to my cabin and lay down, it ain't twenty steps from the kitchen, but I couldn't make it. I lay right down there on the floor. And that's the last clear memory I have till I came to in this place. Is it any wonder what they told me happened don't seem right?"

Judah Daniel clasped her hand and held it a moment. Then she asked, "Last *clear* memory, you said?"

Clara frowned. "I'm a Christian woman. Those things that come to me in that sickness, they come from the devil."

"I know what you saying," Judah Daniel replied, "but it may help you to talk about it."

Clara's frown deepened. "I saw flames, and blood. The cooking fire flamed up, and there was a black man in front of it."

"A dark-skinned man?" Judah Daniel asked.

Clara was shaking her head, her mouth twisted with distaste at the memory. "Blacker than any living man. Black like the devil. I was afraid to look at him and afraid to look away. The light from the fire seemed to burn into my eyes. I must have fainted or something."

"Could it have been Hiram?"

Clara laughed. "Oh, no, Judah Daniel, it weren't *Hiram*. It was the devil. But the Lord done spared me thus far. Anyway," she added, "what I seen weren't real. It was just a part of the sickness."

"Did you see Hiram any time that day?"

"Oh, sure, I seen him. Seen him teasing Hetty about something. He liked to get her going with some of his wild tales."

"Tales about what?"

"I don't rightly know," Clara replied after a moment. Judah Daniel wondered if the white woman's presence was causing Clara's hesitation. "The rest of us didn't pay no mind. But Hetty'd get all worked up. She young and . . . a little soft that way, I reckon. Take things to her heart. That's all. There weren't nothing to it," Clara added in a breezy voice, closing the subject.

"Did you see any strangers around, anyone outside of the family?"

"Well," Clara responded dryly, "I done told you I seen the devil. That's *stranger* enough, I reckon."

"You rest now," Judah Daniel said. "Drink lots of water. If you need, I'll give you something to keep your bowels moving. And keep faith. There's people working to see justice done."

Clara smiled weakly and sat back, clearly tired from the effort of remembering. Judah Daniel withdrew, wondering to herself. Clara's last comment was worded strangely, as if she was putting words together to hide the truth without telling a flat-out lie. Was Clara keeping something back, protecting someone—someone she was calling "the devil"?

When Clara had been led away again, Narcissa said to Judah Daniel, "I am quite sure she knows nothing about it. I shall talk to Dr. Archer about obtaining her release."

As Narcissa hurried away, Judah Daniel thought, She didn't listen too close. Clara, with her mild brown eyes and comfortable plumpness, didn't look like a crazed killer, so she couldn't be one. Well, Judah Daniel had to admit she agreed. But Clara was getting at something with those stories that Hiram told. Might be it was something about Hiram himself, whose anger had shown itself in those stories. Too bad she wouldn't be allowed to talk to Clara alone.

A stiff self-consciousness gripped Narcissa as she sought out Archer to report the conversation between Judah Daniel and Clara. She could not forget the condescension she had heard in his voice when he dismissed her ideas about the murders at Manakin. It was clear he accepted her only as an observer—a spy—in the world of the black women, Judah Daniel and the slaves from Manakin.

Judah Daniel must surely resent being spied upon. Narcissa would have liked to assure the doctoress of her sympathy with the accused women, her conviction that they were innocent. Yet, beyond the few words she had said about Clara, she held back. Why should Judah Daniel believe her? They were the very assurances a spy would give.

In the end she knew that, though neither she nor Judah Daniel liked the arrangement, each would continue to play her part. Their awkward alliance was their best hope to see justice done. If Judah Daniel refused to accept Narcissa's presence, if Narcissa refused to observe and report, Archer would simply get someone else, or interview the women himself— or let Harris and his men beat the women into confessing. She had to accept the constraint Archer put on her involvement, or seem to accept it, even as she summoned her courage to press him a little further.

When she got to Archer's office she walked in unannounced, and before he could speak, she came to the point. "There is something we—Judah Daniel and I—want to try. We might be able to bring Hetty to her senses. But we will need your help."

Archer's reply was cool. "Some physicians' experience with lunatics indicates a fright can bring the sufferer around. Perhaps you could lay her on one of the tables and tell the students, in her hearing, that she is a subject for dissection."

Narcissa caught the slight smile under Archer's neatly trimmed Van

Dyke beard. He expected her to be shocked. Well, she would not give him the satisfaction. Nor would she reveal the anger and frustration hidden beneath her calm demeanor. "I believe that theory, espoused by Dr. Benjamin Rush and others, has fallen into disfavor." She was rewarded by raised eyebrows and a ghost of a nod from Archer.

The irony of her request, and his resistance, did not escape her. Though it was Archer who had sought help from her and Judah Daniel concerning the accused women, the tables had turned. Archer himself seemed barely interested—perhaps he was tired of battling Harris and the others—while the subject obsessed Narcissa. She had to reengage him. "Perhaps you have forgotten the bargain you struck with Judah Daniel," she said, her eyes locked on his. "I have not. Perhaps you are willing to give in to Harris and his idea of justice. I am not."

Archer's silence signaled she had pushed him too far. But then he shifted in his wooden armchair and spoke, his voice almost gentle. "What do you propose, then?"

"Hetty must see the child—little Johnny."

Archer stiffened. "Cantrell has moved household to Manakin to look after things. Colonel Berton will soon be returning to his regiment. I doubt whether he will consent to have the child used in this manner."

"Then you must bring it about without his consent," Narcissa insisted, frowning with the intensity of her conviction. "Hetty saved the child's life! Her mind may be hiding from the idea that something happened to the child she was trying to save. Maybe part of her fear was dread of what Dorothea Berton would do to her if the child were injured, I don't know. But don't forget, she may have seen the murderer."

"And she may have *been* the murderer, or one of them," Archer snapped back. Then he sighed. "But I doubt that is the case." After a moment's silence, he spoke again. "Very well. We will take Hetty to Manakin, concealed in my carriage. If I can talk Mrs. Cantrell into letting me take the child out for a few moments, for some air, I will do it. If your plan works, the effect on Hetty should be immediate. But we must be cautious. It wouldn't do to bombard her with questions. It wouldn't do for the Cantrells to see Hetty, either. If they should set upon her, a suspected murderess in their midst, whatever you might have gained would be lost."

Narcissa nodded, then spoke her own thought. "And Johnny must not see Hetty. Mrs. Cantrell told me he cried for Hetty rather than for his mother. It would be cruel to let him see her, but not let him go to her, stay with her. Ah, it makes me angry! They should be treating her as a heroine."

Archer's gaze kindled a warmth in her, composed partly of gratitude, partly of shame. She had not told him the other motive behind the planned visit to Manakin: she and Judah Daniel would pursue their search for evidence that one or the other of the Cantrells had been behind the Berton murders.

MANAKIN
The next day

Narcissa received word from Dr. Archer that he had been given permission to visit Manakin and check on the health of Colonel Berton's son. She was gratified at the speed with which the request had been made and granted. It was decided that they would ride out that afternoon.

Narcissa requested that the cook, Clara, be allowed to accompany them. She told Archer that Clara's presence would help relax Hetty. She did not tell him that the cook's presence would also allow Judah Daniel to leave Hetty long enough to talk once more to Mrs. Cantrell's maid, Kezia.

Judah Daniel dressed Hetty all in black, with a black shawl covering her head. It proved to be quite a trick to get Hetty, whose slender body had taken on the characteristics of a waxwork figure, into the carriage. Will Whatley, Mirrie's free black driver, half carried the girl, with Narcissa and Judah Daniel supporting her on either side, and bundled her into a corner of the carriage.

An hour later, Narcissa felt her heart pounding as the carriage drove into the shadow-tunnel of cedars, then came out at last only yards from the house. The sun was hot, lacking only the heavy dampness of a summer's day. A sullen-looking young black man, whose clothes were that of a field hand, came to take the reins. Archer jumped out and handed down Narcissa, then reached in for his heavy medical bag. Judah Daniel also stepped down and headed back across the drive toward the kitchen, leaving Clara in the carriage with Hetty.

Cantrell met them at the door and led them inside to the grand hall. He greeted Narcissa offhandedly, then pulled Archer aside and began talking to him in a low voice. Narcissa turned toward the young black girl who had come to the door behind Cantrell and was holding the plump-cheeked Johnny Berton.

Narcissa smiled at the girl and held out her arms for the child. The servant girl placed him in Narcissa's arms and stood watching them. The boy's ruffled white dress was newly ironed and smelled fresh as rain.

Cantrell spoke brusquely to the nursemaid. "The doctor wished to examine the child. But first, have some punch brought. I'm parched. Mrs. Powers, perhaps you would like to take tea with my wife."

The girl inclined her head and reached out to take the child. Narcissa regretted having to trade his company for that of the evil-minded Mrs. Cantrell, but she gave him up and followed the maid across the grand hall to the drawing room. The maid disappeared with Johnny. Narcissa stood, giving the older woman—perforce her hostess—a chance to rise or extend her hand, but she did neither. At last Narcissa seated herself across from Mrs. Cantrell.

What a coldhearted woman she is, Narcissa thought, but she said, "What a lovely tea service." Mrs. Cantrell's gaze followed Narcissa's to the table, where a simple, angular teapot of burnished silver with a wooden handle held pride of place. Then she raised her eyes to Narcissa's face with an expression of satisfied conceit.

"Yes, isn't it? So far superior in design to anything made in this century. It displays the old Yankee workmanship of Paul Revere. I use the term *Yankee* in the true sense, not its current, debased usage."

Mrs. Cantrell picked up a delicate, flower-painted cup in its saucer, then lifted the silver pot and tilted it so that a stream of dark, steaming liquid flowed into the cup. She leaned across the table to hand the cup to Narcissa, then busied herself filling her own cup. At last she spoke again. "It belongs to Manakin, of course, to the inheritors of this house. Yet it seems so out of place here. The South abhors simplicity. Everything must be adorned, covered over, disguised."

Mrs. Cantrell seemed compelled to talk, to pour out the dark thoughts that were poisoning her mind. Narcissa remembered her first encounter with her, the ugly things she had said about young Mrs. Berton—ugly enough, even had the woman not just been murdered. Narcissa probed gently. "I remember you told me you come from New York. It must be difficult to be so far from your family, now that—"

Mrs. Cantrell rose, putting her cup down so abruptly that the delicate china clattered. "You must excuse me, Mrs., uh, Powers. I have many things I must attend to."

Mrs. Cantrell swept from the room, leaving Narcissa piqued. What a shame the woman had suddenly gotten control over the venom that flowed so easily from her mouth. She could only hope Judah Daniel would have better luck questioning Mrs. Cantrell's maid.

Judah Daniel found Kezia in the washroom, sleeves turned back and sweat running down her face, pressing ruffled petticoats with an iron heated at the fire. Kezia smiled in recognition and tilted her head to indicate Judah Daniel should sit.

"Don't you folks have no troubles of your own, that you got to borrow ours?" Kezia asked, slamming the iron down and across the cotton.

"Reckon you knew Dorcas and Zemora, and Hetty," Judah Daniel replied. "You hear Zemora died?"

"Oh, Lord, don't tell me!" Kezia's eyes were wide. "We was the same age!"

"Dorcas and Hetty still real sick," Judah Daniel went on. "Clara sick too, but not so bad."

Kezia was holding the iron aloft now, watching Judah Daniel's face. "Food poisoning?" Then she turned, set the iron on the hearth, and picked up another, wrapping a cloth around the handle to protect her hand.

"Um."

Judah Daniel's failure to answer didn't seem to surprise Kezia, who spoke to the rhythm of her ironing. "Field hands here at Manakin and back at the hall, they got problems too. Most of the ones from Manakin done been sold away. Got a new overseer, and I hear the old one went kicking and cursing."

"Where he go?" Judah Daniel asked with interest. Manakin's overseer, if he had no reason left to be loyal, could supply some good information.

"Went back down south, seem I heard it was Mississippi," Kezia was watching the path of her iron as if she had decided she could learn more without asking directly.

"Sure was a good thing the Cantrells wasn't at Manakin that day," Judah Daniel said. The women exchanged a glance, but Kezia didn't answer. "If they died too, who would be next to step in?"

"Well, just give me a minute to calculate on that!" Kezia smiled her sly smile, and Judah Daniel knew she was getting some satisfaction out of the imagined scene. At last Kezia said, "The Langdons have a big plantation west of here. They ain't related—ain't near related, I reckon all these planters is cousins in some degree, being as they all been marrying each other for more than a hundred years. But I reckon they might step in for a time."

"Well—" Kezia was well aware what she was getting at, Judah Daniel knew, but maybe that was not a bad thing. "How come the Cantrells wasn't here to welcome their cousin Colonel Berton back on his leave? What *was* they doing that morning?"

"Weren't nothing special," Kezia answered with a shrug. "Mr. Cantrell weren't even at home that morning, or the night before. He spend a lot of time in Richmond, playing poker, and losing. Mrs. Cantrell took to her bed the night before with a sick headache. I knocked on the door to take her her breakfast, she didn't even answer me."

"Did you go in?" Judah Daniel knew the swiftness with which she asked the question betrayed her interest.

Kezia gave her a long look, then busied herself exchanging the cool iron for the heated one. She slapped and smoothed again before she answered. "Naw, I didn't go in. Got the whole tray throwed back at me last time I went in with Mrs. Cantrell having one of her headaches. Oh, Lord," Kezia exclaimed suddenly, her sleek face wrinkling with alarm. "There's Mrs. Cantrell now, look like she coming this way. Get out quick, or we'll both catch it!"

Judah Daniel thanked Kezia and slipped out the door. She walked swiftly back to the carriage, hoping her presence in the washhouse would not bring trouble on Kezia. When she had crossed the yard without being hailed, she turned and glanced over her shoulder. Mrs. Cantrell was no-where in sight. Had Kezia really seen her mistress, or had Judah Daniel's questions become too troubling?

Archer came to the door and motioned to Narcissa to follow him. He led her back into the grand hall. "Bring the child outside," he ordered Nar-cissa. "I will complete my examination."

Again Narcissa took Johnny from his nurse's arms and carried him, a heavy, squirming bundle, out the door, following Archer around the side of the house. She knew Archer was looking for a spot that could be seen by the occupants of his carriage—by Hetty.

At last Archer stopped and signaled with a nod of his head to a low bench shaded by a huge sweetgum tree. Narcissa put Johnny on the ground at her feet and began a peekaboo game with a sweetgum ball to keep him occupied. Johnny laughed and reached for the ball, Narcissa whisked it away. He searched for it, holding on to her skirts, until she brought it out from hiding to dangle it in front of him again. Out of the corner of her eye she saw Archer standing, arms crossed, expression inscrutable.

Narcissa thought about Cameron Archer. Bold and self-assured as a surgeon, she knew he was, and brave at facing down other men, she had heard; but when it came to babies and women, he was uneasy. The thought made her smile. Johnny Berton, looking into her eyes, smiled back.

Cameron Archer watched Narcissa Powers play with Johnny. She was so gentle with the child, so assured, as if he were her own. Better far for the child if she had been his mother, or some woman like her. John Berton had confirmed Archer's fears by his reaction to the news of Dorothea's pregnancy. Not that Berton had said anything—he was too much of a gentleman for that. He had bent over as if struck in the gut and vomited the contents of his stomach.

Johnny resembled his father. His paternity should never be questioned. But then, James Cantrell, who was rumored to have been Dorothea's lover, strongly resembled his cousin John Berton. If Johnny Berton ever found out the truth—that his mother had committed adultery, and that the man he knew as his father had killed her for it—it would destroy him.

At that moment Archer, watching the child laughing up at Narcissa Powers, his face bright with innocence—determined to hide the truth. Hiram had accepted the blame for one murder now he was dead; let Hiram bear the blame for all.

Tucking the Berton family's secrets away in his mind, Archer turned his thoughts to Narcissa Powers. It would be better for her, too, that she have a child to care for, instead of expending her youth and strength among sick and mutilated men. She seemed so natural, playing with Johnny, so womanly. It was a shame that hospital work had coarsened her. In their confrontation the other night, he rebuking her and she answering him in kind, she had seemed so mannish. Nature had made her to be a lady, had marked her as such in the strong, smooth curve of her jaw and her large, bright eyes, even though her family was undistinguished. She was made not just to please a man but to inspire him. The death of her brother, a medical student, had turned her away from her natural course, involving her first with the medical school, then with the hospital. And he had to admit that he himself was partly at fault. He had treated her as he would a man—no, worse. Should he apologize?

Women! he thought. *What fools they make of us.*

Judah Daniel leaned over to Hetty, her arm around the woman's shoulder, and gently turned her head to face the spot where Narcissa sat with Johnny. The sound of the child's gurgling laughter came through the open window. "He's all right, Hetty. Look. The baby's safe. You kept him safe."

Judah Daniel felt a tremor pass through Hetty, saw her lift her face so that the sunlight fell upon it. Hetty's lips curved in a slight smile. At last she spoke. "It was so dark."

Pressed up close to Hetty, Judah Daniel could feel her wake up; that was what it was like—but more than that, could feel her come back to life. Little movements of her mouth and eyes, of the muscles in her shoulders and arms, then all down her trunk to her legs, signaled returning life. At last Hetty brought up her right hand, palm in and fingers splayed, close to her face and looked at it as if seeing it for the first time. Then her eyes focused past her fingers, on the face of Judah Daniel. The blank mask that had been Hetty's face crumpled, her lips drew back over clenched teeth as if holding in a sob. She put her face against Judah Daniel's shoulder and wept hot tears.

Chapter Five

On her way to the hospital the next morning, Narcissa went over in her mind what Judah Daniel had told her the evening before. The carriage had been crowded, warm with bodies and breath. Archer had sat next to Narcissa. After a brief and surprisingly gentle examination of Hetty, Archer had pulled his slouch hat down over his eyes and slept, or pretended to. Judah Daniel and Clara, with Hetty between them, had filled the other seat. Hetty, her body relaxed at last, dozed with her head on Clara's shoulder.

Seated across from each other, speaking in hushed tones, Narcissa and Judah Daniel had shared their observations. Narcissa's disappointment at her handling of Mrs. Cantrell had faded when she heard Judah Daniel's news. Both Mr. and Mrs. Cantrell had had the opportunity to do the murders. And James Cantrell was a gambler. Narcissa felt confirmed in her decision to consult Brit Wallace, who had told her of his success at card playing.

As the carriage pulled up in front of the medical college hospital, Narcissa reflected on her different roles. She was accustomed now to working as a nurse. The needs of wounded men kept you going, she reflected, thinking that your effort might make the difference between life and death. But with wounded men, you did your best and left the rest to God. Somehow, in the case of the murdered family and their imprisoned slaves, it felt as if God were leaving it up to her.

Now that it seemed likely Hetty would recover, perhaps remember what she had seen and heard, Narcissa's excitement was electric. But Judah Daniel would not be allowed to speak to Hetty until Cameron Archer gave his permission. While they waited, they would do well to find other ways to get at the truth. Whatever had frightened Hetty—even if she could remember and speak of it—might not hold the key to the mystery.

Soon Narcissa was back in the hospital routine: serving breakfast to those too weak to eat it themselves, dressing wounds and reporting to the surgeons any that appeared inflamed—which was most of them—and writing letters for soldiers whose wounds, weakness, or illiteracy prevented them. At last she took her own midday meal of cold chicken and an apple down to the little room on the first floor in which her shawl and bonnet hung, joined in bad weather by the overcoats of the surgeons and medical students on duty. It was cooler and quieter there, and the ever-present hospital smells of diseased flesh and bodily waste, overlaid with the odor of burning tar, were relatively faint. She had finished bundling up the remains of her meal into the big white napkin and was composing her mind to return to the patients when the door opened.

Jordan Archer stepped into the room, which was so small that the skirts of the two of them took up most of the floor. Jordan was still affecting a mourning style of unrelieved black, yet her hair, this time dressed by hands more expert than Narcissa's own, was topped with a minuscule straw hat.

Jordan looked at her, eyebrows raised. "Narcissa! Whatever are you doing, hiding down here?"

Eating my lunch, she almost said; but a better reply came to her. "My goodness, Jordan, when you wrinkle up your forehead like that, you so closely resemble your great-aunt!"

Narcissa pretended not to notice as Jordan's disapproving expression vanished, succeeded by shock, then by the composing of her face into a serious expression.

"Narcissa, I have come to help the brave boys here in the hospital. I hope that you can find something for me to do. Can you, now? And by the way, I am getting up an entertainment this evening, at my great-aunt's house. I want to invite you. There will be a younger crowd, not so many of my great-aunt's friends." Jordan's small nose wrinkled to show what she thought of them. "But I want you to come."

My jab is well returned, thought Narcissa.

"Your friend Mr. Wallace is invited, and M. Lucien." A coy self-consciousness came over Jordan's face when she said this last name, but she continued talking without a pause. "It's dreadful, having to stay with Great-aunt Caroline. With all her digs and barbs about my behavior—she would wall me up if she could, I assure you! She doesn't care in the least for me—for anyone; but, as I am a girl, she questions me endlessly about places I go, people I see. She did not want me to come here today, but I felt it was my duty."

Narcissa, reading the text behind the words, understood that Jordan was inviting her again to fill the role of chaperone, thus assuring Mrs. Archer Jennings that she could retire to her room and not be troubled to witness the doings of the young people. Narcissa had to sympathize—she herself had seldom met a colder, more repellent individual than Caroline Archer Jennings.

"Tell me about Mr. Lucien. I don't believe I know him," Narcissa said, curious about the expression that had crossed Jordan's face when she said the name.

"*Monsieur* Gerard Lucien," Jordan corrected, softening the G to display a well-tutored French accent. Jordan glanced around and lowered her voice. "He has come to Richmond on a diplomatic mission related to the American visit of Prince Jerome Napoleon. He does not speak of it, but I suppose that is the way of diplomats." Jordan's long, heavy-lidded eyes were wide with suppressed excitement as she added, "I was introduced to him at Great-aunt Caroline's—after you had gone." She said this with mingled satisfaction and pity, like one child consoling another who left the party before the cake was cut.

Despite her slight resentment at being summoned so peremptorily to Jordan's party, Narcissa immediately made up her mind to go. The opportunity to talk to Brit Wallace was too good to let slip. Meanwhile, there was the matter of Jordan's request to help in the hospital. Surely it would not be difficult to find something she could do: young ladies came in to read to the patients and to write letters, and Jordan could help in that capacity.

"Very well," Narcissa said. "Now, if you wish to visit one or two of the patients, let me check with the surgeon on duty."

As Narcissa went out into the hall, she glanced over her shoulder to see Jordan peering into the little mirror Narcissa had hung on the wall behind the bench. She wished that Jordan were a little less high-handed. Perhaps that came from the early loss of her mother, from having been raised by servants.

Cameron Archer came in from the bright sunlight to the dark entrance-way of the medical college hospital. He had decided he would apologize to Mrs. Powers—for his insufferable pomposity of the night before, at least. He could not promise that his roughness in their daily relations would change, though he had vowed to himself to be civil, at least. It cheered him to think of her regarding him with the open, unguarded expression with which she had looked at little Johnny Berton.

As his vision began to clear, he glanced into the office where Narcissa sometimes had her lunch. There she was, in her dark dress, standing with her back to him, apparently adjusting her bonnet in the little mirror she had hung for the purpose. His words came out in a rush. "Mrs. Powers, I apologize for last night. When it seemed that the murders at Manakin could represent the beginning of a slave rebellion . . . well, it horrified me. But that's no excuse, . . . I was rude." Why does she not turn around? he thought. What is it that she wants me to say?

Archer looked more closely at the figure standing there. The right height, dressed in black, wearing a black bonnet similar to one he had seen on Mrs. Powers . . . Then he saw the blond hair, noted the thin shoulders. It was his cousin Jordan Archer. She and Mrs. Powers had made a fool of him! Mounting rage washed away Archer's good intentions. He slammed his gloved fist into his open palm, turned, and stomped away.

Before she could get an answer from Dr. Fielding, the surgeon in charge, concerning Jordan, Narcissa was sent to fetch bandages, instruments, and silk thread for sutures. At last she had her answer, and she started down the stairs to deliver the good news to Jordan. As she did so, she saw Cameron Archer ascending. Thinking he might have news about Hetty, or in-structions concerning some patient at the hospital, she stopped and waited. Archer brushed past her, close enough that she had to hold her skirts out of his way, but with his head down and frowning, acknowledg-ing her with a perfunctory nod. Narcissa hurried down the steps, angry that she had given Archer the opportunity to put her in her place once more.

Jordan had left the little dressing room and was standing in the hall. "You've been an age!" the girl called out. Coming closer, Narcissa could see that Jordan's cheeks were flushed and her straw hat a little askew. Narcissa wondered if Jordan and her cousin Cameron Archer had had words over Jordan's presence at the hospital, perhaps over her wish to serve as a nurse. Strong words they must have been, to have left Jordan so discomposed.

"Yes!" Narcissa said with satisfaction, "you would be very welcome, reading to the patients, or perhaps writing letters."

"Oh . . . ," Jordan responded with surprise, as if she had forgotten why she had come. "I am sorry. I had forgotten another engagement. Another time, perhaps." Then the girl turned and hurried out the door into the street, leaving Narcissa wondering what had changed Jordan's mind in the space of a few minutes.

Mrs. Archer Jennings's house again sparkled with candlelight. Was it the nostalgic old lady or the romantic young Jordan, Narcissa wondered, who preferred candlelight to the harsher, more modern illumination of gasoliers?

A dozen guests were gathered in the less formal of the house's parlors. They were a young and lively crowd, a few more uniformed youths than glossy-haired girls. They talked and laughed, their enjoyment unhampered by the presence of Mrs. Archer Jennings, who dozed slack-mouthed in her thronelike chair.

Jordan, in a gown of leaf green over which she had draped a light shawl with a pattern of vines and flowers, advanced to meet Narcissa and drew her over to the corner near the piano where the only two men in the room not in uniform were standing. Brit Wallace greeted Narcissa warmly, then turned and said, "Mrs. Powers, may I present M. Lucien?"

Lucien met Narcissa's eyes and bowed, smiling slightly. She was surprised to recognize the man she had seen here at this house on the night of the reception in Jordan's honor—the man who had stood with Beaumain Newton and had spoken French to Von Wulfen. The man whose look had been flattering—to Jordan, as well as to her, she imagined, remembering how Jordan had spoken about the Frenchman.

Lucien's manner conveyed pleasure to be in her company but without suggesting, by a too-long look or a press of the hand, an overly personal interest. His manner toward Jordan, too, was relaxed without being forward, correct without being formal. But for some reason Jordan seemed shy of Lucien, immediately attaching herself to Brit Wallace and teasing him in a way that brought out his dimples.

Lucien addressed a remark to Narcissa. "I never drive here on Church Hill, never pass St. John's Church, without remembering the words of Patrick Henry: 'Give me liberty, or give me death.' " He gave the word *liberty* a hint of its French pronunciation.

"Which inspired *liberté, egalité, fraternité*," Brit Wallace broke in. "And now the Confederates sing the 'Marseillaise.' "

Narcissa saw Jordan Archer steal a glance at Lucien, then look quickly away to smile at Brit Wallace.

Lucien's expression was thoughtful. Then he turned to Brit and smiled. "Do you find it ironic that slave owners should raise a call to arms in defense of freedom? Or that they should fight for the freedom to own slaves? You are young, Mr. Wallace. When you have seen as much of the world as I have, you will accept that the most basic human truth is self-interest. Except in the cases of a few madmen, 'Give me liberty or give me death' is merely a rhetorical flourish. But of course, it is those few madmen who, perhaps once or twice in a millennium, change the course of human history."

Narcissa saw Brit's face stiffen and smiled to herself. Lucien's assumption of superior age and experience—and he himself looked to be no more than thirty, less than a decade older than the Englishman—was obviously galling to Brit. How funny, she thought: I am piqued because Jordan treats me like an old woman; he is piqued because Lucien treats him like a young man!

"What about the example of my own country, which freed its slaves in the British West Indies?" Brit spoke coolly, as if Lucien's answer was of no concern to him.

Lucien straightened his shoulders like a soldier anticipating the call to charge, though his tone was still offhand. "For whose benefit did your country purchase the manumission of those slaves? The slaves themselves? Subsequent history says no. Ask a former slave how he exercises his rights as a citizen of the British Empire! The British aristocracy freed the slaves, and compensated their owners at tremendous expense to the nation, for the sole purpose of fomenting antislavery feeling in the northern United States, thus driving the wedge between the free states and the slave states."

Brit preserved his expression of mild interest. "And why so?"

"So that the great democratic experiment that was the United States of America would fail at last, and cease to be an example of what a nation could achieve in the absence of a privileged aristocracy."

Narcissa took a deep breath, then turned back to Lucien. "You are so familiar with all the details of other countries' history—what of your own?"

"I am a Frenchman," Lucien replied. "My country has seen its downtrodden peasants rise up to overthrow its aristocracy, mow them down like so much ripe grain. During the last century many members of my family were planters. I bear in my heart, and on my family crest, as it were, the horrors of the slave uprising at St.-Domingue. The Reign of Terror in Paris was a *divertissement* compared to the butchery of men, women, and children in St.-Domingue. Whites, blacks, mulattoes, all tortured and killed each other. And what brought it on? What but the talk in Paris of *freedom?* You here in the Confederacy should have a care how you use the words of Patrick Henry and the 'Marseillaise.' "

Jordan was now staring at Lucien, her face pale. The Frenchman smiled apologetically, shrugged, and said, "Voltaire's advice was the best. 'We all must tend our own gardens, and avoid the world's corruption as best we can.' "

An odd philosophy for a diplomat, Narcissa mused. But his description of the killings in Santo Domingo pressed on her. Had she been too quick to dismiss her fears of a slave uprising behind the murders at Manakin?

Brit folded his arms across his chest and smiled. "I myself never drive on Church Hill without thinking of *Pawnee* Sunday."

"Pawnee Sunday? An Indian attack?" Lucien asked.

"Ha! Not so long ago as that, don't you know. Back in April it was rumored that the *Pawnee*, a Federal sloop-of-war, was coming up the river to attack Richmond. The rumor was false, obviously," Brit said with a shrug. "But I won some little notoriety with the account of the event published in my paper."

Again Narcissa smiled. Certainly Brit had won notoriety in Richmond; in fact, he had won himself an invitation—fortunately temporary—to leave the city of Richmond and the Southern states.

Jordan spoke up suddenly. "There *was* an Indian massacre—a massacre of Indians, that is—very near this house, at Chimborazo Heights, where they are building the new hospital. It was almost two hundred years ago now. The creek that runs along there is named after it: Bloody Run. As children we used to go there to look for arrowheads, when we visited my

great-aunt. It was just as you said of St.-Domingue." Narcissa noted Jordan
had used Lucien's French pronunciation of the name rather than Santo
Domingo, which the Americans and English used. Jordan was looking at
Lucien, her eyes wide with horror. "They killed us, we killed them. But we
won, and they are gone."

"And are there ghosts?" Brit asked, dimples signaling his willingness to
be charmed.

Jordan turned slowly toward Brit. Suddenly her eyelids fluttered, and her
thin frame went limp. Narcissa stepped forward and caught her around her
shoulders. Brit reached out a moment later, putting his arm under Jordan's
elbow and supporting her weight.

Jordan leaned on him a moment. Her face was white, her eyes closed.
Then she straightened and put her hand up to her forehead. "I'm sorry! I
felt faint for a moment. This headache . . . I thought it was gone."

Jordan's near faint attracted the attention of the others in the room, and
she was soon surrounded by a crowd of solicitous acquaintances who
helped her to a chaise longue, fetched pillows for her head and feet, and
brought several glasses of brandy to stimulate her nerves. Great-aunt
Archer Jennings slept on in her chair, unaffected.

M. Lucien stationed himself in a side chair near Jordan's head and
leaned over her, talking to her in a low tone. Narcissa saw Jordan, her shy-
ness of the Frenchman now forgotten, speaking earnestly to him and gesturing with her hands about her face—describing, Narcissa imagined, the
headache. Lucien said something, to which Jordan shook her head, looking away. Lucien spoke again, pressing some point, until at last Jordan
nodded.

Lucien stood up and, in his appealing voice, addressed the dozen or so
young ladies and gentlemen gathered around. "My friends, join me in
applauding Miss Archer's recovery. She is feeling much better now." He
paused to allow appropriate congratulatory remarks. "Miss Archer has
informed me she suffers greatly from headaches. I have informed her of
my success in relieving headache sufferers through mesmerism. She has
agreed to permit me to mesmerize her now."

Lucien held up his hand to stem the flow of delighted commentary that
greeted his announcement. "I know mesmerism is sometimes performed
as a parlor trick, but I view it as a serious undertaking. You all must agree
to remain silent from the time I begin until Miss Archer has been fully
awakened. Now, please give us some room." Those who had been crowded

around Jordan moved away, the men carrying chairs for the ladies. In a few moments they formed an orderly ring around Jordan's chaise, the ladies seated, the men standing behind them.

Narcissa turned to see Brit Wallace standing with his arms folded across his chest, frowning as if he would like to disrupt the proceedings. But he did not. Should I try to stop it? she wondered. But Jordan had agreed to it, and Narcissa's objection would likely make her more determined to go on. Anyway, despite what M. Lucien had said, and despite its sometimes flamboyant portrayal in novels and the stories of Edgar Allan Poe, mesmerism was a parlor trick, and harmless enough.

Lucien helped Jordan to a sitting position on the chaise and slipped her shawl down from her shoulders, then placed his chair facing her with a distance of about a foot between them. His eyes fixed on hers, he took both her hands and held them, palms together and thumbs up as if in prayer, level with her chest. He covered her hands with his and pressed his thumbs against hers, all the while fixing her with an unblinking gaze. After a few minutes he placed her hands, palms down, on her lap, then raised his own hands to rest on her shoulders. He paused a few moments as if waiting for some internal signal, then ran his hands down her arms to the tips of her fingers. Lucien's touch was light and measured, Narcissa noted, her discomfort receding. There was nothing of the wooer in his touch; in fact, he resembled a doctor performing a difficult operation.

"That's called a 'mesmeric pass,'" Brit whispered in Narcissa's ear, sounding as if curiosity had won out over disapproval.

Lucien repeated this action a half-dozen times. Then he raised his hands above Jordan's head and, after a moment, drew them down before her face, at a distance of one or two inches, and along her body to her feet. Jordan remained staring at the place where his eyes had been, and if she knew his eyes no longer looked into hers, she gave no sign of it.

At last Lucien straightened, his eyes again on Jordan's. Slowly he eased his hands in front of his face, palms toward Jordan, then brought them down slowly in front of her eyes. As he did so, Jordan's eyelids drooped, then closed.

"Do you sleep?" Lucien's voice was so low that Narcissa strained to hear.

"I sleep, and I do not sleep," Jordan responded in a light, slightly puzzled tone.

"Are you well?" Lucien asked then.

"I am very well, but you must not leave me."

Lucien slipped back in his chair and picked up a glass of brandy. He put it to his lips, then put it down. "What do you taste?"

Jordan drew her bottom lip in slightly; the tip of her tongue touched her upper lip; then her lips parted to speak: "Brandy."

The silence in the room grew expectant. What would be Lucien's next trick?

"There is something in your head that pains you. What is it?"

"At Champs-Elysées," Jordan said, as simply as a child answering her mother.

Lucien hesitated, as if this were not the answer that he had expected. "Can you tell me about it?" he said at last.

"I see a shining in my head. It is too bright, it hurts my eyes. Diamonds, gold, so shiny, so pretty. Why does it make my head hurt?"

"Where are these things?"

"In my head."

"Is there anything else?"

"I see the bride, there on the stairs. Her dress, her veil."

An intake of breath jarred Narcissa as if she herself were coming out of a trance. She looked toward the sound to see Mrs. Archer Jennings standing there, leaning on her cane and staring at Jordan and Lucien, her eyes wide with horror. A little tremor of reaction ran through the assembled onlookers. Lucien himself turned away from Jordan and held his hand up toward the old woman as if to warn her.

Jordan's body jerked as if in seizure. Her eyes flew open, her hands went to her face. "Oh, God, a skull! A skeleton!" Jordan jumped up and was tearing at her face, her hair. Lucien, knocked off balance by her sudden violence, got to his feet and took her hands in his again. She twisted this way and that, trying to break free of him. "Be calm, be calm," he was saying. Narcissa went over to them and helped Jordan to sit next to her on the chaise. Jordan's pale face was tear-streaked, but her expression was puzzled. "What happened? Did he mesmerize me?"

Above the din of voices, Narcissa could hear Mrs. Archer Jennings shrieking, "Get out! Get out!"

The party came to an abrupt end, with Mrs. Archer Jennings ordering Jordan to her bed and sending the guests away.

"Why was the old lady so angry at that Frenchman?" one young man in a lieutenant's uniform remarked as he strolled past with a girl on each arm.

"Yes, it was her own fault, breaking in like that," a pretty, dark-haired girl replied. "Her face must have come into Jordan's mind, and she took it for a skull!" They laughed. Then the other girl said, "The wonder is, Jordan wants to go out in society at all, considering what everyone is saying about her father."

Narcissa wanted to hear more of their conversation, but Brit was offering his arm to her. "Allow me to accompany you to your carriage." His manner was formal, but Narcissa could tell by his erect posture and bright eyes that his journalist's interest had been aroused by the curious, strangely frightening scene they had witnessed. She took his arm and they moved, just enough to count as walking rather than standing, toward the Powers carriage.

"Before you arrived," Brit said in a low voice, "Miss Archer told me the most extraordinary thing. Some slaves have turned on their masters and murdered them, quite close to here apparently! I couldn't believe Lucien, speaking so brutally about the massacres in Santo Domingo. He doesn't know about it, obviously, or he would not have been so tactless. I suppose that was the source of Miss Archer's distress."

Wallace watched her for her reaction. Narcissa felt all the shock he could have expected her to feel, though not, she knew, for the reason he would have expected. How on earth had Jordan learned about the suspicions of an uprising? The deaths at Manakin had been explained as the result of accidental food poisoning, with the fact that slaves had been affected lending credence to the story.

Brit went on eagerly. "There's been nothing about this in the papers. Of course, the Witherspoon case down in South Carolina, everyone knows about it, but nothing whatever in the papers. The authorities fear a panic, don't you see. And that was just one old lady, smothered in her bed by servants afraid of a beating. If I could find out the particulars . . . I promised Miss Archer I would tell no one, but if I could find confirmation of the story from another source, it would knock the blockade right off the front pages."

Though she had planned to tell him about the murders, enlist his help, Narcissa was dismayed. Having found out this way, Brit viewed the story as subject matter for one of his dispatches. They had reached Mirrie's carriage now.

"Did Miss Archer tell you where she heard this rumor?"

Brit nodded energetically. "That's just the thing. She said she heard it from Cameron Archer. I can't imagine that he, being a medical man and all that, would spread such a story if there were nothing to it. You and he are very much in each other's pockets at the hospital, are you not? Can you find out anything about this?"

Narcissa knew she could not hide her dismay. "We must speak about this," she said quickly and emphatically, then mounted into the carriage for the drive back to the Powerses'.

As Narcissa puzzled over what Brit Wallace had told her, her anger against Cameron Archer grew fierce. What had possessed Archer to tell his young, reckless cousin Jordan about the Berton murders? Had he wanted so badly to impress her?

Jordan was not old enough, mature enough, to understand what public knowledge of these murders would mean. That was obvious from the fact that she in turn had told Brit Wallace. If the Berton murders gained full-blown notoriety, everyone would suffer: the accused slaves hustled perhaps to execution; slave owners subjected to the horrors that haunt the aftermath of slave insurrections; their slaves suddenly objects of baseless suspicion; slave-owning soldiers torn between their military duty and their fears for their own parents, wives, and children. Look at what had happened to Jordan as a result of hearing the rumor, then being invited to dwell on the horrors of slave revolts. The nervous sensitivity that existed in Jordan side by side with reckless impetuosity had brought her to the brink of collapse.

THE NEXT DAY

Cameron Archer mounted the steps to the city jail at a trot, but his head was bent as if he had to watch his feet, and there were dark circles under his eyes. He pushed through the door of the jailer's little office, then halted. Seated at the table were Major Harris and another man, in civilian clothes of the finest fabric and cut. Both men froze at the interruption. The apology Archer should have made went unspoken, pushed aside by alarm. The last thing they needed was another civilian involved in the

Berton murders. Perhaps this man was here about some other subject—but Archer didn't think so. He and Harris held each other's eyes for a long moment. Then Harris rose, and the other man followed his lead.

"M. Lucien, may I present Dr. Cameron Archer?"

Lucien smiled and extended his hand. Archer shook it, wondering who the Frenchman was and why he was here.

Harris explained. "M. Lucien has offered his expertise in helping resolve the Berton case." Harris turned to look at Lucien, who smiled still, watching Archer.

"And just what is your expertise, M. Lucien?"

The Frenchman continued to eye Archer a moment, then said, "I have . . . dabbled in the subjects of mesmerism and galvanism. The application of electrical current in the treatment of disease."

Archer drew himself up to make a response, but Lucien anticipated him.

"The electromagnetic machine, the galvanic battery that drips acid on to metal to release electrical current—no. I do not quarrel with the proven success of many who use such devices to treat patients. But I do not claim to be a physician, versed in anatomy and pathology, as you yourself are, doctor."

His quick response thus deflected, Archer was silent.

"I am sure you know, as well, that some individuals possess, and are able to communicate to others, a very high degree of animal magnetism." Lucien's eyes held Archer's. "It is an ancient practice, the art of healing by the laying on of hands, only recently understood in the light of modern scientific principles. Electricity—that agent by which the Almighty moves and regulates the planets—is used by the mind to move the feet, arms, limbs, and perform the various functions of the animal mechanism. In what are termed the nervous diseases, the brain, stimulated to painful activity, consumes more than its due proportion of the nervo-electric fluid, and the remaining organs are deprived. It is the interruption or partial withdrawal of the nervo-electric circulation which causes nervous diseases. I have been told—and I have seen it to be true—that I possess a very high degree of individual electricity. In my native country, I have been called on by individuals I am not at liberty to name, who—"

"And why do you suppose us to be in need of your . . . services, M. Lucien?" Archer broke in.

Harris stiffened in his chair as if anticipating an angry reaction from

Lucien, but the Frenchman crossed one leg over the other, brushed away some invisible speck from the fine wool fabric, then looked back at Archer.

"I do not wish to be indiscreet. I cannot tell you from what official I came by this information. Let me simply say I understand there was some trouble, involving slaves—trouble that needs to be traced to its root and eradicated. I understand there were slaves, women, who might have witnessed the . . . incident, but that severe nervous collapse has prevented them from giving evidence."

Archer tried to conceal his shock. Lucien was in possession of more information than he had thought possible. Harris looked impressed: Lucien could not merely be repeating what Harris himself had told him. So, what "authorities" had given him the information? Winder? Or had Winder himself passed the information on to higher government authorities, even the president?

"Animal magnetism," Lucien said again, pronouncing the words carefully, as if they themselves would have an effect on Harris's mind through his ears. "The application of nervo-electrical current has been shown to awaken, as it were, subjects suffering from mental disorders. If I were permitted to come into contact with these slaves, to lay my hands upon them, there is a very good chance it would bring them to their senses, make them able to tell what they have seen."

Major Harris had put his head back and was looking through narrowed eyelids at Archer. "Are you aware of these methods, Doctor?"

"I am aware of galvanism, of course, Major," Archer replied in the drawl of the Richmond gentry. "I do not think it warranted in this case. The prisoners are not insane, they are suffering from datura poisoning." *Damn!* Archer thought. Now he had given away important information. He had to get his emotions under control.

"In your opinion, sir," Harris retorted.

"In my opinion," Archer repeated. "And actions affecting the mental and physical state of the prisoners are taken with my permission."

Harris looked as if he would argue, but in a moment he recovered himself. "M. Lucien, I appreciate your offer of assistance. Dr. Archer is . . . *at present* . . . in charge of the prisoners' medical treatment. And now, you must excuse me," Harris added, his manner suddenly brisk. "M. Lucien, I bid you good day. I look forward to seeing you again." Harris offered his hand, and the Frenchman shook it. "And you, doctor." Harris nodded curtly to Archer and walked past him out of the room.

Lucien turned a smiling face toward Archer. "Please pardon me. I have to go as well. I hope you will consider my offer. The stability of your government is very important to my country. I assure you I have no intention of interfering with your handling of the . . . suspects." He bowed and departed.

Archer hesitated a fraction of a second, admiring the man's coolness. Then he strode after Harris, who was standing at the far end of the hall, riffling through a sheaf of papers, and did not look up.

"How did he hear about the murders?"

Harris sighed. "M. Lucien is in Richmond on a diplomatic mission connected with the French government. Back in the time of the uprisings in Santo Domingo, his family's plantation was ransacked by marauding slaves. Many of the household were killed. Obviously he will have given much thought to the question of slave massacres."

Archer frowned. "So he has said, perhaps. But don't forget: two white Frenchmen helped Gabriel Prosser rise up against us, in our grandparents' day. We have only Lucien's word that the stability of our government concerns him, not its overthrow."

Harris's look of horror gratified Archer. But no other explanation for Lucien's knowledge was offered, and Archer did not press the point. It was hopeless to trace the source of rumor in Richmond; the provost marshal's men would sell the most sensitive information for the price of a drink. But the fact that the news was out alarmed him.

In a moment, Harris had recovered and taken the offensive. "What about that—Negress you brought in to question Berton's wenches? Turns out she's been in jail herself, brought in for performing abortions. She calls herself a conjure woman. You think those women were poisoned? Well, she could be slipping it to them, keeping them sick."

Archer replied coolly. "She is never alone with them, she's watched every minute—"

"By a nurse!" Harris broke in. His curling lip revealed what he thought of the profession.

Archer said nothing, making the threat with his eyes: one word more, and Harris would find himself on the floor.

Harris shifted his weight away from Archer and said simply, "I will be waiting." Then he turned and hurried away.

Archer stood frowning, arms crossed over his chest to hide the shaking of his hands. It had been a close call. Harris had cornered him, forced him into going ahead with Judah Daniel's questioning of Hetty. He told himself it was unlikely Hetty had seen anything that would implicate John Berton in the killings; but if she had, better it be told to Judah Daniel and Narcissa Powers than to this stranger, this foreigner. Anger was rising in him at the interfering Lucien, the officious Harris. The roots of the anger ran deeper, he knew: he was angry at John Berton for having killed his wife and parents, for having put him, Cameron Archer, in the position of lying to protect him. But most of all, he had to admit, he was angry at himself for so obscuring what ought to have been clear as day. Now that he had begun it, he could not see a way out.

Judah Daniel walked down the steep road from Church Hill. The sweat of her exertion cooled quickly in the fall air. The days were getting shorter; she'd have to hurry to get back to the Chapmans' before twilight. She hadn't wanted to rush through her visit with Auntie Lora. As she'd expected, the old woman had sniffed suspiciously at the blue-flag-root tonic she'd brought. "Smell like liquor," was her comment.

"Just take a spoonful at morning, another one at bedtime," Judah Daniel responded carefully. There was a little homemade wine in the bottle, just to give it some flavor.

The old woman laughed. "Some folks I know, they'd have that spoon just a-going." Auntie Lora mimicked quick action with the spoon.

"Well, it don't taste that good, and there ain't enough in there to get you happy even if you drained the whole thing at one time."

Auntie Lora looked disappointed. Then she put the spoon and bottle aside and looked at Judah Daniel. "Do you believe in healing with the laying on of hands?"

"Yes, I believe in it. It's in the Bible."

"Do you heal that way?"

Judah Daniel hesitated. Was Auntie Lora testing her powers by calling for a miracle? She thought for a moment. "Well, yes, but not above maybe three or four times in my life. The power come from God when and where it will. I can ask for it and not get it. Then, other times, I ain't thought to ask for it, but it's there. It's in me, like a thing I know, but I can't tell how I know it. And I put my hands on the sick one, and it go through me, and it's gone. It's a good feeling though."

Auntie Lora nodded slowly. "That's what it be like. My momma, she was a midwife, she told me about getting that feeling sometimes. Well, Miss Jordan, she suffers something awful from the headache. Ain't nothing could give her no ease until"—Auntie Lora lowered her voice—"she say this Frenchman she met, name of Lucien, got the ability to cure the headache by animal . . . something. She said he put his hands on her, pull the headache right out of her, right through her skin. You know what I told her?"

"What did you tell her, Auntie Lora?"

"I told her, she better see to it he don't pull her right out of her clothes!"

"Ha!" Judah Daniel's laugh was abrupt. Auntie Lora's deep chuckle shook her soft body until tears rolled down her cheeks.

Auntie Lora went on. "She got all huffy, said she ought not to of told me. I tell you, there's all sorts in this city. It's a sign of judgment, the things that go on here."

Narcissa's stated reason for paying a call on Jordan was to inquire about her health following the ill-fated party. Jordan herself seemed fully recovered, though she confided that her great-aunt Caroline had taken to her bed, complaining of the assault upon her nerves and forbidding Jordan to see Gerard Lucien again.

Narcissa got to the heart of the matter. "Brit Wallace has told me you relayed to him a . . . rumor of some slaves who had killed their owners. May I ask you where you heard the story?"

Jordan Archer responded with a slow smile and a glance from her long eyes. "Did he? Well, I heard the story from a close acquaintance of yours—my cousin Cameron Archer. I am surprised he did not tell *you*, since you are so intimate."

Narcissa felt the gentle, tactfully worded speech she had prepared blown away like dry leaves by the force of Jordan's words. Could Jordan really be implying an improper relationship between her and Cameron Archer? She sat in shaken silence for a moment before she could formulate a reply.

"Yes, I did know about the deaths," she said at last. "Since I have been engaged as a nurse at the medical college hospital for some months now, it is natural that Dr. Archer and I discuss confidential matters, bearing on the patients. We trust each other." Narcissa looked into Jordan's eyes as she uttered this lie. She had not trusted Archer before, and she was confirmed in her decision now that he had told Jordan about the murders—Jordan, who viewed a secret as a means to make herself the center of attention.

"But," Narcissa went on, "it is not clear that murder was done, or if it was, that it was done by the slaves."

"But you think it is true, don't you? Otherwise you would not be so angry," was Jordan's disingenuous response.

Narcissa brought her face down close to Jordan's and spoke in a low voice, as if to a misbehaving child. "I will not enter into this—contest of wills with you. I simply say this: do not repeat what you heard. If you do so, great harm may be done, both to the people wrongly accused of these . . . deaths, and to the soldiers fighting to defend our country. Only tell me this one thing: have you told anyone else besides Mr. Wallace?"

Jordan looked away, as if made uneasy by Narcissa's earnest tone, yet unwilling to give up the game. At last she shook her head no. It was possible she was telling the truth, but it was also possible that Jordan, afraid of further rebuke, was lying.

Hours afterward, sitting with Mirrie and Professor Powers *en famille* in the back parlor, the dissatisfaction of her interview with Jordan still clung to Narcissa. She had a book open in front of her, and at regular intervals she turned over a page. It would not do to be seen moping.

Had she failed, she wondered, by not putting herself more in Jordan's place? Much more than she herself, Jordan had grown up with slaves far outnumbering the whites not only in her own household but in the surrounding countryside. The idea of a slave rebellion could have a horrific power upon the mind of an impressionable girl like Jordan. Then, too, the slave Auntie Lora seemed Jordan's closest connection. The rest of her family had abandoned her one by one, first her mother by death, and now, it seemed, her father. Now would Jordan be watching her old servant, doubting her? It was impossible to imagine Auntie Lora lifting a knife to kill Jordan. But did the old slave long to be free, to walk away from the needy young girl who had never grown beyond the three-year-old in her dependence upon her?

Pity for Jordan welled up in Narcissa. She is a child who needs a mother, Narcissa thought. Then: I am a mother who needs a child. But it was too late. Jordan was a young woman, capable of having her own child, though not yet of loving it, raising it, putting its needs before her own. How I wish

I could help her, teach her, she thought. But, she reminded herself, Jordan was more interested in trying her own wings than crawling under someone else's. Perhaps Jordan did not need a mother. But what about her, Narcissa Powers—what did *she* need?

She looked over the top of the book she was holding, glanced around the room as if seeing it for the first time. The room's proportions were graceful, the furniture—what could be seen of it—and rugs of good quality. But every inch of space was crowded. There were shelves full of objects for study: flints chipped by ancient races into ax blades and arrowheads; bits of animals, plants, and shells that time had turned to stone; dark, specked engravings of old churches and classical sites—and everywhere, books, newspapers, the artifacts of life being not lived but studied, withering into history.

Just for a moment, she allowed herself to imagine that this was her house. The place would be cleaner, and fresher. The artifacts could go to Hampden-Sydney College, where both the professor and his son, her late husband Rives, had taught. And most of the books would go to the college as well, so that those who were so inclined could spend their days among them. The newspapers, once they had been read, could be used for kindling.

If this were her house, she would throw open the dusty windows. Sunlight would pour in. Children would run, and laugh, and her husband— Why couldn't she see his face? Because, she realized, he wasn't Rives, dead for almost three years now. Rives was Mirrie's brother; he would have loved the house just this way. And if he were still alive, if it were *their* house, she would love it too. But she had changed. And the face of the man who would be her husband and her children's father was in shadow.

Narcissa came to with a start. Mirrie, her own book neglected in her lap, was watching her. Narcissa feared some teasing comment, but Mirrie's voice was gentle. "Your face is as good as a play, Narcissa—anger, ennui, elation, sorrow. What is it you are reading?"

Narcissa looked guiltily down at the book she was holding. "It's a volume of Dr. Hoge's sermons."

"Oh—that explains it," Mirrie responded with a wry face.

Just then, Beulah came into the room with a little paper packet, a folded-over note or an envelope, which she handed to Professor Powers. Mirrie's eyes followed the paper, and Narcissa breathed a sigh of relief for the distraction. The professor opened the paper and read the contents silently, then held it out toward Mirrie, who rose to take it. Mirrie glanced at the contents, then hurried over to Narcissa.

"It's from Mr. Wallace. He has heard Colonel Cohen was wounded. Not in an engagement with the enemy—some kind of accident, apparently."

"Oh, Mirrie!" Narcissa dropped the book of sermons and held out her hand for the letter. "Is it serious?"

"He doesn't say. He heard it in the street and promises to let me know more when he is able to find out. How is it no one in his family sent to tell me?"

Narcissa could not give the answer, though Mirrie knew it herself: *Because you would not be his wife.*

Professor Powers looked troubled. "I am sorry," he said hesitantly. "I had hoped—"

Mirrie's chin came up, and she looked at her father. Narcissa knew an angry retort was coming. But Mirrie must have seen something in the old man's face that softened her. She went to her father and knelt by his chair, her head on his chest. He spoke again, very softly. "I had hoped, when I die, that you would not be alone." He stroked her hair a moment. At last he said, "Never mind. It is probably not so serious, after all. Tomorrow you may call on the Cohen ladies."

Mirrie looked up and nodded. Her eyes were dry, but it seemed to Narcissa all the sadder that Mirrie was denied the release of tears.

THE NEXT MORNING

Narcissa had slept badly and woken late; now she had to hurry to her meeting with Judah Daniel at the jail. This was the day appointed for Judah Daniel, accompanied by Narcissa, to question Hetty. God willing, Hetty's restored memory would answer crucial questions concerning the murders at Manakin. But answers to questions would not pave an easy path to justice. Even if Hetty had seen James Cantrell slit the throats of the old couple and their daughter-in-law, she—a black woman—could not testify against him in a court of law.

Judah Daniel was conversing with Hetty in the same office where Clara had told her about seeing the devil. The quiet presence of Narcissa Powers seemed quickly forgotten by Hetty, whose back was to her.

"There was a terrible thing happened at Manakin," Judah Daniel said in a soothing voice. "You fell sick at the time, don't recollect much about it, I expect. What can you tell me about the last day you can remember—the day Master John supposed to come home?"

Hetty twisted in her chair. She looked like the young, frightened girl she was—thin for her age, which Judah Daniel guessed to be about twenty—instead of the wax doll she had appeared to be when in the grip of catalepsy. At last she began to speak in a low voice. "Johnny was fractious. Woke up in the early morning, wasn't nothing I could do to quiet him. Finally Miss Dorothea told me if I couldn't keep him quiet, she'd whip us both."

"You . . . and her son?" Judah Daniel asked. "Had she done that before?"

"Slapped Johnny and me sometimes, had me whipped once, bad." She grimaced at the recollection. "But it was just mostly threats, I reckon."

"Where were you and Johnny?"

"Up on the third floor, in the nursery."

"What about the young master, Colonel Berton? Did he whip you and the child, too?"

"No, ma'am. He loved his son, and he was pretty good to me. But it was like the whole house was edgy. Hiram started in teasing me. Used to be, when I was little, he'd tease me about Indians coming and killing everybody, or some such. I had nightmares.

"When I started working in the big house, when Johnny was just born, Hiram'd go back to that every now and then, to scare me. He was doing it that day, he was talking about an angel coming to kill"—Hetty's voice dropped even lower—"the white folks." She looked up at Judah Daniel, her face creased with the effort not to cry. "Should I have warned them?"

Judah Daniel shook her head. "He talked that way before, and nothing ever come of it. Weren't nothing to tell you this day was different."

Hetty relaxed a little. "I tried to laugh it off, I said to him real smart-like, 'Then what you going to do when they dead? Who going to put the food in your sorry mouth?' He got real quiet and answered, 'Reckon I be dead, too. But it'd be worth it.' After that, he shut up about it. And I forgot about it, till—" She shuddered, then gave a nervous laugh. "I didn't expect no angel to be driving no carriage."

Judah Daniel repeated the word, her tone mildly questioning. "Carriage?"

Glancing beyond Hetty for a moment, Judah Daniel saw Narcissa sit up straighter, knew she shared her own excitement. Was it Cantrell in the carriage?

Hetty went on. "Miss Dorothea done sent me and the baby up to the nursery, so it wasn't like I seen him face to face. I looked out the window and seen the driver taking the carriage on around back. He done let his master out at the front of the house, I reckon. It was too far away to tell anything about it. Then I fed Johnny and laid down on the bed next to him, and he went right to sleep."

Judah Daniel tried to keep the disappointment from her face. "So, you never seen the white man, then?" she asked.

"Oh, I seen him—a little part of him, anyway."

Judah Daniel put a hand on Hetty's arm to reassure her and said, "What do you mean, part of him?"

Hetty took up her account again.

"Well, after a while I woke up. I heard strange noises on the second floor, faint-like: things being moved around, and groaning and crying. . . ." Remembered fear was showing on Hetty's face, and she pulled the shawl tighter around her.

"I heard Hiram's voice coming up through the chink in the floor by the chimney, and I went and looked through the chink down into the old master's room. At first I couldn't see nobody, but I could hear. I heard another voice—not Hiram, but a younger, stronger voice. It was a colored man, the same one as drove the carriage, I reckon. He was talking low-like to Hiram but I couldn't make out any words. That's when I seen the other man, the white man. He reached up over the mantelpiece right under the chink. His hands was so close it scared me. I was afraid he would hear me breathing. He took down the sword that was hanging there.

"I seen his white hands take that sword." She shuddered. "I was so scared. I thought he was the angel Hiram told about. I feared he was coming for me."

"The white man's hands," said Judah Daniel, "what did they look like?"

"Not real fat nor real thin. Not real old nor real young."

"What was he wearing?"

"Seem like it was a dark-colored coat, black or blue, maybe."

Judah Daniel closed her eyes for a moment, imagining what Hetty had seen when she looked down through a chink between the bricks in the hearth, down into a room whose ceiling was probably twice the height of a man. Dark sleeves, light skin; what had Hetty really seen?

"Could it have been Mr. Cantrell?"

Hetty looked surprised. "Could have been, I reckon."

"Could it have been a woman—Mrs. Cantrell, maybe?"

"I—it weren't a woman's clothes," Hetty answered, shaking her head.

"What happened next?"

"After the white man lifted the sword down I heard the black man speak again, then Hiram say something back to him: 'I been waiting for this moment a long time, Gabriel.' " Hetty shuddered at the memory. "Then I remembered another story Hiram used to scare me with, about Prosser's Gabriel over to Henrico. I was still half-asleep, but it was like I was in a bad dream. I don't know, I got real scared. I got it in my head they was killing the old master, and they'd be coming for the baby next. I went back over to the bed. Johnny looked like an angel with them blond curls. If they was to come for him . . . I picked him up and went to hide under the eaves. I don't remember nothing after that."

Judah Daniel put Hetty's words together with what she already knew. On that day two men had been with Hiram, one black—maybe the "black devil" Clara had seen in front of the kitchen fire—and one white. The white man had handed the Berton family sword to Hiram to use on old Mr. Berton. But it seemed like the black man, the one Hiram had greeted as Gabriel, had been giving the orders. And the most interesting thing was, Hetty seemed to think Hiram had been greeting Prosser's Gabriel, who had been dead—hadn't he?—for half a century.

Judah Daniel dropped her voice and leaned forward. "Do you want your freedom, Hetty?"

Hetty's dark brown eyes seemed to fill with visions. "Yes, but—if they killed Johnny, run him through with a sword or cut his throat, and him holding out his arms to me—what kind of freedom would that be?"

Narcissa's hands tightened on the wooden seat of the chair. She had to keep still, so as not to distress Hetty further, but the slave's words struck fear in her like the ringing of the tocsin. Gabriel, the slave from nearby Henrico, had enlisted and armed hundreds of slaves, maybe thousands, from Louisa County to the Tidewater. Since that uprising at the beginning of the century, Richmonders had had to accept the fact that the unthinkable was possible. Prosser's Gabriel was a blacksmith, young, strong, literate. Being hired out as a blacksmith enabled him to spread the word of what the slaves had achieved in Santo Domingo—what he wanted to achieve in Richmond—a murderous overthrow of slave-owning whites.

The rebels, more than a hundred—including some whites—had poured out of the neighboring plantations, armed with farm implements sharpened into blades. Their numbers might have been greater, had not a torrential rainstorm washed out bridges and transformed roads into rivers of mud. As it turned out, slaves loyal to their masters had given away the plot. Gabriel and his followers were caught, tried, and hanged. There could be no doubt that Gabriel was dead. Even if he had escaped execution, he would be a feeble old man by now. Whom had Hiram called by that name?

The black man had driven the carriage up to the house; the white man had ridden inside. A carriage implied wealth. Was the white man an abolitionist like John Brown, but with wealth and cunning to go along with Brown's fanaticism? The black man, was he the "devil" that the cook, Clara, had seen dancing in front of the fire? Devils, angels, angel's trumpet . . . Gabriel was an angel's name.

She had to send word to Cameron Archer. It was out of her hands now. Winder's men would seek out and question blacks with a reputation for troublemaking, as well as whites who had a reputation for abetting them. Their methods would be rough, no doubt, and that was a shame, since most of the men they would question would no doubt be innocent. Still, it had to be done, to save defenseless women and children.

White women, she thought, with a tiny pang of shame; what has happened to my resolve to see justice done for those black women in jail? Hetty had saved Johnny's life. Should Narcissa herself do less for Hetty?

Thinking again of Hetty's words to Judah Daniel, she could see another way to understand them. Two people—one black, one white—had come to the house and, with Hiram as their accomplice, killed three members of the Berton family. But what if the white had been Mr. Cantrell? He had a body servant he relied upon; Mrs. Cantrell had said so. Was the servant named Gabriel? No, it was a short name. . . . Ike, that was it, short for Isaac. But Hiram could have called him Gabriel, in a horrible sort of homage to the rebellion's leader. Or Mrs. Cantrell, who prided herself on being better able than her husband to *control* their slaves, could have bribed and threatened one of them to do her will. Hers could have been the hands that lifted down the sword.

If Judah Daniel were to question Ike . . . But there Narcissa stopped in confusion. The possibility of a slave rebellion cast her trust of the free black Judah Daniel in a different light. Once she had thought that, if she and Judah Daniel could find the real culprit, Cameron Archer would see to it that the women would be released. But suppose Judah Daniel was sympathetic to the idea of an uprising to free slaves?

Judah Daniel, Cameron Archer. Neither of them could she trust wholeheartedly.

Chapter Six

Early the next morning, Judah Daniel joined Narcissa and Archer in the little office on the ground floor of the medical college hospital. She thought that Archer would question her about what Hetty had said. When he did not, she realized Narcissa must have told him already. Of course they would have talked about the possibility of a slave uprising among themselves, decided what was safe to say in front of her and what was not. Why would she expect any different? Her plan, too, was already made: to find out as much as she could from the free black and slave communities about any brewing storm of rebellion. Her plan did not necessarily include telling Narcissa Powers and Cameron Archer what she found out.

Being a woman was a hindrance. Slave plots were usually men's business. A woman might kill her master or her mistress, if driven to it. But Hetty's quick, almost unthinking decision to save the life of the child who depended on her was probably more common. Maybe it wasn't always love for the child; maybe it was fear of what would happen to their own families when the rebellion was put down. Anyway, if slave men didn't always tell their secrets to their own women, for fear they wouldn't have the stomach for it, she couldn't expect them to open up to her easily.

Judah Daniel put aside these thoughts and listened with interest as Archer again played his lecturer's role, describing what he had found in the postmortem examinations. His findings confirmed their suspicions: old Mr. and Mrs. Berton and Dorothea Berton had been poisoned with doses of datura sufficient to cause death even had their throats not been cut. The slave Zemora had died of the poison, and even now the life of Dorcas hung in the balance. Clara and her granddaughter Litabet were recovering.

"Angels, devils," Judah Daniel mused. "Once we got it figured out about the jimsonweed, it weren't so hard to understand. The poison make your eyes—and your mind—play tricks on you. The women thought they saw those things, most likely because Hiram put the idea in their heads. But I got the feeling somebody's behind Hiram in this, pulling *his* strings. And then we come to Gabriel, and the other man, the white man. Hetty saw him take down the sword Hiram used to cut the old master's throat. All she could say about him was, his hands was white and his coat sleeves was dark."

Archer was silent for a moment, then said, "There is often some misguided white man who gets swept up in these uprisings. Or even leads them himself."

Narcissa recalled the madman John Brown. The way he'd been hailed as a hero by some in the North, his acts could inspire imitation. But if Hetty's recollection of seeing a white man raised the possibility of a John Brown, it certainly made more probable her own belief that James Cantrell—or his wife—was behind the murders. The white man hadn't spoken, not that Hetty had heard, anyway. Was it because he knew she was concealed somewhere in the house and feared she might recognize his—or her—voice?

"Let us hope the witness is better placed the next time," Cameron Archer snapped. He wheeled around, nodding to them and placing his hat on his head in one swift motion, and was out the door.

Narcissa put her hand to her left temple. The gesture had become her habit when troubled, since being struck there by a man whose cruelty still haunted her dreams. "Gabriel Prosser, the angel Gabriel—I think those stories would have appealed to Hiram. Clearly the message he took from his Bible was 'An eye for an eye.' "

Judah Daniel's shoulders slumped. "I been figuring and figuring," she said, "how Hiram could let the women be blamed. Let alone be killed if they took too much of the poison. Because Hiram must have give them the poison, all of them, with their breakfast: the blacks before the whites. The one called Gabriel must have told him how to do it, maybe got him believing the women was winning their salvation. He got close to Hiram, told him the time for retribution was come, give him the jimsonweed to mix in with the breakfast. Maybe the coffee was bitter that morning!"

Judah Daniel laughed dryly. "It was a nervy thing to do: Gabriel and White Hands must have hid until the poison made them all good and sick. The white folks probably went to their rooms to lay down. Then Gabriel and White Hands done the killing, got the maids into the mistresses' rooms, set the knives near to the maids' hands. They saved the old master for Hiram, gave him the sword and let him take his revenge. Then they throwed out any food that was left over, cleaned up the breakfast dishes, and set the table for dinner. And that's what the cook seen: a black man, feeding the breakfast leavings into the fire. In her crazy state of mind, she thought it was a devil."

Judah Daniel paused a moment. "It was bad luck for them that we figured out about the jimsonweed. Ninety-nine out of a hundred would have just said the slaves went crazy."

Narcissa was puzzled. "What they did, Gabriel and White Hands"—she shivered a little repeating the nickname—"they murdered four people directly—five, if Dorcas dies—but they as much as murdered all the house servants, by putting on them the blame for the crime. If a mob of whites had been raised, or a few dozen armed soldiers brought from the training camps, they might have killed every slave at Manakin." She thought some more. "It was so tidy, so nearly perfect. If Dr. Archer hadn't been called in, and then us . . . But even more, if Hetty hadn't been able to see, and hear, and tell what she saw . . . Hiram must have known she was in the house. Why did he let her escape?"

"Well," Judah Daniel said slowly, "I reckon he thought she took the poison and crawled off to the nursery, too sick to know or care. But maybe he had a soft spot for her, protected her."

Narcissa felt her anger rise once again. Hetty had chosen to save the life of John Berton's son. Taking the child with her into hiding was a risk: he could have cried out and given them away. Hetty deserved to be rewarded. The other women had been drugged into insensibility. Cameron Archer must not forget the women, must continue to let her and Judah Daniel investigate. But would he?

CAMP HAVOC, NEAR LEESBURG

"That old plantation house, Champs-Elysées . . . I had guard duty there last night, and . . . it's true, what you said. The place is haunted."

Archer Langdon looked up, hiding his surprise. If the words had been spoken by one of the boys his own age, Langdon would have accused the speaker of pulling his nose. But it was O'Donnell, the rugged Irishman, who had always watched the escapades of the younger men with detached amusement. Now, speaking in a whisper, his eyes darting around, O'Donnell looked—well, like he'd seen a ghost. Still, one of the boys might have put him up to it. Langdon remained circumspect. "Why do you say so?"

O'Donnell squatted on his haunches next to Langdon and spoke in a low voice. "You know," he prompted impatiently. "It was in that stack of broadsides you got printed up and sold around. The woman fell down the stairs and died, dressed in her wedding dress. And the man she was going to run away and marry got buried alive under the house. A tunnel caved in on him. The woman makes a moaning noise, and the man . . . scratches." O'Donnell curved his sun-browned right hand into a claw and raked the air. Langdon—who was not immune to the story's effect, despite having made money on it—felt himself shiver.

"I knowed the boys didn't like to pull picket duty there," O'Donnell went on. "Captain ain't going to send more than one, and it's a lonely place. In the dark, sometimes, a man gets to seeing things ain't really there. But I didn't think nothing about it. I just shouldered my rifle and rode on over around sunset. I looked around in all the windows. It's a fine old place, sure enough. Then long about time it got real dark, I heard the scratching. It went through me like a knife, I can tell you." O'Donnell shook his head at the memory and managed a smile. "I know what you thinking, but it weren't no animal. It was a long, slow scraping, like—" O'Donnell drew his lips back in a grimace and blew out through his teeth. The noise was like that made by hot iron plunged in water. "It was a long ways away," O'Donnell went on, "muffled, like it was under the house."

Archer shot him a doubting look. But the Irishman held up his hand to forestall him. "I jumped up and looked all around me. Then I went up to the parlor window. The moon was up by this time, throwing shadows in the room. I could tell wasn't nobody in the room. The scratching stopped, and I was telling myself not to even be thinking about no moaning. Then all of a sudden the piano commences playing, all by itself, just like a madman was at the keys." O'Donnell raised his hands with fingers curved again, but this time brought them down hard on an imaginary keyboard. "Then it went off in a sort of trill, like, and was quiet again. I picked up my rifle and fired into the room, right through the window. Then I hightailed it out of there. Did the rest of my picket duty from down the road."

Telling his story must have helped O'Donnell, Langdon decided. He was looking more himself, not so chalky in the face or white around the eyes.

"Don't you go telling nobody about this," O'Donnell added, rocking back on his heels. "I wouldn't never hear the end of it."

The broadside had been written from the point of view of a believer, Langdon realized—in ghosts in general and in the Champs-Elysées ghosts in particular. O'Donnell had chosen him as his confidante because he expected Langdon to take him seriously. And in truth, Langdon had to admit that a dark night on lonely picket duty could turn the doughtiest skeptic into a believer in the supernatural. "You have my word," he said, with a formal little nod.

O'Donnell was getting up, the look on his face now distant. Wondering if the man regretted having revealed his fear, Langdon cast around for a way to ease his embarrassment. "Let us, you and I, find a way to go over there in the daylight," he said. "Find out if your shot winged anything."

O'Donnell looked at him suspiciously, then smiled. "Yeah."

MANAKIN

Brit Wallace whistled tunelessly as the hired carriage clambered along the drive to Manakin, each of its four wheels seemingly engaged in a separate struggle to ascend, then descend, the mounded clay ruts. He had been in an exhilarated state since Mrs. Powers had confided to him the truth: that there had been a massacre, just as Jordan Archer had told him. Not a slave uprising, perhaps; Mrs. Powers seemed fairly sure the murders had been more domestic, more personal, than that. She had also urged on him her belief that a white man, conceivably even a white woman, was behind the deaths. Well, he would see. Now that he had the name of the plantation, the names of the people, involved, he would winkle out the truth on his own.

He had decided to start with the scene, with Manakin, and with Mrs. Cantrell, its current mistress. He had written to her, with a letter of introduction from an eminent member of Richmond society, requesting a tour of the historic mansion with a view to writing an article for the London *Weekly Argus.* He knew better than to allow her time to respond: he had hired the coach and set out early the morning after the letter was sent. After his interview was concluded and he returned to Richmond, he would call on the Powerses, with some good news concerning their friend Nat Cohen. Cohen's injury—a kick in the stomach from a horse—could have been serious but apparently was not, and he was expected to return to Richmond in a day or two to complete his recovery. Brit had also heard some interesting rumors concerning an offer of a diplomatic position that the Confederate government was making to Cohen. Finally, once this news was delivered and rumors speculated on, Brit hoped to speak with Mrs. Powers in sufficient privacy to tell her his impressions of Mrs. Cantrell.

Brit felt his luck hold when the young, bland-faced servant who came to the door at Manakin took his card and disappeared, leaving the door open. He could see the servant hold out the card to a lady—the frills silhouetted against the light identified her as such—could see the "lady" snatch the card from the servant's fingers with a word that made the girl recoil as a slap would have done.

His luck had not run out. The slave did not come to dismiss him. Instead, the lady—it was Mrs. Cantrell, Brit felt sure, from Narcissa's description—came to the door. Brit had stationed himself so that she would have to step out onto the porch to address him. He could tell by the switchings of her skirts—rather like the jerking movements of a cat about to pounce—that she was angry, but that disturbed him not at all. Angry people were often most talkative.

"Young man—" she began.

"Have I the honor of addressing Mrs. Cantrell?" Brit bowed. "Perhaps you did not receive my letter. I am William Wallace, a correspondent employed by the *Argus*. Of London."

Mrs. Cantrell put out her hand to give him back his card. Brit clasped his own hands behind his back and gazed around him, up at the house, into the yard, anywhere to avoid meeting Mrs. Cantrell's eyes. "A lovely old place," he said admiringly. "What scenes these ancient trees must have presided over! And the house! Why, this door is most quaint, most curious—what unusual cross-panels, reflecting the old custom of the cross warding off evil. Do you mind if I—" He took a step closer to the door.

Mrs. Cantrell made a curious noise, like a strangled cough. Brit looked into her face, his patter silenced. She had laughed. The trace of it was still on her lips, and in her eyes. It was the glee of a witch whose hex had done mischief pleasing to its creator.

"Ah, but it didn't work, did it, Mr.—" she glanced at the card in her hand, read it, then let it drop from her fingers and fall unheeded to the ground. "Mr. William Wallace. It didn't ward off evil."

Brit raised his eyebrows in mute inquiry. He had to force himself to stand his ground, not to back away from her.

"I know what brought you here. You heard about the deaths in this place. The old master, the old mistress, the heir's young wife. All dead. *Food poisoning.*" She emphasized the last words as if inviting him to challenge them. "It comes from the debased institution of slavery." Mrs. Cantrell was looking into his eyes now, determined to be heard. "The generations are debased, the wise lose their knowledge, and the ignorant sink deeper into their ignorance. Cover it up, cover up the *bad smell.*" Her lip was curling as if she were truly in the presence of a bad odor. "They consumed poison, and they never even knew it.

"Stop by the graveyard on your way out." Mrs. Cantrell gestured with her head. Brit looked east in the direction she indicated, saw a high wall of rose-colored brick. "They are rotting there now."

Brit leaned against the door frame, crossing his legs at the ankles. He came up with another question Narcissa had asked him to put to Mrs. Cantrell.

"I understand your husband, Mr. Cantrell, has a body servant named Ike?"

Mrs. Cantrell stared at him, her pale blue eyes cold. "Sold off. To pay Mr. Cantrell's gambling debts. I cannot imagine why that would be of interest to you."

Mrs. Cantrell stepped back into the house and swung the door so hard Brit had to jump aside. He stood before the closed door for a moment, then shuddered and turned away. Though the selling of Ike was suspicious—perhaps Cantrell had feared his "loyal" servant would betray him—Brit now found himself doubting that Cantrell had done the murders. Why would the man who had Mrs. Cantrell for his lawful wedded wife bother with killing anyone else's?

RICHMOND

Cameron Archer felt an ugly anger roiling, the pressure of it building inside him. It was not an unfamiliar feeling. It came to him whenever he saw himself to have failed—to have made a mistake or simply to have lost. Most times, he was spared the sight of the grave's victory over his surgeon's skill. But when he had to witness it, he usually cursed whoever was handy: the assistant surgeon, the orderly, the patient himself sometimes. He could not sit like a nurse—like Narcissa Powers—and hold the hand of the dying, and pray. If he tried to pray with the dying, he knew he would end up cursing God.

He was headed toward the city jail, to confirm Harris's fears about a slave rebellion. He had examined Hetty himself the night before. Her recovery seemed virtually complete—although he could not say for sure, not having known her before—and it pleased him as much as if it had been his doing. But her answers to his questions, reiterating what she had told Judah Daniel, did not please him. "White Hands" had to be John Berton, but he could not tell Harris that: he had vowed to save some future for Berton's son. And what if he did tell Harris? He had no evidence; Hetty had not identified "White Hands" as her master. If Archer were to go in and charge Berton with the murders, Harris would think he was crazy. No, Harris would fasten on the idea of a slave rebellion. He would report it to General Winder. And what came of it then . . . It was too bad, though, that Hetty's testimony would not clear those damned women with the damned little bloody knives.

Mounting the steps of the jail, Archer willed his inner voices to silence. Then another voice took him in its grip, raising prickles on the back of his neck. A woman was screaming. As he listened, the scream died in an anguished wail. Then he heard the thwack of a lash, and the scream again. He rose on the balls of his feet and ran down the hall toward the sound.

The largest cell, a room roughly ten feet square, stood open. A dark-brown-skinned woman—Dorcas—was half standing, half hanging from the shackles that held her wrists high above her head. A Negro man was whipping her, his face impassive. Harris stood, arms folded, a few feet away. In the far left-hand corner was Hetty, who lay with her eyes closed, openmouthed, as if in a deep sleep.

The black man doing the whipping paused at Archer's entrance and looked over at Harris as if in doubt what to do. Archer saw the look they exchanged, saw Harris nod, saw the black man draw his arm back to drive the lash again. Archer felt hot blood rush into his head. He took two strides and tore the whip stock from the hand that held it, dropped it onto the ground. Then he turned and strode past Harris to where Hetty lay. He felt the pulse in her throat—there was one, though faint—then slipped his arm under her shoulders to lift her up. There were ugly welts on her back, oozing blood. Blood streaked his uniform sleeve.

Archer rose and walked back to Harris. "What is the meaning of this? These women are my patients."

"And they are my prisoners," Harris answered smoothly. "I heard you had that conjure woman questioning Hetty, but you've made no report to me. I wanted to know what she said."

Something about Harris's words, or the expression on his face, told Archer that Harris had not succeeded in getting any information from Hetty. Judging by her present state, it might be quite some time before he did. Without thinking very much about it, Archer growled, "She saw all the killings. Hiram acted alone."

Harris's response was quick. "The conjure woman may have lied to you. When Hetty recovers sufficiently, I will question her again. And this one"— he gestured toward the elderly Dorcas—"I doubt she ever gets her sense back, if she had any in the first place."

Archer restrained himself. He despised the man's callous attitude toward the women, but he had to admit there had never been much hope of better treatment for them. Getting himself court-martialed for attacking Harris would be too much of a distraction from what he had to do. At last he said, "Don't bother these women again until I tell you their recovery is complete." And that will be never, he added to himself. "If you do, I will take my complaint to Jefferson Davis himself." He saw Harris's eyelids flutter and knew that his threat had found its mark.

As Archer passed from the jail's stinking miasma into the fresh air, the full import of what he had done hit him. Suppose there was a slave rebellion brewing, and he had failed to give the warning? He did not believe it, but now that so much depended on the question, he was taking a terrible risk to protect one little boy.

His thoughts directed inward, Archer stepped into the street, into a near collision with a hack. Archer could feel the horse's breath in his face, hear the black driver cut short an oath in deference to his white skin.

Having crossed safely, headed now for his home on Marshall Street near the medical college, Archer returned the salutes of soldiers he passed. Chilly raindrops pelted his face, and a bitter laugh was rising inside him. If only they knew the ugly state of his soul, how they would despise him! He knew John Berton, aided by Hiram and perhaps by some other servant, had killed his own mother, father, and wife. How did he know it? Only because, in the depths of his own soul, he could understand it. He could even imagine having done it himself. Berton's beautiful wife an adulteress, pregnant with another man's child. His father, whose autocratic nature left John Berton lingering as a middle-aged crown prince. His mother killed, perhaps, because her grief at the old man's death would be a reproach. His son saved because, of all of them, Johnny was the one John Berton truly loved. Maddened by shame and held-in anger, as Berton must have been, could he himself not have done the same?

What Hetty had seen only made his conviction stronger. Hetty had been asleep on the third floor of the house until the moment of the old man's murder. After it, she had been unconscious, cataleptic. The carriage she had seen, who knew how much earlier in the day, may have had nothing to do with the murders. John Berton had come into the house alone, unseen by the field hands who were working far from the house. Someone, probably Hiram, had poisoned both the family members and the house servants but had allowed Hetty to hide herself away with Johnny. John Berton could have made the fatal cuts himself, or he could have left it to Hiram, or another, to commit the acts. Berton's own body servant was said to have run away, but no one knew that for a fact. Maybe Berton had gotten him to do the killings, then helped him to run, so that he could not be questioned.

Justice, and his own honor, demanded that he get the slave women out of jail. But he would not sacrifice John Berton, and Johnny, to save them. If he clung to his insistence that Hiram acted alone, would Harris eventually come to accept it? Or was there another way?

TWO DAYS LATER

Judah Daniel dreamed she was being shut up inside something, a coffin or a box or just a hole in the earth. Must be wooden, whatever it was that was closing on her, because she was banging on it with her fists, and it made a thumping sound like wood. She woke up in a panic, sweat-drenched. It took her a second to realize she was lying on her pallet at John Chapman's. Her forearm was across her face; maybe it had been cutting off her breath. In another second she realized the thumping she had heard was someone pounding on the door of Chapman's house.

She pulled her shawl around her shift and ran barefoot into the hall. Inside the doorway, two men were supporting a third between them. John Chapman was replacing the bar at the door. Their forms were visible in the light of a tallow candle in the hand of John's daughter-in-law, Elda. When Elda saw that the man being half carried into the house was her husband, Tyler, the light jumped and danced with the shaking of her hand. Judah Daniel reached out and took the candle from her. Elda went over and put her hands on Tyler's face. Judah Daniel could see him smile, though his face was drawn with pain.

"Take him into my room," John Chapman ordered. "Is there anyone after you?"

"No," replied one of the men. "But he needs a doctor bad. He got shot last night. In the flesh of his side."

"Dear Jesus," Elda whispered.

"We got the doctoress right here," John Chapman said in a clipped voice.

The two men supported Tyler to the bed, then faced Chapman. "We'd best be going."

"Elda, why don't you fix them something to take with them to eat?" Judah Daniel said in a low voice. Elda drew her gaze unwillingly from her husband and went out of the room. The men followed her. John Chapman looked vexed—no doubt he was eager to get the men out of the house—but Judah Daniel said to him, "It'll calm her down. Best she not get too upset in her condition. Light that lamp, John, and bring it over here. Now, let's see this wound."

Grimacing with pain, sweat beading up on his face, Tyler allowed her to pull off the blood-stiffened bandage, made of a man's tattered shirt, and examine the wound. The bullet had carved a trough in the flesh right below the ribs on his left side, a handspan away from his heart.

"When did it happen?" she asked Tyler.

"Two nights ago." He whispered, probably because it hurt to talk.

Judah Daniel felt around the wound. No sign of broken bones or hidden damage. No heat or smell of infection. Still, it had to be cleaned, and that would hurt like hell.

Elda came back in the room and, pressing her hands tight over her stomach, looked down at her husband.

"Get me some hot water and clean rags," Judah Daniel told her. "And some whiskey."

Tyler looked up at this and smiled a little. "Things is looking up."

Judah Daniel mock-frowned at him. "You ain't going to drink it. And what I'm going to do with it, like to hurt more than getting shot."

While Judah Daniel worked at cleaning Tyler's wound, John Chapman stood over the bed on the other side and questioned his son. His voice was rough with anger and, Judah Daniel knew, with fear.

"You best tell me how you come to get yourself shot."

"Got shot by some damn-fool soldier."

This rocked John Chapman back on his heels and froze Judah Daniel's hand for a moment.

"Didn't even know he hit me," Tyler continued. "Just fired through a window into a dark room. At a ghost."

"Hold it right there." Chapman walked out of the room at an unhurried pace and came back a few moments later with a three-legged stool that he positioned near the bed, then sat on. "Now go on."

"The Loyal Brethren's using some of the houses left empty by folks refugeeing from the war. They done found this place called Champs-Elysées right near the Potomac, not too far from where some Quakers live."

Judah Daniel looked up with a jolt, met Tyler's eyes. She had told him about Champs-Elysées. But she hadn't intended this.

Tyler was still talking. "Folks stay clear of it now that it's empty because they think it's haunted. Local folks, white and black, and the soldiers too. And just in case anybody got too close, we—oof!" Tyler flinched as Judah Daniel trickled whiskey over the wound she had reopened. The pain silenced him for a moment. "We thought, there's this old-time spinnet, standing all by itself in the parlor. One of the boys got this tame raccoon. We put food on the spinnet and taught the raccoon to jump on the keys." Tyler was grinning. "When we saw this soldier snooping around, we let the raccoon out. Done his trick on the keys and about scared the fellow to death. But he let off a shot through the window, and it came right through the curtain and hit me."

Reaching around Tyler to secure the fresh bandage, Judah Daniel imagined the scene. The heavy cloth of the drapery had slowed and deflected the bullet enough to save Tyler's life. She sent a thought of gratitude to God. On the other hand, though, what chance a shot in the dark by a frightened soldier would have hit Tyler at all?

John Chapman's eyes searched his son's face. "What if that soldier comes back, in the daylight, and looks to find out if he shot anything?"

Tyler's face fell. "We thought of that. We killed the raccoon, left his body there near where the ball stuck in the wall. Mangled up like rats got to it, so they couldn't tell wasn't a shot killed it."

"Was this all your idea, this raccoon business? Training it to play on the spinnet?"

"Yes, sir," Tyler said. He wasn't smiling now.

John Chapman sighed. "We Chapmans got to be big men, got to get folks looking up to us, trusting us. I ain't blaming you, son, reckon you can't help it. But why's it got to be the Loyal Brethren? We got enough to do here just to survive and keep what we built. You got a wife and child depending on you, and another one on the way." John Chapman couldn't keep the pride out of his voice, but worry wrinkled his face. "I ain't telling you to quit, you a grown man. I'm just telling you to think about it, that's all. Think about what you risk being out at night, soldiers everywhere, just itching to use those guns and make some noise. And you, taking a chance like that—"

Judah Daniel finished the sentence in her own mind, as she knew Tyler was doing. Something that could get you sold off into slavery, or killed. She would bear some of the blame, too, for having told him about that ill-fated house, Champs-Elysées. No, she corrected herself. If not there, somewhere else.

"And now I got to replace you driving the wagon for the fourth day."

Tyler squeezed his eyes shut for a moment, drew in a breath, and let it out slowly. Then he braced his forearms and slowly raised himself to sitting. "No. I'm going."

Judah Daniel tied up the bandage, then rose and left the room without protesting Tyler's decision. It might be better for him to rest, but it was important to both Tyler and his father that the younger man carry out his duty to the family. She went to lie down on her pallet for a few minutes. Ordinarily she slept till sunup, a couple of hours past the rising time of the Chapmans, who had to have their baking done and deliveries made by the time their customers were sitting down to breakfast. She frequently had calls to doctor someone late at night, after the Chapmans were asleep. But today she would be at the bake shop with them. A fear was simmering in her head, a question. Did this seeming upswing in activity among the Loyal Brethren have anything to do with what happened at Manakin . . . with the "miraculous" reappearance of the dead man, Gabriel? And if it did, where did her own loyalty lie—with the Loyal Brethren, or with the women accused of murder?

Spurred on by the knowledge gained from Mrs. Cantrell that her husband was a gambler, Brit Wallace was making the rounds of the gaming dens on Main Street, partaking of the free food, wine, and cigars spread for the high-stakes players in the upper rooms. At the Star Saloon on Main Street he chanced upon an acquaintance from the Exchange Hotel. Thomas Yancey was a pleasant young man whose deformed spine had kept him out of service and who had a trusted position with the War Department as a telegraph operator.

Yancey had his eyes on the cigar he was lighting. At Brit's greeting, Yancey looked up, a frown on his usually genial face. He looked Brit over, at first coldly. Then his features relaxed.

"Wallace," he said, waving away the smoke from the now-lit cigar, "just came in, did you?"

"How do you do, Yancey? Yes; looking for a game, as a matter of fact."

Yancey's mouth twisted in a shy, self-deprecating grin. "Come, join me." He pointed toward the empty seat across from him. "I didn't know you foreigners still mingled with us small fry."

Brit accepted a glass of claret from a passing servant, sipped on it—not the best nor the worst he had had at one of these places—and turned back to Yancey. "What do you mean, 'us foreigners'?"

"Oh, it's all the talk about the Frenchman who's winning everything in sight, there in the back room. They say he's a blockade runner. He's got the luck for it, I'll say that." Yancey gestured with a sideways nod of his head toward the end of the room, which was partitioned off, its unpretentious door shut tight.

"Has he run afoul of you, swamped you, with his luck?" Brit asked, lifting an eyebrow.

"It's not that," Yancey said laughing. Then his mouth puckered with disapproval, and he nodded again toward the door at the back of the room. "It's the company. They play for high stakes back there. Speculators, whoremasters, and bribe takers, that's about all can afford it." Yancey sighed, his young face tired. "At least the Yankees draw blood in a fair fight. But we're being drained from within, Wallace, and that's a fact. I wouldn't like to think of you joining in with them . . . even if you *were* winning!"

"Sounds too rich for my blood, Yancey," Brit replied lightly. "But tell me: do you know a James Cantrell? Is he among that company?"

"Yes, he's one of them," was Yancey's terse reply.

Brit pressed for details. "A speculator?"

Yancey spoke so low that Brit had to lean over him to hear the answer. "Not that I know of. He's a planter, old Virginia family, so it's his own money, I reckon. But he's a traitor all the same, by acts of omission. If he wanted to give his money away, it would better go to our troops than to the leeches who are sucking our strength."

Brit draped his arm around Yancey's mismatched shoulders. "A closed door to a journalist is like a red flag to a bull. I have to get a look at this mysterious foreigner. Come along, you can point him out to me." Brit fastened his bright blue eyes on Yancey and smiled a determined smile. He had no reason to distrust Yancey; still, he thought it best to disguise the extent of his interest in Cantrell.

Yancey hesitated, then acquiesced with a sigh. "Very well. No harm in looking, I suppose. You won't use my name, will you, when you write about this?"

Wallace laughed and tugged him toward the closed door. It was easy enough to open the door and walk through it. The surprise was, there was nothing on the other side but a cluttered, dusty storeroom, at the end of which a staircase rose to the third floor of the building. A massively built Negro rose from the bottom step at their approach and stood, arms crossed over his chest, blocking their way.

"Lord William Wallace ... and guest," Brit announced in what he thought of as his high-and-mighty, British Empire voice, and stood, his arm through Yancey's to prevent the timid young man's flight.

The black man chewed his lip in indecision for a moment, eyeing Brit's expensive clothes. Then he stood aside and let them pass up the rickety staircase.

The next door opened into a different world. The most obvious difference was the presence of women, beautifully gowned and coiffed, languidly posed, the highest of that class the Richmond newspapers referred to as Cyprians. Gasoliers along the ceiling cast a low light that set their own crystals atwinkle; despite their dazzle, the room itself, which looked to be about fifteen feet deep and twenty wide, was rather dim. Brit's feet sank into thick carpet. He glanced around the room, then drew Yancey along with him to long, narrow tables on which crystal decanters reflected the light of the gasoliers. Heaps of oysters on their shells, enticing patés, rich, layered pastries, were free for the sampling. The house take would have to be considerable for these delicacies to be given away. Yet no one's attention was on the refreshments. Two games were in progress, and the one drawing the larger crowd of onlookers, including several of the women who had taken Brit's breath away, was at the near end of the room.

Brit filled a glass for Yancey and one for himself and, sipping appreciatively, allowed his eyes to rest on that table.

Yancey followed Brit's gaze, nodded toward one of the men, and whispered, "That's Cantrell."

Cantrell was red-faced and portly, with unusually small and prominent ears that looked like teacup handles unsuited to his mug of a face. He was scrutinizing his cards, leaning back, to the danger of the dainty gilded chair, the delicate rims of his ears fiery red. Three other men sat about the round table covered in green baize. One of them had a rougher look than the others. A prosperous farmer, no doubt, thought Brit Wallace, come to the city to sample every vice available, and perhaps to enlist in the Rebel army should the effects of the whiskey last long enough. Flanking Cantrell on the other side was an older gent, his muttonchops shot through with gray. The other man still left in the game had his back to Brit Wallace. He was dressed in a black tailcoat, and he seemed more relaxed than any of the other three. Now and then he turned to whisper something into the coiled blond hair of the Cyprian who had draped herself onto a low cassock at his side. Brit strolled a few yards deeper into the room to get a look at his face. It was Gerard Lucien.

Clearly Lucien—judging from the pile of money in front of him—was the foreigner whose good fortune was inspiring gossip. Brit blinked at the stout stacks of gold coins in front of Lucien and understood Yancey's indignation. An image formed in Brit's mind, like a cartoon from the papers: Richmond, the entire South really, had cast off from shore on a raft of paper money buoyed up by bales of cotton. Still safe on shore, grinning and waving at the imperiled vessel, were men like these in this gambler's hell. And Lucien? Likely his winnings would go back into the pockets of the same speculators, poured through the hands of whores.

Muttonchops offered the deck to M. Lucien. Lucien cut it with a movement that showed his hands to be as familiar with the cards as were those of a professional gambler—though to call a man by that name was highly insulting. Then the starting stakes were established—one of Lucien's gold coins, a mix of coins and paper money from the other players. The irregularity of the currency reminded Brit of the games he played at Camp

Havoc. But there the men were passing time and willing to pay for the privilege. Here the money was the thing.

Muttonchops dealt, and the cards slithered across the cloth. Cantrell could hardly wait, picking up each of his cards as it was dealt. Brit watched his face and thought he saw a wince. M. Lucien seemed to pay no attention, chatting softly with his shapely friend till all five cards were in front of him. Then he drew them close to his patterned vest. As he fanned the cards, Brit waited. Was that a smile that flickered there for a moment? The dealer looked a question at Cantrell, who plucked three cards from his hand, snapped them facedown, and accepted the three replacements from Muttonchops. The farmer took two, as did Muttonchops. Lucien, his smooth face revealing nothing, took only one card.

"Damn," said Cantrell. "You're bluffing, Lucien. Nobody gets as many good first hands as you appear to hold tonight. Nobody."

"Quite," said Lucien.

Cantrell looked hard at Lucien, then at the Cyprian on his arm, hoping for a betraying look from either of them. Finding none, he pushed forward bills for twenty Confederate dollars. The farmer and Muttonchops matched the bet. Lucien drew from his paper cache to meet Cantrell's bet, then gently pushed another gold coin into the growing stakes. Muttonchops and the farmer folded their cards. They had lost too much to the Frenchman already. Cantrell matched Lucien's bet, thought for a moment, and raised it another twenty dollars. Lucien smiled then, dropped his paper twenty on the pile, and this time slid two gold coins out.

Cantrell was sweating. His face threatened apoplexy. He leaned forward, brought his cards up to his mouth as if he were about to kiss them, then threw them down on the table in a fury as he stood. The gilded chair thudded against the carpet. "I'm not contributing another damned dollar to your funds tonight, Lucien. But sooner or later you're going to be on the losing side, and I mean to be there when that day comes." Cantrell stalked off to the bar, nearly knocking Yancey to the wall as he passed.

Lucien folded his cards and dropped them on the table. He had sat through Cantrell's outburst without comment, without gloating. As he looked after Cantrell, Lucien shook his head, as if in pity. "He does not seem to enjoy the game," he said, "which limits his ability to play it well."

The table was done for the time being. The farmer had begun to make loud advances toward a raven-haired Cyprian, who seemed to be sizing up her opportunity. Muttonchops was in a corner, speaking to a man who looked to be in charge of the room. Brit had kept an eye on M. Lucien's cards, and now he stepped forward to the table, turned them over, and fanned them out. A pair of fours was all he'd had, almost surely an inferior hand. Wallace reached for Cantrell's cards, but he felt a firm hand on his arm. Lucien was at his side.

"Ah, ah, Mr. British Journalist," he said, "bad form. You've seen my hand, but that is enough."

Brit was embarrassed. He made an awkward half-bow and stepped back. "My curiosity got the better of me, M. Lucien," he said. "And what I saw confirmed my suspicion that you are brilliant at the bluff."

"It is knowing when to bluff that matters, don't you think, Mr. Wallace?" Lucien eyed him for a moment, then turned to his lush companion, who was arriving with two glasses of the claret. Lucien took one and offered it to Brit, who waved it away.

"You have me at a disadvantage," said Lucien. "You discover me at my vice, and now I must wonder if you will portray me in one of your dispatches."

"Not likely," said Brit. "The readers of the *Argus* want stories of the common man. It is obvious to me that you are an accomplished . . ." Brit hesitated, apparently about to say the offensive word *gambler*. "Diplomat," he said at last.

Lucien acknowledged Brit's witticism with a smile. "There is little more common than this: money won and lost, men consumed by lust for one thing and another."

"Well," said Brit, "in my experience it is altogether uncommon that a man's vice is so profitable as yours seems to be." He made a little bow to the Cyprian, who fluttered her eyelashes and tried to blush.

Lucien's eyes were bright in his unsmiling face. "I am Fortune's son."

Brit, taken aback by the seriousness with which Lucien made the statement, didn't see the source of the words hissed just loud enough to hear: "Son of a whore, more likely." Cantrell had come back to their end of the room. Brit's glance caught Cantrell turning away.

Lucien gave no sign of having heard. The Frenchman made a formal bow and turned away. The girl on his arm cast her eyes back at Brit. He saw but didn't respond. How very like she was to Jordan Archer—and how very different.

When Yancey whispered, "Let's go," Brit followed him out.

At breakfast, Narcissa was distracted with thoughts of Hetty's revelations concerning the Berton murders. She had the impression that Mirrie was excited about something, and she forced her attention back to what Mirrie was saying.

". . . quite an agreeable invitation from Mrs. Cohen. I hope that you will come with me. Though, would it be discourteous to leave Jordan alone, on her first night staying with us?"

"Jordan—*what?*" Narcissa's hand halted in the act of bearing a piece of biscuit to her mouth.

"I thought you would be pleased," was Mirrie's answer. "Miss Archer has become one of your charges, as it were; why should she not become at least a temporary member of our household?"

"Jordan asked you if she could stay here?"

Mirrie nodded, eyebrows raised as if in mild rebuke at Narcissa's strident tone. "For a while. I made no promise to house her for the duration."

She should have asked me, Narcissa wanted to say. *I'm the one who knows her; I'm the one who's—what?—persecuted by her!* But she said nothing. What Jordan had done was technically correct. Mirrie was the mistress of the house and made the decisions as to whom she would invite to stay. And of course, as Jordan surely realized, Narcissa would have said no. Now she could say nothing, without putting Mirrie in an uncomfortable position.

"Does her great-aunt Caroline approve?" Narcissa asked.

"I doubt it," Mirrie responded with a smile. "But she has not forbidden it." Mirrie took a bite of biscuit and returned her attention to the copy of the *Examiner* folded in her hand.

"Will Auntie Lora be staying as well?"

Mirrie shook her head. "Perhaps later. Jordan seemed reluctant—I don't know why."

Narcissa stifled a sigh. Let loose from both her great-aunt and her servant, Jordan could be hard to handle.

At last Narcissa put down the biscuit and slowly wiped a trace of butter from her fingers with the linen napkin. "I think it's good of you, Mirrie. Really. Jordan seems to feel herself very alone, much more so than she truly is. Her father's situation—he has not yet come back south, you know—has something to do with it. She feels there is gossip about him, even within their own family. She has aunts and uncles all over Virginia and South Carolina, some with daughters her own age, who would gladly take her in. But perhaps the quiet here with us, the retirement from city life, will revive her spirits."

Mirrie glanced at Narcissa, then away, sipping from her water goblet before responding. "I am so pleased you think I did the right thing. She should be here in"—Mirrie consulted the little gold-cased timepiece hanging at her waist—"a half hour."

Narcissa retreated to the back parlor to wait. She did not want to be accused of moping, but . . . the thought of Jordan coming here . . .

Narcissa and Mirrie, with old Professor Powers between them in his wheeled invalid's chair, watched as Mrs. Archer Jennings's coachman helped Jordan down from the carriage. Jordan lingered, giving instructions to the coachman and the Powerses' own driver, Will Whatley, who were wrestling with an enormous trunk. At last Jordan turned and walked slowly toward the house, holding her shawl around her, although the day was not cold.

Narcissa glanced at Professor Powers, who seemed to be assessing Jordan as a prospective student, and at Mirrie, who was holding herself very straight and wearing a tight, uncomfortable little smile. Maybe she is afraid she made a mistake, Narcissa thought. But any misgiving on Mirrie's part had come too late.

Then, looking back at Jordan, she noticed how the shawl was bunched up in the crook of her arm. Surely it had moved, that bundle of cloth, on its own. Jordan shifted its weight onto her left arm and raised her right hand to settle it. As she touched it, a small, dark snout poked out, then a head with floppy ears. A puppy! Mirrie must have seen it at the same time. Her intake of breath was so sharp that Jordan, close now, raised her head toward them and smiled. As she did so, the puppy jumped up and began licking her chin.

"Oh, the darling!" Mirrie said under her breath. Together, Mirrie and Narcissa moved toward Jordan and the puppy.

"I hope you don't mind, Miss Powers, Narcissa," Jordan said as she stroked the dog's sleek head. "My cousin Archer Langdon brought her to me. One of the 'dogs of war' at Camp Havoc became a mother!"

"A genuine *fille du regiment*." Mirrie put her hand out to pet the little animal. "Has she a name?"

"Friday," Jordan replied, her chin up a little as if expecting ridicule.

"That's a wonderful name!" Mirrie exclaimed. "So you've read Defoe?"

Jordan looked from Mirrie to Narcissa and back. "Robinson Crusoe was all alone until he found his Friday. Now I have mine. I hope your father will not object?"

"Not at all!" Mirrie responded. "Come and meet him. May I—?"

Narcissa watched as Mirrie gently slid her hands under the wriggling animal and drew it to her. The puppy promptly transferred her kisses to Mirrie's face. Jordan and Mirrie walked up the steps to Professor Powers's chair, and the three began to talk. She saw Professor Powers take the puppy onto his lap. Friday, gentle with the old man, snuggled under his arm.

Narcissa followed, shaking her head in wonder. Knowing how deeply Mirrie had mourned the death of her spaniel, Shandy, a few months back, still she herself would not have thought to advise Jordan on this way to ensure her welcome. Never in her life, Narcissa mused, had she met anyone more charming than Jordan—at least, when she wanted to be.

Jordan declined the invitation to accompany Mirrie and Narcissa to the house on Franklin Street where Nat Cohen shared his home with his mother, a brother and his wife, his widowed sister, and several children. Arriving at the Cohens', they found Nat Cohen propped up in a chaise longue, surrounded by the ladies of the family. Nat raised himself a little to shake hands with Mirrie and Narcissa, then fell back, grimacing with pain. His spirits seemed high, however.

"Kicked by my horse!" he explained. "Damned embarrassing! Oh, pardon me, you see how camp life has coarsened me."

For a moment Nat's brown-bearded, high-colored face looked regretful. Then he smiled again. "So, as you perhaps have heard, I have decided to accept our government's offer of a diplomatic mission." Mirrie's face lit up with interest.

Narcissa listened for a few minutes as Nat talked of the appointment. Then she murmured, "Pray excuse me," and drifted away, leaving Mirrie and Nat to their political discussion. Across the room, the three Cohen ladies—Nat's mother, his sister, and his brother's wife—carried on their own conversation, with every comment repeated at least once for the deaf ears of *maman*. In the moments of quiet, meaningful looks were exchanged by the women. Narcissa knew that they were as conscious as she herself was of the conversation between Mirrie and Nat.

A half hour later, Narcissa had eaten more cake than she wanted, and drunk more tea, and exhausted every conversational topic that she could think of. She was stifling a yawn and wondering whether she might tell Mirrie it was time they were going, when she heard Nat speak, his voice low but urgent.

"May I write to you at least?"

Mirrie must have replied, too softly for Narcissa to hear.

"Ah, how little you know yourself!" Nat's voice boomed into the silence. Narcissa glanced nervously at the Cohen ladies, but they sat, eyes on their knitting needles, expressions blank. "You have written to me since first I saw you, and you have never stopped. You write to me with your eyes, that say so much more than other people's. You write to me with your hands in the air, how much they have to say! You write to me with your walk. Alas, my dear, even your silence these past months has written to me, has pierced my heart like no one else's words could ever do."

"So, Mrs. Powers, I believe I have heard you are a nurse at the hospital?" deaf Mrs. Cohen shouted gaily.

There was a little gasp from across the room. Narcissa could imagine Mirrie's embarrassment at the sudden reminder of others in the room. A few minutes later, Mirrie stood and beckoned to Narcissa.

Narcissa came over to Nat Cohen and gave him her hand. "I do hope we have not overstayed our welcome," she said with a sly smile. Nat Cohen looked very pleased with himself, and Mirrie's flurried eagerness to be away heightened Narcissa's suspicions that Nat's warm words had not met with a cold response.

On the carriage ride home, Mirrie talked with infuriating glibness on every topic except her conversation with Nat. At last, as the carriage rolled up the driveway to the Powerses' house, Mirrie said, "I believe it will do us good to have Jordan staying with us for a while. We are too set in our ways, Narcissa. It's time we opened up a little more—opened up our hearts."

THE NEXT MORNING

The damp chill of an early autumn morning was warmed off Judah Daniel the minute she walked into the oven-heated room behind John Chapman's bake shop. She didn't usually arrive so early, but she knew she would have to watch for a time to question Reverend Truesdale in private about the Loyal Brethren. Tyler Chapman had told her Truesdale was involved with the Brethren, at least carried messages for them. Truesdale preached God's love and mercy. But the Brethren were loosely organized, and some members, frustrated with the small number of runaways they could save, might feel driven to stir up a rebellion. She would ask the Reverend about Gabriel, too. Old as he was, he would remember.

Meanwhile she set herself to helping Elda. Young John slept on a pallet in the corner. Often an older cousin looked after the baby, but Judah Daniel knew that, after the scare of Tyler's wound, having her son nearby was necessary to Elda.

The sun was well up and the day pleasant when the old men came to the room behind the store that was the unofficial gathering place for the free blacks in Richmond. Honus Chapman, John's father, leaned on Webb Clark, who was still strong enough to do some smithing despite his years. Truesdale was led in by a young boy who then disappeared into the street. The old men greeted Judah Daniel with the respect due a healer, and she greeted them with the respect due their years and the troubles they had survived.

Judah Daniel hesitated to call attention to Reverend Truesdale by drawing him away from the crowd. She felt protective toward the old man, weakened by age and blindness but strong in spirit, strong as a leader of his people. So she pretended she had nothing else to do and nowhere else to go. She helped Elda beat biscuit dough and listened to her bemoan the effects of the Yankees' blockade on Southern ports—flavorings were hard to get, especially chocolate and vanilla, and too expensive to buy even when they could be found. No one had seen an orange or a lemon in weeks. Even so, the Chapman bakery was busier than ever, supplying the needs of a town whose population had outgrown its kitchens. Though Elda kept loving lookout on her son, Young John, she didn't mention Tyler, who should be back from his deliveries by now. Elda's discomfort seemed to touch the others there, for one by one they took their leave, all save old Honus Chapman, who'd fallen asleep where he sat, and Zed Truesdale.

"Why don't you take Young John out to play in the cool?" Judah Daniel said at last. "I'll be here a while longer." Elda smiled gratefully, dusted the flour off her hands, and scooped up her son, who laughed with pleasure.

Then she said to the Reverend Truesdale, "I got something special I need to talk with you about." She seated herself next to him on the plank bench. "It's about the Loyal Brethren."

Truesdale inclined his head but said nothing.

"Is there a head of the Brethren?"

Truesdale smiled gently. "No head, nor no foot neither. We is all equal, all of us in the Brethren. It's like a spiderweb, all knit together. When one strand is pulled, the whole web quivers with it."

"But there ain't no spider? No one person directing the work?"

Truesdale gave a full-bodied bass laugh that seemed too strong for his frail body. "Well, now, maybe I picked the wrong creature. The spider is the slave-owning white man. Or, in those places where slavery's not allowed, the slave-catching and slave-selling man. The Loyal Brethren, we just flies helping the other flies."

"Would the Loyal Brethren ever kill?" Judah Daniel asked.

"What you mean, sister?" Truesdale leaned toward her, not just with his ear but with his whole upper body, as if to feel through his skin what she might be driving at. Then he exhaled and relaxed a little, understanding there was no hostility or fearfulness in her question. In a minute, he said, "Them that goes out at night, meeting the runaways, got a knife or a strong staff at least. I ain't saying it ain't possible some Brother knock some slave hunter on the head to save a life. But—"

"Would the Loyal Brethren ever kill a slave-owning family, or help a slave to do it, promise him freedom?"

Truesdale frowned. "That would be a foolish and a sinful thing to do. Wouldn't get him his freedom, more likely get him killed, and stir up the white folks so the chains get tighter." He sighed. It looked to Judah Daniel as if weary old age was pulling down his spirit.

"What about King?"

Truesdale laughed a little. "King took a blow would kill another man, rose up and killed the ones who give it to him, then run for the swamp. I seen him once before I lost my sight. He got a scar in his forehead a half-inch deep. Men and dogs gone in after him, and those that come back, never would go again. Used to be, the white folks feared him: some drunk fall off his horse and stove his head in, folks would say King got him. But King smart. Too smart to be caught by liquor or women. Too smart to steal so much they'd have to come after him. After a while, folks forgot he was there."

Judah Daniel pressed a little harder. "Would he come out to kill whites, now? To lead a rebellion?"

Truesdale considered. "I reckon King come to accept his lot by now; just like I come to accept mine." Then he sighed. "When I was a young man, I prayed God would raise up a Moses from our people to destroy Pharaoh and his charioteers and lead us to freedom. I come to accept it that God love the white folks, too. But many's the time I've said to myself, 'Whoso shall offend one of these little ones, it were better for him that a millstone were hanged about his neck, and that he were drowned in the depth of the sea.'"

Judah Daniel felt the blood rise in her face, thinking of the simple, kindly women who had been the servants of the Bertons', and who had been betrayed by someone's greed or hatred. She, personally, was going to hang that millstone. The thought of those women led her to ask, "What about Gabriel?"

"Gabriel?" The old man's voice was sharp. "The angel Gabriel prophesied to Daniel, and to Zacharias. Gabriel foretold the coming of the Messiah."

"Well, now, I ain't talking about the angel Gabriel. I'm talking about the man Gabriel, belonged to the Prossers."

Truesdale reached up his left hand to his face. The hand, finger joints knotted like galled twigs, shook so that Judah Daniel wanted to take it in her own. She admired Truesdale, had never thought to pity him before, but his hand betrayed the helplessness that was conquering his strength.

As if reading her mind, Truesdale brought his left hand down to the table and covered it with his right. He seemed to draw himself up.

"Gabriel Prosser was a prophet too. Least I thought so, when I was a young boy, about fourteen year old. He was calling on us, on every black man, to rise up, rise up with him, rise up and strike down the devil with the whip. I seen him. He was a big man, tall, arms like links in an anchor chain. He was a blacksmith. His head was all scarred up—they said he been cut by one of his owners. I was there, with the others, and he come up to me and put his hands on my shoulders and told me to follow him to freedom. To freedom. To everlasting freedom."

Truesdale was rocking back and forth on the hard bench, his voice coming from the cradle of his soul.

"I wanted to follow him. I was ready to lay my burden down and follow him anywhere."

There was a little sound behind them from the door that led to the yard. Judah Daniel glanced over to see Tyler push the door closed behind him and stand, listening.

Truesdale, caught up in his memories, did not seem to hear. "Gabriel's plan was strong. We would be a trusted band, and we would march. As we marched we would grow to hundreds, then thousands. We would form three regiments and fall on Richmond while it slept. The Quakers, the Methodists, the French people, we would not harm. The poor people, those that loved freedom, would follow us. They would follow Gabriel's flag with the words 'Death, or Liberty.'"

The light went out of Truesdale's face, and his voice got quiet. "I went out that night. But the rain came pounding down, such a rain as I never seen before. I couldn't see my hand in front of my face. I tried to go on, but the rain beat me back. Knocked me down, came near to drowning me right on the road not a mile from the cabins. Then I felt strong arms gather me in and pull me from the water. I knowed it was Gabriel.

"It was my father. He half-carried me back home. Then he went back out again. Later I found out he'd gone to the master. My own father was one of them betrayed Gabriel. He got his freedom for it . . . and mine."

A shudder went through Truesdale, leaving him bent over. His eyes were shut tight, keeping out remembered sights, holding in tears. His voice, when he spoke again, surprised her with its strength. Not for nothing had he been a preacher all these years.

"I hated my father for that. I hated God, for sending the rain. We couldn't fight against it. Wind, lightning, rain like the end of the world. It was like Daniel walked into the lions' den, unafraid, trusting in God—and the lions ate him! What kind of God is that, give up his prophet to be destroyed? I even hated my freedom.

"More than two years passed before I got peace in my heart. I was reading the Bible, even in my hatred, wanting to know Why? why? And Jesus touched my heart. We been told to love our enemies. Ain't no way given for us to get around that. Gabriel's uprising was a sin. God sent the rain to stop it. When I saw that, I went to my father and was reconciled to him. And the love that came into my heart has not departed from it."

Truesdale raised his face toward heaven. Judah Daniel saw him smile through tears he could no longer hold back. She squeezed his arm, then looked back to where Tyler was standing, his eyes narrowed, body stiff with the pain of his bandaged wound. When he met Judah Daniel's eyes, he frowned and went back out the door to the yard.

"Is anyone there?" Truesdale asked Judah Daniel. The ecstasy had left him, and his face looked troubled.

"Tyler," Judah Daniel replied lightly. "He didn't want to break in on your thoughts. You know how he always look up to you."

"I worry about that boy," Truesdale said sadly.

"I'll go talk to him," Judah Daniel reassured him as she rose to go after Tyler.

She caught up with Tyler just outside the door, where he sat on the plank bench watching Elda play with Young John. Tyler was slumped against the wall, hands in his pockets, but he sat up straight when Judah Daniel came up and sat next to him.

"God made the storm," Tyler said in a hoarse whisper, "but men made the meaning of it. Reverend Truesdale gave it a meaning that's kept him safe, kept him from having to raise his hand against the oppressors. Now he's old, I ain't blaming him for it. But when he was young . . . Just think, Judah Daniel," he said, turning fierce eyes on her, "if it wasn't for that storm, we might all of us be free. We might all of us have what is ours by right, and not be terrified of losing it."

"Reverend Truesdale a brave man," Judah Daniel said thoughtfully. "He could be arrested just for preaching the Gospel. And helping the Loyal Brethren—that could get him killed." She looked into Tyler's bright brown eyes to see if he understood her warning.

His frown deepened, cutting a harsh line between his brows, but his words were thoughtful. "I believe in the work of the Loyal Brethren. I know I'm taking a chance." He glanced over to where Elda and Young John were playing, but his look did not lighten. "But how come Reverend Truesdale chances his life, I chance my life, so as to free a few slaves without having to hurt no white people?"

Judah Daniel met his eyes but could think of no answer to his question.

Tyler went on. "Jesus said a lot of things, Judah Daniel. 'I come not to bring peace, but a sword.'"

His fingers flexed as if wrapping themselves around the hilt of an imagined sword. Judah Daniel pictured a sword, used to slash an old man's throat. Someone with Tyler's anger could have cut the throats of the Berton family. But to poison the slave women, fix them to take the blame—that took a different kind of heart.

⁘

In the afternoon of the day following Jordan's arrival at the Powerses', when Narcissa returned from the hospital, she followed the sound of voices and excited yapping out into the back lawn of the Powers home, be-yond its formal gardens to the washhouse. The Turkey carpets from the back parlor were hung over the clothesline, and Mirrie and Jordan were flailing them with woven wicker carpet beaters. They were laughing, and Friday, who stood less than a foot high on her stubby hind legs, was jump-ing, now and again catching the rug between her teeth and hanging, swinging, falling off, then jumping again with redoubled energy.

At last they caught sight of Narcissa. Friday bounded over. Narcissa scooped her up, but the puppy quickly wriggled away to return to the game. Mirrie came up, pushing strands of hair away from her face, which was bright pink and damp with perspiration.

"Have a go!" Mirrie said, laughing, and thrust the carpet beater into Narcissa's hand.

Jordan called out, "You can pretend they're Yankees—or newspaper editors," she added, glancing at Mirrie, who blamed the Richmond editors for inciting Virginia to secede, "or my cousin Cameron Archer, or any de-spised species you may choose!"

Narcissa felt her own face blazing. Had they been talking about her and Dr. Archer? Had Mirrie voiced her opinion that Narcissa knuckled under to him, and had Jordan insinuated that Narcissa's acquiescence might have a sentimental motive? Stiff with self-consciousness, Narcissa handed the carpet beater back to Mirrie.

"No, thank you. I've done my share of work today." How pompous I sound, Narcissa thought. Why could she not join in the fun? The remark about Archer was more likely inspired by Jordan's own resentment of his occasional high-handedness. She became aware of Mirrie's eyes on her, their expression serious, though her mouth still smiled. Jordan came up, too, and looked at Narcissa as if eager for her approval of what they had done.

"Well, come and see what we've been doing," Mirrie said. "We've given the back parlor a thorough turning-out. We've dusted, tied up newspapers and carried them down to the kitchen, polished the furniture—"

"I thought Beulah did those things for you, when you wanted them done. I would have been glad to do it, if I had thought—" Why could she not just go along with their enjoyment? Narcissa wondered. Why did it seem a reproach to her? Narcissa, born to a less privileged life than Mirrie—and certainly than Jordan—knew very well how to mix wax and white sap into furniture polish. But she had always assumed Mirrie liked

the house the way it was and viewed more than the most necessary cleaning as a source of disturbance, best to be avoided. "How did you even
know what to do?"

Mirrie pushed her spectacles up on her nose, reached into the deep
pocket of her apron, and pulled out a small, dusty volume. "Read about it
in a book, of course!"

At that, Narcissa laughed. Mirrie and Jordan laughed too, and Friday
danced around them, yapping as if she knew to what use a book should
be put.

Mirrie and Narcissa, arm in arm, walked into the house, Jordan following behind with Friday. "You may be the salvation of that girl," Narcissa
whispered.

"She adores you," Mirrie whispered back. "She wants you to be her
mother, she wants to *be* you. And of course, for those very reasons, she
hates you fiercely."

"Did she tell you that?" Narcissa asked, alarmed.

"Of course not!" Then, in a louder voice, Mirrie added, "Wait until you
see what we've done with the arrowheads—"

Chapter Seven

No battle had been fought in recent weeks, but not a day passed that death did not win its battle against life somewhere in the city. And hardly a day passed that the Dead March was not heard accompanying the slow ride to one cemetery or another. The dirge's drawn-out first note, thrice repeated, blown on a horn that was sometimes clear, sometimes quavering, caught at Narcissa's throat as often as she heard it. To drown out its relentless summons to grief, she hummed to herself. *The strife is o'er, the battle done, the victory of life is won*—the new hymn they had learned at Easter mounted to a joyful *Alleluia!* But it was hard to raise her mind from the grave, the mourning family, the empty place at the table, in the heart. Was she growing numb to the greater meaning of death, that most fearful, most wonderful aspect of all: the passing of the soul to God's judgment?

Narcissa's eyes blurred with tears over the letter she had written to one such family. Sergeant Turner, son, husband, father of three children. He had spoken proudly about his family until the fever left him too weak to talk. She had struggled to give them some words of love and hope, but the yearned-for, sometimes-realized faith that was in her withered on the page to conventional phrases of condolence.

She sealed the letter, unsatisfied, and looked up at the figure that had entered the room. It was Jordan Archer. The line between her brows spoke of pain, not of petulance. Narcissa felt a stab of concern and rose to greet her.

"Walk with me, Narcissa." Jordan's voice, too, was strained. Narcissa let herself be led down the stairs and to the little room where her bonnet and cape hung.

They walked out and headed up the street toward Jefferson Davis's "White House." The streets were crowded, some soldiers but many civilians, armed men from who knew where, come to get what they could from the city.

Jordan seemed unaware of their jostling and their stares. She walked with her head down, looking off into some middle distance, seeing something invisible to Narcissa.

To lighten Jordan's spirits, Narcissa asked, "Why did you not bring Friday with you?"

The mention of the puppy failed to make Jordan smile. "I . . . I hoped to see M. Lucien, to give me some ease from my headache."

"M. Lucien!" Narcissa was surprised. "How . . . what led you to think you might see him?"

"We have mutual friends; I thought he might call upon them. That is what I am forced to, now that Great-aunt Caroline and Cousin Cameron have taken against him so."

"And did you see him?" Narcissa asked. She could see that Jordan was getting her hackles up. Was Jordan's behavior her responsibility, now that Jordan was staying at the Powerses'? Cameron Archer would think so, as would Mrs. Archer Jennings. Jordan herself, she knew, would not.

"Yes, I saw him!" Jordan stopped so quickly that the old man behind them had to dodge to keep from stepping on Narcissa's skirts. "Only the hostess insisted on some childish games, and there was no time. . . . I hope *you* are not going to watch me, and question me!"

Narcissa told herself this was neither the time nor the place to argue the appropriateness of Jordan's behavior. "I am sure you know how to use good judgment," she said, feeling like a coward.

Jordan accepted this assurance and changed the subject. "Great-aunt Caroline is driving me mad. Moving out of her house has not freed me from her. She keeps sending me notes. She's threatening to sell Auntie Lora! I don't see how she can, Auntie Lora belongs to Father—and to me. But I'm afraid." Jordan lowered her voice. "She's accusing Auntie Lora of trying to poison her. I'm afraid she will make an accusation to the police! I dare not . . . do you think I should ask Mirrie if Auntie Lora can come to stay as well?"

Narcissa felt a surge of anger against the old woman. There were people in this world with real problems, like the family of poor Sergeant Turner. What right had Mrs. Archer Jennings to fabricate dangers, just to get attention she had not earned through charm, generosity, or even simple kindness?

But hadn't Jordan herself been unwilling for Auntie Lora to come with her to the Powerses'? She put the question to Jordan, who replied, "Auntie Lora opposes my seeing M. Lucien, as well—and she has never even met him! She will like him, though, when she does. I'm sure of it."

"Did Will Whatley bring you?" Narcissa asked. Jordan nodded. "Then let us go and talk to your great-aunt," Narcissa said gently. "I think we can persuade her to let us take Auntie Lora back with us to the Powerses' house. Mirrie is against slavery, but she would not turn Auntie Lora away because of that. Given the choice of protesting the institution of slavery or helping a slave, she would choose the latter."

Jordan looked hopeful at that, and the two turned back toward the medical college, where the Powerses' carriage was waiting.

It was a short ride down Shockoe Hill and up Church Hill to Mrs. Archer Jennings's. Will Whatley drew the carriage up at the bottom of the long flight of stairs leading to the house. Narcissa noted that Jordan's stride as she mounted the steps was vigorous enough. She hoped that the girl's youth and spirit were reasserting themselves. But only a few steps into the front parlor, Jordan sank heavily onto a low chaise and waved a hand at Narcissa. "My head aches abominably. Please, find Auntie Lora."

Narcissa, piqued by her tone, considered making an excuse and walking away. But Jordan had convinced her that Auntie Lora might be in danger of being sold, if not arrested. Something had to be done.

The entire bottom floor of the house was dark and chilly, no fire or lamps yet lit against the coming night. She tried to remember if she had seen any lights from the kitchen or the servants' quarters behind the house. Where was the dignified butler that she had seen in attendance on Mrs. Archer Jennings, the night of that ill-fated party honoring Jordan? Narcissa walked slowly up the stairs to the second floor.

Through a half-open door at the head of the stairs shone a faint light, as of an oil lamp burning low. Narcissa walked up to the door, her footfalls muffled by the carpet, and knocked quietly. A voice rose in response to the knock, a servant's, she thought. She pushed the door open and walked in.

Mrs. Archer Jennings's bedroom, she supposed, from the elegance of the furnishing. A huge bed, its carved, twisted posts extending twice her own height, dominated the room. It was unmade, as if recently vacated, the bedclothes tangled, white with something dark, something that gleamed faintly. Narcissa took another step, drawn to the strangeness of it even as another impulse was rising in her, pushing her back. It was blood, so much of it . . . *the old woman had so much blood in her?*

But whose blood was it? The bed was empty. No, there, something . . . In the bedclothes, light and dark, forming a pattern at once familiar and horrible: the pale dome of a human skull with scurfs of reddish hair clinging to it, shadowed holes of eyes and gaping mouth.

Narcissa forced herself to look again. It was the face of Caroline Archer Jennings, slack-mouthed and hollow-eyed in death. Her nightcap had slipped off, revealing the nearly bald head she had covered with false hair. The head seemed to lie separate from the body, on a piece of dark cloth. No, that was the blood that had flowed from the wound in her neck. There was her nightdress, and there, lying on the counterpane, one of her hands, clawlike, deformed with arthritis. Narcissa felt her heart beat again. The woman's death was horrible; why did she feel so relieved that her head was still attached to her body?

Narcissa heard that sound again, barely recognizable as a voice, coming from beyond the bed. Narcissa felt her skin tighten again. Too frightened to move, she could only look. There was Auntie Lora, sitting in a big carved chair, staring at the glowing embers in the fireplace. Her lips were moving. In a moment Narcissa realized that she was singing. On the floor next to the chair lay a big, broad-bladed kitchen knife, stained with blood.

A crazed killer, a knife . . . Narcissa could feel every muscle taut, ready to run if Auntie Lora looked her way. A few moments passed with Narcissa blind and deaf to anything else in the room. Then, as the fear began to ease out of her a little, she became aware of another sound. She turned. Why had she forgotten about Jordan? She should have kept this sight from her young eyes. It was too late. Jordan was staring, her hands over her mouth, holding in a scream.

At last Jordan spoke. "Help her." Somehow Narcissa knew it was Auntie Lora whom Jordan meant. "She didn't do it." In the whispered words Narcissa could hear Jordan's hysteria rising. She put her arm around the girl.

Jordan sagged into her. "Help her," she said again.

She agreed with Jordan: Auntie Lora had not cut the throat of Mrs. Archer Jennings. But that meant the killer could still be in the house. They had to get out, get to safety. But Jordan had to recover herself first, enough to walk down the stairs and out of the house.

Narcissa helped Jordan to a chair and stood next to her, holding her shoulders with a reassuring pressure. She looked over the girl's bowed head toward the light of the old-fashioned oil lamp burning on the side table—the lamp that had beckoned her into this room. Narcissa glanced, then stared. What was that irregularity in the rose pattern of the wallpaper? She kept up the pressure on Jordan's shoulders as she strained her eyes to make it out. A dark stain, its shape suggesting—oh God! Narcissa felt her heart leap, hoped Jordan did not feel her fear. It looked like a handprint smeared on the wall there, still a little shiny. A handprint in blood. The print had been placed carefully, where the light would fall on it. She didn't think either Mrs. Archer Jennings, wounded, or Auntie Lora, ill as she seemed, could have placed it there. It had to be a signature left by the murderer.

Gabriel was growing bolder, demanding to be noticed.

She dared not tell Jordan that she must hurry, that the killer could still be in the house. "Come, Jordan." She spoke firmly. "We must get Will Whatley to take us to Dr. Archer."

"What about Auntie Lora?" Jordan started toward the old servant.

Narcissa caught her arm. "She's ill—maybe poisoned. We can't carry her. Come—now!"

"You think someone's here, hiding, don't you?" Jordan's eyes searched Narcissa's as if seeking permission to escape into hysteria. It seemed Jordan got her answer, for she fell silent, and her agitated movements quieted. Slowly the girl rose and stood for a moment, clinging to Narcissa. She took one hesitating step, then another.

Hurry, hurry. Narcissa held in the words. She forced herself not to look again at the lamp and the stain behind it. Jordan was not ready to confront that sign of stalking evil that had passed so close to her.

———————

Judah Daniel stepped through the strong wooden door of the jail cell that held Clara, her granddaughter Litabet, and Hetty. As she heard the bolt sliding, locking her in, she had to force herself not to turn around, not to pound on the door and scream to be let out. She had to talk to Clara, and who knew when she might have another chance.

Litabet shrank behind her grandmother, frightened of the stranger, but Clara's words put the girl at ease, and soon she was tugging on Judah Daniel's sleeve, eager for a smile and a kind word. Clara and Hetty crowded around, eager too to know what had brought the doctoress.

"I been wanting to see how y'all was doing. So I been hanging around down here when I could, looking to see when some trouble someplace drew off the guard. There was trouble somewheres this afternoon, 'cause about twenty minutes ago the men done poured out. They's left the place guarded by a couple old men, near about deaf and blind by the look of them, and the women. I talked to that one woman who ain't so bad as the rest, and she let me in. No, baby," she said, stroking Litabet's head. "I ain't sure when they's going to let you out. Keep praying to Jesus."

Litabet nodded solemnly, swallowing her disappointment.

After examining Hetty's wounds, which an attendant had treated at Dr. Archer's orders, checking on the others' health, and gently probing around any new thing they might have remembered, Judah Daniel drew Clara aside.

"Something you said about your son—Litabet's father. Seemed like you'd have said more if we was alone. What was it happened to him?"

Clara put her face close to Judah Daniel's. It occurred to Judah Daniel that Clara probably couldn't see very well: old age had clouded the brown of her eyes with a slight fog like breath on a windowpane.

"He ran away," Clara said at last. "He went up to the army camp with young Mr. Berton. He stayed there for weeks, learning how things was done, watching and waiting. Then one night in late summer he took a boat and rowed across the Potomac. He made it up to Philadelphia, where they's sheltering him." Now pride was bright in Clara's eyes. "He's going to find a way to get us up there, me and Litabet. Then we going to Canada."

"You hear from him?" Judah Daniel asked.

"I got a letter a couple months ago, smuggled in by the Loyal Brethren." Soft as Clara was speaking, her voice dropped to a mere breath on the last words. "Hiram read it to me. Then I tore it up and dropped it into the privy. They could still catch him and bring him back. And I reckon that would about kill him. Quintus always said, since he was a little boy, he was going to be *free*. I reckon it's my fault, giving him the notion. But I ain't sorry."

Cameron Archer rode out to the Powerses' house to inquire about the health of Jordan and Narcissa. Narcissa helped Jordan to a low sofa, then sat supporting her as Archer administered a draft of laudanum and brandy. Soon Jordan drowsed, then slept, her head in Narcissa's lap.

Speaking in a low, tense voice, Archer told Narcissa that Harris had had men combing the streets and a half-dozen uniformed soldiers searching the mansion itself. They had found no concealed killer. At last they had taken Auntie Lora with them to the jail.

Narcissa felt her heart give a sickening lurch. "Do they think Auntie Lora did this?" she whispered. She regretted now her decision to leave the old servant in the murdered woman's bedroom while she summoned Archer. But she had not thought Archer would be so quick to alert Harris. Now, judging by the look on his face, Archer had come to regret his own decision to call in the provost marshal's men before he himself had examined the scene.

Archer's voice in response was roughened with anger. "Harris questioned the cook, Tildie. Found out Auntie Lora had been taking a tonic. They found the bottle; there are seeds in the bottom. The butler must have taken a little as well. Tildie found him sick just before you and Jordan arrived. She helped him back to his room."

Archer sat heavily on a dainty rosewood chair across from Narcissa. "At last they have accepted my explanation of what happened at Manakin." Narcissa's fear mounted at the distress in his face. "They are not ready to release Auntie Lora until she comes around and can give an account of what happened. But they think the woman who supplied the tonic is responsible for both the poisonings, here and at Manakin. They are looking for Judah Daniel."

Narcissa brought her fist up to her mouth, pressing her knuckles hard against her lips to keep in the shout of anger and frustration.

"I know it is not true!" Archer spoke for them both. "But it will be hard to disprove. The poison could have been mixed up at any time and given to some slave to administer to both victims and witnesses before he killed."

Narcissa shook her head. Her fist was still pressed against her mouth, and tears of suppressed rage welled in her eyes.

"We have to get at the truth," Archer went on. "It may be that this murder is connected to those at Manakin. It may be that there is a slave rebellion brewing. This house was an easy target, the mistress and the servants being elderly."

Narcissa glanced down at Jordan, who slept with the abandon of a child. "What about Jordan?" she asked. "She is young and beautiful, like Mrs. John Berton. Perhaps the man—or men—who did this thought that

Jordan would be at home. You examined Mrs. Berton's body. Was she raped?"

Archer shook his head. "She was not."

Narcissa thought for a moment. Then she spoke, keeping her voice low. "Then you may have put Jordan in danger yourself, when you told her about the Berton case. Perhaps someone heard that she knew something, and made this attack upon the household to get at her, not knowing she had come to stay with the Powerses."

"Told her!" Archer almost jumped from his seat. "*I* did not tell her!"

"Brit Wallace learned about the Berton murders from Jordan Archer. She told him she heard it from you!"

Archer stared in disbelief, then sagged back into the chair. He was cursing under his breath. At last he spoke, his voice halting and bemused. "I wanted to blame her. I wanted to blame *you*. But I suppose it was my own fault. One day, just after the Bertons were killed, I was coming into the hospital and I caught sight of you in the coat room. You were turned away from the door, looking into that little mirror, and you had your bonnet on as if you'd just come in, or were going out.

"I stood in the doorway, looking up the stairs in case anyone should come. I spoke to you, something about the murders at Manakin, the accused slaves. Then I caught sight of blond hair in the mirror and . . . it wasn't you, it was Jordan, dressed in your clothes or near enough."

When Jordan came to ask me to her party, Narcissa remembered. *I went upstairs, and Jordan stayed behind. She was dressed like me, all in black save her straw hat. She must have taken off her hat and put on my bonnet, tried it on in front of the mirror. I saw her afterwards, her hair disarranged . . .*

"Her expression showed nothing when she looked at me," Archer was saying. "I consoled myself by thinking she had not understood. But now I know that she not only understood, she told Mr. Wallace . . . and, I suppose, that interfering Frenchman, Lucien."

"Lucien was here that night, at Jordan's party," Narcissa broke in. "That's when she told Mr. Wallace. She may well have told Lucien as well."

Archer grimaced. "Ah, yes, the night of the mesmerism. I hadn't heard about that when Lucien showed up at the jail, playing detective and offering to bring the slaves to their senses through animal magnetism. He made some shadowy claim to represent the French government, though I've heard some say he is getting up funds to outfit a blockade-runner. The one thing sure is, he's an opportunist, come to Richmond to feast at the table we've so incautiously prepared for spies, speculators, and out-and-out thieves."

Archer struck his open palm with his fist. "I could whip Jordan for a foolish child. But it's my fault for speaking so incautiously. Lucien must have taken that germ of information from her and paid one of Winder's men for additional details. At any rate, when I heard about that mesmerism trick he had played on Jordan, I forbade her to see him."

Narcissa hesitated, then said, "But she *has* seen him. In fact, if it had not been for her going to see him earlier today at the house of some friends, she could have been at Mrs. Archer Jennings's house when the killer struck." *And so could I,* she thought to herself.

Archer's brow darkened at his cousin's defiance. "So . . . she is still seeing him, then?" He paused. "I can't, for the life of me, figure out what he has to gain from it. The only secret of any importance that she'll ever be in possession of, he has already wormed out of her."

"She's a very lovely young woman. Is not that enough?" Narcissa said lightly. "His interest need not be so very calculated."

Archer shook his head as if dismissing the thought. Then he sighed and said, "Well, if Jordan's infatuation with Lucien kept her safe, perhaps it is for the best. A least he has not interfered again in the investigation of the Manakin murders—not to my knowledge. And Mr. Wallace, I suppose, has succumbed once again to your management."

Archer rose from his chair.

"Wait!" Narcissa held out her hand to stop him. "The bloody handprint in your aunt's room. What did you think of it?"

Archer lowered himself back onto the chair, nodded at her to speak her mind.

Narcissa want on. "I think . . . The sight of it was chilling, printed in blood as it was, like the mark of an animal—or a madman. But I am sure it was made deliberately. First of all, the 'madman' would have to lean over that table, covered with little leather daguerreotype cases and china figurines, to place the print just where the light would fall on it. Or, he would have to move the lamp to show up the print, then rearrange the little things on the table, as a servant would do if something got broken, so the mistress would not notice."

Archer nodded, his face attentive.

Narcissa continued. "The poison, the slit throat: just like the murders at Manakin. Then the handprint: deliberate, defiant. It's as if Gabriel and

White Hands are tired of the secrecy surrounding the murders at Manakin. Whichever one of them is the instigator, he, or she, wants to cause a panic."

"You know . . ." Archer spoke slowly, his face intent. "I mocked Harris for his trust of Lucien, reminded him about the Frenchman who aided Gabriel Prosser in his plans for rebellion. Perhaps I spoke the truth without knowing it. Perhaps Lucien's goal is to stir up instability in our government. If Lucien was meeting Jordan when Aunt Caroline was killed, he could have arranged with some henchman to come in and cut the poor old lady's throat. If that henchman should happen to be a black man, there we have them: Gabriel and White Hands."

Narcissa felt a tingle of excitement, though she could tell from Archer's tone that he himself put little credence in the scene he was sketching. After a moment, she spoke. "Lucien bears watching, for many reasons. But I think the real purpose of the attack, the bloody handprint, is to stop us looking for a personal motive for the murders at Manakin. Despite the attempts to put the blame for the murders on slaves—and free blacks, in the case of Judah Daniel—the slaves in each attack have been injured as much as the masters, or nearly so. If rebellious blacks are behind this, they show a terrific callousness for their own."

"Well, insurrectionist slaves aren't known for tenderheartedness," Archer responded wryly. "So you've not given up suspecting the Cantrells?"

"Not at all," Narcissa answered.

Archer got to his feet, bowed, then spoke again. "Well, Mrs. Powers, I must confess you've half-convinced me. My thanks to you for your thoughts and observations."

Archer bowed again, turned, and walked away. Narcissa stared after him. If it hadn't been for Jordan asleep in her lap, she would have run after him and forced him to tell her what was in his mind. There was something he was not saying—something he knew or suspected—she was sure of it. She was glad to learn he intended to help Judah Daniel, but his assertion did not give her peace. She, too, must find a way to help. It would be easy enough to send Will Whatley with a note to John Chapman's house, where Judah Daniel had been living since her house was burned the past summer. Somehow she felt that, given the warning, John Chapman and Judah Daniel between them would know what to do.

Gently she withdrew her hands from underneath Jordan's head and shoulders, easing herself free.

Judah Daniel was walking up from the jail toward John Chapman's, deep in thought. One possible explanation of the Bertons' murders was that John Berton, angered by his wife's involvement with Cantrell, had done the killings, helped by his body servant, Quintus. It fit what Hetty had seen and heard: Berton as White Hands, Quintus as Gabriel. Quintus's letter, which Hiram read for Clara and which Clara had then destroyed, was no real evidence. Or Cantrell could have been helped by his servant Ike. Or Mrs. Cantrell . . . though she did not seem to trust her servants enough to make an accomplice of one.

But what if the murders weren't a white man's plot for which a black man had been used? What if Gabriel himself was the key? It wasn't always easy to tell whose hands, whose mind, held the power. Things on the outside—the color of a person's skin, the clothes he wore, the way he carried himself and spoke—were distracting. Could Quintus, taught by his mother to love freedom, have made himself into a vengeful "Gabriel"?

She could believe it. But she could not believe that, whatever else Quintus might have done, he had let his mother and his child be poisoned and led off to jail.

She had come through the white part of town now, into the section where many free blacks, including the Chapmans, made their homes. It was not like coming home to her own house, she thought, not quite, though all the Chapmans were kind, and John had on occasion shown himself willing to be more. If she went to his bed, would they grow closer, or would it be too jarring, given that neither of them was young, and both were strong-willed? As she pondered on it, there was a little scuffle of dust, and Darcy was beside her, moving with her, silent as her own shadow.

"Judah Daniel, they's been a murder up in Church Hill—a poisoning, and they's looking for you. Mrs. Powers and Dr. Archer from the hospital, they both sent word to warn you." Darcy pressed a packet of papers into Judah Daniel's hand.

Judah Daniel caught Darcy's hand and held it tight.

"They sent some money, too. Tyler's holding some of it. He say he got a plan. Go to the Reverend Truesdale's," Darcy went on. "Tyler'll meet you there and take you someplace to hide."

Judah Daniel looked down, wanting to assure Darcy that everything would be all right, that they would be together again soon.

Darcy looked up at her, frowning a little. "Don't be scared," the girl said. "Everything going to be all right."

This is my child, sure as if she come from my body, Judah Daniel thought. She bent down and hugged the girl with all her might. Darcy put her arms around Judah Daniel's neck and hugged back. Then she was gone, and Judah Daniel was turning down the alley to the Reverend Truesdale's house.

<hr />

That night, having failed to turn up witnesses who had seen anyone or anything unusual at Mrs. Archer Jennings's, Cameron Archer sat back in his favorite chair, a glass of brandy at his side, and tried to clear his mind. By the time he drained the last drop from the glass, it seemed to him that he could see both scenes of murder, as if he were looking down on them from some removed height. It came to him that, for all their apparent bloodthirstiness, both sets of killings had been carefully arranged. There was no overwhelming attack; the victims were rendered helpless in advance. Neither rape nor robbery had been committed. It was as if the victims had been maneuvered into position, their lives taken, like captured pieces on a chessboard. Not only the major pieces, but the pawns—the slaves, sacrificed for the sake of the game.

His initial sense of relief had faded. John Berton, returned several days back to his regiment in northern Virginia, could not have murdered Mrs. Archer Jennings. But what of the black man, "Gabriel," who had helped commit the murders at Manakin? If Berton's body servant had been Gabriel, perhaps the killings had given him a taste for blood, inspired him to strike out on his own. Maybe Aunt Caroline's killer had thievery in mind, but Mrs. Powers and Jordan had interrupted him before he could make good his intention. The thought was chilling.

Archer rubbed his eyes. They felt gritty: the clock had struck two long before. He had done the postmortem examination of his great-aunt and found no evidence of datura poisoning. What did that mean?

A chess game: but whose hands moved the pieces? That was the question on which more lives may depend. He had to go up to Leesburg to talk to John Berton. But he hated leaving Judah Daniel, as well as the Berton servants, at the mercy of Harris. He would have to see to Judah Daniel's safety, and force another dose of threats down Harris's throat, before he could leave for Berton's encampment.

What questions could he ask that would coax helpful information from Berton without revealing his suspicions? It wasn't a job for a straightforward surgeon-soldier: better for that fool reporter, Brit Wallace, always making notes in his little pocketbook. Archer set the brandy glass down so hard that the delicate stem snapped in his fingers. Then he picked the pieces up and threw them into the fire, watched the flames blaze up for a second as they tasted the trace of brandy left on the glass.

CHICKAHOMINY SWAMP
THE NEXT DAY

In the gray light before dawn, Judah Daniel slipped down from the bakery wagon into a world where denser fog blurred the lines between land, water, and sky. She entered the swamp near where the Chickahominy River crossed the Mechanicsville Turnpike and made her way in, guided by the bright-white bark of the huge sycamore. But the sycamore was too exposed for her to wait near it. She would find a place to hide, near enough to the tree for King to find her—if he wanted to find her.

The first mile or so she had to walk was familiar: she had come here many times to gather healing plants. But as she walked farther, her steps slowed, and she walked placing one foot in front of the other, Indian style. Her feet in their wooden-soled shoes felt for ground that would support her weight. If she put a foot wrong, she could find herself in water up to her waist. She looked around her, at dead trees whose blackened skeletal branches were aimless fingerposts. Some time years back, when drought had subdued the swamp, these trees had grown tall, many times a man's height. Then the water had returned, drowning their roots. Now they rotted, but slowly. Maybe one day the cycle would come around again, the land would dry out, and new trees take root and grow. What then would become of King and his kingdom?

King. It seemed like one of God's crueler jests that only a few days ago she had doubted the existence of the outlaw. Now her life might depend on King's willingness to save it. To keep warm, and to eat, she had her shawl, and a knife. The swamp grew rank with roots, bark, cattails, and nuts that could serve as food, and it teemed with game that could provide both food and skins. It was good that the first frost had come, quieting the mosquitoes and sending the snakes to their holes. But she would need a shelter, and belly-filling food, to stay alive. What tricks did King know to keep himself and his fellow runaways alive, to keep them hidden from the white world?

Anything—prison!—would be better than this. For it would be prison, at the least. If only she had been working at the hospital, under the watchful eye of Cameron Archer, on the day of the killings at Manakin. But she'd been here in the swamp, doctoring the boy who'd been bitten by a slave chaser's hound, and that she couldn't tell. And on the day Mrs. Archer Jennings had her throat slit, she'd been listening to Zed Truesdale talk about Gabriel Prosser—and King—with no white person as witness.

She turned away from the drowned trees into deep, concealing woods. It felt safer here, though the carrion-vine briers caught at her skirts and scratched her ankles. Raised ridges in the ground, covered with dead vines like matted gray hair, could be firm earth or half-submerged logs that would turn under her foot.

A quivering in a thicket about fifty yards ahead and to the left made her hold up. Birds, probably. But she had a feeling the watcher was human. She pushed back the shawl to show her face and stared into the bush as if expecting it to hail her. The rustle came again. Then a shadow in the bush detached itself and rose. It resolved into a very dark-skinned man, younger than King must be, dressed in a ragged homespun shirt, hair overgrown by about a half-year from its last cut in the slave quarters. He looked cautiously around and then started toward her, feeling carefully with his feet before each step.

Judah Daniel exhaled a breath she hadn't known she'd been holding.

The young runaway had tied a blindfold around her eyes before leading her deeper into the swamp. Their progress was slow, but at last she knew they were nearing a camp. There was a trace of smoke in the air, spiced with a delicious smell of burned animal fat. There were the sounds and smells of people, too—how many, she couldn't tell. Her guide stopped, took her by the shoulders, and placed her, his hands neither rough nor gentle. She raised her hand to the blindfold and, when no one stopped her, pulled it off.

She had been brought to stand a few yards away from where King was sitting, an old musket across his knees and a knife at his waist. She knew him from the deep scar on his forehead. He wore a tattered blanket around his shoulders, a pair of ragged breeches, and boots. His graying black hair fell to his shoulders and tangled with his beard in a kind of lion's mane. His bulging, bloodshot eyes, the brows drawn low in a frown, gave him a fierce expression. But Judah Daniel saw pride in King's face as he glanced around him, inviting her to look.

Behind King, raised on stilts to almost a man's height above the dry tussock of earth, stood a house made of logs daubed with clay. It looked big enough to hold ten people or more. They would have to stoop to pass through the entranceway, but could stand at the center. Lying close together near the fire, wrapped with the deerskins that now hung around in profusion, fifteen or twenty desperate souls could survive the fiercest of Richmond winter nights.

King was watching her. At last he spoke, in a voice that sounded rusty with disuse. "Welcome to Scratch Hall."

Judah Daniel was holding herself very straight. There was no point circling around the reason she was here. "Let me hole up here for a while."

King looked at her for a minute, then said, "Won't be long. They needs you back there, and you needs them."

CHAMPS-ELYSÉES

Private Langdon had asked his captain that Private O'Donnell be allowed to accompany him on picket duty at Champs-Elysées. The captain had mocked him for appearing reluctant to guard the house alone, and Langdon had accepted the jibes with a shame-faced grin, keeping O'Donnell's secret. At last, permission had been granted. Now the two men were entering the mansion through a latch that had been broken but refastened on the outside. If they were caught, they could be court-martialed, since they were trespassing at least. Langdon was aware of this danger, but not much concerned by it: the Archers of Champs-Elysées were his cousins, after all. O'Donnell seemed jumpy, though whether it was human or ghostly punishment he feared, Langdon did not know.

The broken latch fastened a simple plank door securing the narrow entrance used by servants carrying dishes from the kitchen into the dining room. So it was the dining room they entered first. Langdon, who was in the lead, looked back at O'Donnell, The Irishman looked puzzled for a moment, then gestured with his musket, which he held at the ready, to the left. Langdon walked that way, stepping quietly—he noted his own reluctance to be heard in this house, and O'Donnell seemed hardly to be breathing—and soon entered an elegant entrance hall into which the staircase flowed like a cascade into a still pool. Again Langdon looked back, and again O'Donnell jerked his weapon forward and to the left. Langdon, then O'Donnell, entered the parlor. There was the spinnet. Across the room was the window whose glass had been shattered by O'Donnell's shot. Their eyes followed the line the ball would have taken. There, against the wall, lay a pile of fur and bones so thoroughly gnawed that there was not even a smell. Langdon walked over and stirred the pile with the toe of his boot. He looked up at O'Donnell, careful not to smile.

"Ha!" O'Donnell said, disgust covering his relief. "Just an old coon." He kept looking, though, until he found the splintered hole left by the ball, about waist high. O'Donnell looked back at the spinnet. The raccoon had been on the keys: it made sense, or near enough. He looked back at the wall, then down. O'Donnell saw it too, and bent down to peer at the mark, a faint powdering of reddish brown. O'Donnell touched his forefinger to his tongue, dipped his finger in the powder, rubbed it between his finger and thumb. "It's brick dust," he said. "Thought for a minute it was dried blood."

"Come on, let's get out of here." O'Donnell was speaking in his normal tone of voice, and his words echoed loud in the empty rooms. Speaking softer, he said to Langdon, "This was a grand idea you had, coming here like this. I reckon I won't be such a blazing fool no more after this. You know I ain't no coward."

The look he gave Langdon was more belligerent than grateful, but Langdon understood. "No more to be said about it," he replied carelessly. O'Donnell smiled and thumped him on the back.

RICHMOND
THE NEXT DAY

Narcissa awoke shivering, with a slight soreness in her throat. In a restless sleep she had pushed the covers off, and her nightgown was bunched around her thighs. The window was open, and the October night had cooled. She reached to pull down her nightgown and pull up the covers, then resettled herself, wondering if sleep would come again.

Narcissa had retired to bed early, hoping sleep might rescue her from

the nightmarish images that thronged her waking mind. Today, the day after the murder, Narcissa had stayed home from the hospital so that, between herself and Mirrie, Jordan would not be left to brood on horrors.

Auntie Lora was in the city jail, still unable to give an account of what
she might have seen, and still under suspicion of having killed Mrs. Archer
Jennings, possibly with poison provided by the doctoress Judah Daniel. A
message brought back by Will Whatley from John Chapman thanked Narcissa for her warning, and as far as she knew, Judah Daniel still went free—
though Narcissa feared every moment to hear of her arrest.

Meanwhile, the laughter and ease were gone out of Jordan's face. Even
Friday's playfulness could not drive the haunted look out of her eyes. Jordan had spent most of the day in bed. Mirrie had come in at regular intervals, bringing a book or periodical she thought might interest her. While
Mirrie struggled to cheer Jordan, Narcissa rushed off to attend to a chore
or consult with Beulah in the preparation of a dish. When Narcissa returned, hopeful of improvement, and settled to needlework, she watched
out of the corner of her eye as Jordan opened the offered book, frowned,
sighed, fidgeted, and finally put it down.

"Has Mirrie not found anything that interests you, Jordan?" Narcissa
had asked at last. "Perhaps you had better tell her what you like to read.
She thinks your taste is *Robinson Crusoe*—that is why she is bringing you
Marco Polo and Sir John Mandeville."

Jordan had turned toward Narcissa, lines of worry furrowing her brow
and her words coming almost in a sob. "I don't want Mirrie to hate me. I
never even read *Robinson Crusoe*. A boy I met at a party once told me the
story of it. Now my head aches so. M. Lucien told me I should not read. It
is very bad for my nerves. Oh, if only I could see him! Ask him to come,
Narcissa!"

Not raising her voice, not ever expressing outright denial of Jordan's request, Narcissa had resisted until at last Jordan gave up and turned away,
burrowing into the covers. To summon M. Lucien to the house—to mesmerize Jordan!—so soon after her great-aunt's murder would have scan-
dalized even Mirrie.

Now that she was beginning to feel warm again under the covers, Narcissa tried to ease her mind, breathing deeply and repeating the Twenty-
third Psalm. *The Lord is my shepherd, I shall not want* ... Then, from
downstairs, she heard Friday yapping. The puppy had already learned to
go in and out of the little hinged opening in the back door, so she was not

crying to be let out. Surely someone had remembered to feed her. But given that the whole household was distressed by Jordan's tragedy, perhaps no one had.

Narcissa jumped out of bed and, holding up her long cotton nightdress so as not to stumble, felt her way down the steps. Friday had quit barking, she thought; no, there it was again, but the sound was muted now, as if the dog were closed up in one of the back rooms. Why had it seemed louder upstairs?

At the bottom of the staircase she stopped, hand on the railing, suddenly confused as to which way to turn. She was not at Springfield, she reminded herself, chiding her distracted brain. Curious how the home of your childhood stays in your brain, the compass to which you return—but why tonight? There was no lamp lit in the hall that led to Professor Powers's first-floor room, where there had always been before, in case the old man should need help in the night. Who had put out the light?

A floorboard creaked in the hall. Someone gasped. Narcissa, listening, could hear the blood beating in her veins. Fear had turned her ice-cold. "Who's there!" she called out.

The held breath came out in a sigh. "It's me." Jordan's voice sounded tiny, and almost as frightened as Narcissa felt.

"Jordan! What happened to the light?"

"Nothing. I just closed the door." In a moment, the hall door was open again. In the lamp's glow Narcissa could see Jordan in her long white nightgown, a dark shawl wrapped around it. Narcissa crossed over to Jordan and put her arm around the girl's thin shoulders.

"What were you doing down here in the dark?" Narcissa asked as gently as she could. "Did you come to feed Friday?"

The rueful look on Jordan's face told Narcissa that was not the explanation.

"Poor Friday!" Jordan sighed. "Let me let her back in." Jordan hurried away and after a few moments returned. "I put her in her basket in the back room." Jordan stood, holding her shawl tight around her, swaying a little.

"Come back to bed," Narcissa said.

"I can't," Jordan answered. "He may come. I dreamed he was coming." There was urgency in her voice, not fear.

"Who may come?" Narcissa asked.

"M. Lucien. I am sure he knows how I am suffering. And he will come. But if I am not here to let him in—"

Narcissa's voice was sharp with alarm. "Has he written to you? Have you written to him?"

"No!" Jordan pulled away from Narcissa's embrace. "He knows me. Our souls have touched. It began with the mesmerism, but now . . . if I come into a room, and he is there, I know it, even before I see him. And then he turns, and I know he felt my presence! You wouldn't understand."

Narcissa smiled inwardly. Once she had known that feeling very well. Even now, sometimes . . . "That feeling you speak of is very natural, Jordan. It's the attraction between a man and a woman. But—"

"No!" Jordan shook her head vehemently. "It's not that! Not a *romance*. You don't understand! And now he cannot hear me, he will not come!" Jordan turned and ran up the stairs.

Narcissa stood looking after her. Despite Jordan's denial, she was sure the girl was in love with Gerard Lucien. Narcissa had to admit she knew no real harm of him—knew nothing much at all, come to that. Would it be so wrong, after all, to invite Lucien to the house, after some little time had passed? Better that Jordan should meet him in safety, among people who cared about her. Yet Jordan seemed determined to break free of those who cared about her. She had snubbed her cousins; run away from Mrs. Archer Jennings, whose care had been unsentimental, but protective, and from Auntie Lora; flouted Cameron Archer. To Mirrie, Jordan was now only polite, afraid of giving offense.

As for Narcissa herself—from her, Jordan seemed to expect endless interest, patience, understanding . . . and to be constantly disappointed.

Chapter Eight

Brit Wallace, riding out of Leesburg on a hired horse he had dubbed Auburn, was composing in his head, gathering images and fitting phrases to them. Soon—less than a half hour's ride, now—there would be an engagement to observe, then report; he had best unlimber his rhetorical guns.

21 October. I ride north through the Virginia countryside toward the Potomac, where rumors of some impending action have been rising, gently bursting, rising again, like the bubbles in a glass of champagne.

"Oh, God," he groaned. Well, forge ahead.

The day is such as would bring the gods down to earth. The air is pure and clear to the dome of heaven. The sun streams through hickory leaves, the light thus gilded falling to earth like Zeus transformed into a rain of gold for the love of Danaë. The maples are a mellower fire, wine and honey. The oaks, rich antique garnets set in old gold. Closer to the ground, sumac, red as the blood of Actaeon, spilled as he runs from the hounds of chaste Diana . . .

Auburn's sudden shies left Brit half out of the saddle, clinging to the horse's scraggly neck. In the road just ahead stood two pickets, whose clumsy rising had startled the horse. The privates raised their muskets with fierce frowns, but their nervously jittering feet gave them away. Brit righted himself, called out the password he'd been given, and watched as the youths hesitated, then relaxed. One came up to Brit, scrutinized the pass, then pushed back his forage cap and grinned.

"Reckon you'll be luckier than we are, stuck out here away from the fun."

"Reckon so," Brit responded amiably. "Which way do you recommend I take?"

"Follow this road about a mile till you come to a path off to the left. Take it, it'll bring you up into the woods behind our men—at least, behind where they were last time we heard."

"Who's in command?" Brit asked.

The picket replied, "General Evans. But he's not on the field. He's at Fort Evans"—the youth waved his left arm to indicate the direction of the fort—"on the Leesburg Pike, holding off reinforcements from Arlington or Edwards Ferry."

Brit thanked them and pressed on, his excitement growing. So the reports were true: the Federals had crossed the Potomac from Harrison's Island just above Leesburg in the early hours of the morning, met by stiff resistance from the Confederates encamped near there.

He rode on until the undulating fields ended. Ahead was rough terrain: jagged hills and deep ravines covered with close-growing trees and tangled undergrowth. He could hear the crackling of artillery fire and the occasional boom of a twelve-pounder, muffled by the thick woods and the rise and fall of the land. Brit dismounted and tied Auburn to a tree. Guided by the sound of the guns, careful of his footing on the uneven ground, Brit hiked an uphill course toward the river. All at once he saw them: gray-coated men coming up over the rise, pushing through the brush in the direction he was coming. A retreat? He stopped. Some of the men saw him; there were gestures back and forth, then one powder-blackened face split open in a grin. The slender soldier made his way to Brit's side. It was Archer Langdon.

"Retreat?" Langdon's voice rose to a squeak in response to Brit's question. "By God, no! We charged 'em hours ago, gave 'em the yell, drove 'em toward the river. Since then we've been fighting, driving them, retiring, over and over. Thing is, we're running low on ammunition. But 'Shanks'— General Evans, you know—ordered us to fight till every damn man falls! They say he's been partaking of 'liquid reinforcements.' " Langdon laughed uproariously at this soldiers' jest. "Come on up!" he added, looking around to where his comrades had positioned themselves near the crest of the hill, standing behind stout trees so as to see as much as possible without presenting a target. "You'll see some fun!"

Brit followed Langdon up the hill, chose an oak bigger around than his arms could reach, and peered from behind it down into a cleared field of a few acres rimmed with woods. There the dead and dying lay so thick that a man could cross the field without touching the ground. Firing flared, died, flared again. Through the smoke Brit could just make out where the

Federals were drawn up in the woods on the other side of the clearing. Remembering the map he had studied the night before, he knew the Federals had their backs to the river, though it was not visible through the woods. The Confederates had them ringed—though, judging by the ease with which he himself had penetrated to the center of the action, the ring was a narrow one, perhaps a thousand men spread out over a distance of a mile or two. Although the Confederates held the stronger position, their shortage of ammunition could force them to fall back.

Activity among the men drew Brit's attention. A lieutenant was passing down the line, motioning to the men, giving some order that caused little groups to gather, fumble with cap boxes and cartridge boxes, then return to their stations among the trees. Brit darted over to Archer Langdon.

"They're about to order a charge. We've been told to divide up our cartridges, so that each man has one. When we've used up all our ammunition, we're to rely on the bayonet."

Archer Langdon dashed back to his place. Brit watched the grim-faced soldiers load their rifles. For a moment the ramrods waved like batons conducting a discordant symphony. With only one shot for each rifle, it would be the sight of them, and the sound, that must carry the day. The order to charge sounded along the line. For the moment that the call hung in the air, the men performed their individual rituals, pulling down their caps, tugging at their belts. At the next moment there swarmed down from the ridge and into the field a new creature, crying out in a bone-chilling ululation that was the voice of war.

Brit Wallace, standing incautiously at the crest of the hill, saw the blue-coats across the field hesitate, then break. The creature that was Berton's men drove its prey before it, pushing the Federals into the woods that skirted and concealed the bluff just above the bank of the river.

The shadows lengthened: twenty minutes, a half hour maybe, since the charge. The Federals attempted a rally on the Confederate right but were driven back. Some had surrendered and been taken prisoner. Colonel Berton had pulled his men back to give them some rest, the first, they said, since noon. Brit picked his way through the exhausted men, following the directions given by first one and then another, to find Colonel Berton. At last he caught sight of the colonel, in the act of turning his horse around and riding back in the direction from which Brit had come.

"What's afoot?" Brit called out to a lieutenant.

"Stand aside, or be trampled!" the man called back. "We're going to push them over the bluff!"

Brit thought for a moment. What he needed was a vantage point from which he could view the opposing forces but not get caught up in their movement. Get behind the charging soldiers, follow the wood ring in the direction of the river. He started off at a run over the rough land toward the river, clutching at saplings to steady himself. Above the roar of the muskets a cry rang out—from Jove himself, it seemed: "Charge, Mississippians, charge! Drive them into the Potomac, or into eternity!"

Brit forged onward. At last, as he came out of the woods above the bluff, he looked down into the near-darkness to see Union soldiers, maybe a thousand of them, gathered at the verge of the steep cliff that fell a hundred feet to the swift, rain-gorged river below. As he watched, it seemed a shudder ran through the men. Those nearest the verge tumbled over it, pushed by those behind them. Brit grabbed a tree the size of his forearm and leaned out as far as he could to look down the bluff. The river's muddy bank provided a merciful landing for those who did not fall on top of their comrades. But there they were stranded, with fifty feet of river between them and safety on Harrison's Island. He could see a couple of big, flat-bottomed boats and a few smaller ones. Altogether they could have held a hundred men, perhaps; to transport the men already gathered would take hours. But death bayed at the Federals' heels, and they would not wait. Men were throwing themselves onto the boats, heedless of those trying to maintain order. And still the dark wave came, over the precipice and onto the men trapped below.

Now came the Confederates, pushing forward, the first line firing, then dropping back as a second line replaced them, firing and dropping back in turn. So the ammunition had not run out. Soon the graycoats had possession of the bluff. Soldiers knelt and sighted their muskets on the figures massed below.

A flatboat shoved off, loaded beyond capacity, and still men flung themselves onto it, on top of the wounded who had been loaded first. It floated out—shot raining down from above, pocking the water like hail—about fifteen feet, tipped to the right, and, with excruciating slowness, emptied into the river its cargo of what looked to be about one hundred souls. The men surfaced, writhing in a knot, fighting each other and the current. The flatboat floated free of them and was gone.

Men were stripping off their coats and boots, jumping into the water to swim for the island. In the dim light, with the swift brown river water churned to froth by the hail of bullets, Brit could not single out any one figure whose progress he could follow. He thought he saw a few make it across, to the island itself or to one of the little islets of mud that straggled out from it. The entire stretch of river between the shore and the island was filled with the bobbing heads of men, swimming and drowning, the weak pulling down the strong.

Brit, sick and exhausted with the horror of it, looked on until darkness shrouded the scene.

RICHMOND
TWO DAYS LATER

News of the victory at Ball's Bluff gave a lighthearted mood to the gathering of patriots in the lobby of the Marshall Theater on Broad Street. The occasion was not a professional theatrical performance but a number of charades and tableaux vivants featuring Richmond notables. It was said the town's leading citizens had given family treasures to be used as props in the tableaux, then donated to the Confederate cause. Jordan had been in high spirits: she was to have a starring role in a tableau that Gerard Lucien was getting up. By appearing in public so soon after her great-aunt's murder, Jordan was showing her indifference to society's opinion. And society, Narcissa knew, would have its revenge. She hated to see the girl isolate herself further from the circle of relatives and friends that ought to keep her safe. But Jordan either wilted in pain or flew into a rage whenever Narcissa brought up the subject.

Brit Wallace escorted Narcissa into the theater, saw her to a seat, then rejoined the crowd in the lobby as it traded anecdotes of the recent engagement. At last he broke away and slipped into the seat to Narcissa's left.

"Has my beard gone quite white, Mrs. Powers?" Brit asked facetiously, stroking his smooth-shaven chin. "I am beginning to feel like the Ancient Mariner, telling my tale again and again." Then he lowered his voice. "Cantrell is here. Look, he has taken a seat down near the front, on the aisle. His wife is not with him. I hear she has left town, gone back to her family in the North."

Brit reverted to a more normal tone. "I heard an interesting thing just now. The story comes from a New Yorker of the Tammany regiment who was taken prisoner at Ball's Bluff. You know the battle went on after the sun had set? Well, about that time, an officer stepped out in front of the Tammany men, waved his sword, and ordered the men to charge. Some of the men, maybe a hundred, advanced, but then two other officers came up and gave the order, 'Hold your ground.' Most of the men pulled back, but the dozen or so Tammany men who had been the first to charge were shot to pieces. And later—this is a strange thing—some said it was not a Union officer but a Confederate officer who had ordered the charge! It was too dark to discern the uniform, you see. And then—you would be surprised at the credulity of soldiers, they assert the truth of things that would make a Hindu fakir scoff—the story went up that it was a phantom who ordered those men to their death!"

"How terrible," Narcissa said softly. She could see it in her mind's eye, another of those ironies of war that mocked humanity's belief in its own importance.

As the lights dimmed, a uniformed young man slipped past them, bowing and smiling, and sank into the seat Narcissa had been saving for Mirrie. She recognized Jordan's cousin Archer Langdon, whom she had met at Champs-Elysées. Where was Mirrie? Narcissa wondered as she watched the stage curtain rise to reveal a pair of silver candelabra, each with a dozen twisted arms holding white tapers. Their light struck answering sparks from the scene behind them, from brilliant silver- and gold-colored objects that seemed suspended in dark emptiness. The crowd responded with admiring murmurs.

Narcissa held her hand in front of her face to shield her eyes from the candles' glare. Then she could make out the scene: a dozen figures, men and women, wearing flowing robes in dark, rich hues of purple, wine red, emerald, and indigo reclined gracefully on low "sofas" that in fact seemed to be pallets and mounded bales of straw draped with cloth. Behind and above the others sat Dr. Stedman, wearing a false beard of stylized curls that seemed to have been made of wood shavings. A golden tinsel crown marked him a king. Each posed figure held some sort of silver vessel—a heavy, carved goblet, a two-handled loving cup, a slender-spouted teapot of elegant simplicity. Narcissa scanned the faces, looking for Jordan and Lucien but not finding them. Then she leaned forward, staring at the teapot. Was it not identical to the one from which Mrs. Cantrell had poured tea for her at Manakin, the one she had said was made by Paul Revere? If it was as precious as Mrs. Cantrell had said, what was it doing as part of a stage set? She could not imagine her lending the object for such a use. Mr. Cantrell was present, sitting close enough to recognize the familiar treasure. If he had made the gift, it must have been against his wife's strenuous objections. Besides, she remembered, the teapot belonged not to him but to Colonel Berton, who was since his father's death the master of Manakin.

Narcissa leaned over and whispered to Brit Wallace. "That teapot: Mrs. Cantrell showed it to me at Manakin. She said it was priceless. How did it come to be among these things?"

Brit sat up straight, as if to bolt out of his seat, then restrained himself. "I have an idea," he whispered back. "I'll tell you later."

Narcissa looked more closely at the other items on the stage. On a low table in front of the revelers was piled more silver, and gold-colored objects too, their tinsel gleam showier but cheaper-looking than the silver. All but one of the revelers were staring at these real and false treasures, grinning with exaggerated greed.

Suddenly Dr. Stedman turned his head slightly. He looked, then stared, mouth open and eyes wide, at a point to Narcissa's left. She followed his gaze to a high side table covered with a dark cloth that was the only other piece of furniture on the stage. On it stood a row of candlesticks whose glow fell on a "wall" of light-colored muslin stretched on a frame that ran diagonally across the stage. Within the spot of light made by the first candle floated a hand. It seemed suspended there, unattached, though it was easy to guess someone hidden behind the tablecloth, dark sleeve concealed in shadow. The fingers of the hand grasped some kind of implement that left red marks on the canvas.

"The handwriting on the wall!" someone in the audience called out. "Belshazzar's Feast!"

Narcissa watched transfixed as the hand moved from the first spot of light to the second, the third, then the last, forming those letters that had spelled doom to the Babylonian king Belshazzar in the Old Testament book of Daniel. MENE . . . MENE . . . TEKEL . . . UPHARSIN. The mysterious words had appeared on the wall of Belshazzar's palace, and Daniel, prophet of Israel, had interpreted them: *Thou art weighed in the balance, and found wanting.* Daniel's interpretation had proved true. Belshazzar had been killed that night, his kingdom lost to the Medes and the Persians.

Brit jerked in his seat, his eyes following the swift steps of a man who was walking up the aisle. Brit rose and, with a muttered apology to Narcissa, began to make his way down the row to the aisle, greatly hindered by the women's hoops. *Cantrell,* she thought. Archer Langdon, seated on her other side, turned to look after Brit. After a moment he too rose and made for the aisle. The woman two seats down jerked her skirts out of the way of his boots, expressing her annoyance with an audible *humph.*

The audience was applauding vigorously, happily convinced that the verdict of guilt and death depicted in the tableau applied to the Union and its army. But Narcissa felt an almost superstitious horror. The wall, the lamp, the bloody writing: someone had incorporated into the tableau a scene from the murder of Mrs. Archer Jennings. She had tried to keep Jordan from seeing the bloody handprint on the wall of the old woman's bedroom. But Jordan not only had seen it; she had described it in detail, most likely to Lucien, who had designed the tableau.

Was Cantrell's hasty exit from the theater the reaction Lucien had been trying to provoke? Where had Cantrell been heading, and what would Brit do once he caught up to him? And above all, where was Jordan?

Lucien came out from behind the draped table. His had been the handwriting on the wall, scrawled with red paint into the haloed pool of light from the candle. An awkward position, holding his arm above his head, flat to the wall; he probably hadn't even been able to see what he was writing. As the assembly applauded, Lucien walked to the front of the makeshift stage and bowed.

Narcissa heard Mrs. Stedman, seated in the row in front of her, turn to the lady next to her and remark, "M. Lucien is quite an actor, is he not?"

Where *was* Jordan?"

Lucien held his hands out in front of him, and the crowd grew quiet.

"Thank you . . . thank you all."

"Tonight I bring you a very special message from Mademoiselle Jordan Archer, who is in mourning for her great-aunt and could not join in the festivities."

Could not join? Narcissa felt a jolt of alarm.

"Miss Archer wanted me to tell you all, her friends and neighbors—her family, some of you—of a special gift she is making in memory of her great-aunt, Mrs. Caroline Archer Jennings. A gift to the Confederate States of America, to the cause of freedom so cherished by Mrs. Archer Jennings and by Miss Archer herself. A gift—I will praise it, since she is not here to prevent me— Thanks to her generosity, all these precious objects are to be donated to the Confederacy."

It seemed to Narcissa that the insightful Mrs. Stedman had seen through at least one layer of Lucien's facade. In his poise, in his sonorous voice and elegant gestures, most of all in his ability to command attention, he was an actor. As Narcissa watched, Lucien bowed and grasped one of the candelabra around its base. He extended his arm and turned slowly so that the candles' light played across the lustrous silver heaped on the table. The actors came forward one by one and added the items they had been holding to the rich display.

"And now—" Lucien turned again with a movement that began gracefully but ended clumsily, with his heel knocking against the candelabrum that had remained on the floor. It fell against one of the straw pallets. In a moment the straw was smoking, then flaming. Lucien turned back to the audience, mouth open in surprise, and the candelabrum in his hand brushed against the muslin curtain. It too began to burn.

Men and women fled the stage and mixed with members of the audience, who had jumped from their seats and were surging toward the doors, some shrieking with fear, some calling out to those in front to raise the alarm. A few were trying to put out the fire. Dr. Stedman, his tinsel crown askew, tried to stamp out the flames. Instead his long robe caught fire at the hem. He pulled it off his shoulders and stepped out of it, then joined the others clambering down from the stage. His wife pushed through the crowd to him and draped her paisley shawl around his shoulders.

Narcissa walked to the end of the row of chairs and stared at the stage. The thin muslin had been quickly consumed, with no damage done, but the straw bales were feeding foot-high flames. Narcissa wondered if the bales had been in contact with lamp oil, paraffin, or some other flammable substance. Where was Lucien? She was sure he had not gone past her. And where, where was Jordan?

It was time to decide. Would she follow the crowd into the street, or would she follow Lucien, in hopes that he would lead her to Jordan?

There was a door, now standing open, that led backstage. If she moved quickly, she would be in no danger from the flames. In an instant she was running for the door.

———

"Colonel John Berton sends his regards to Major Cameron Archer," the note began. It went on to say that Colonel Berton had returned to Manakin for a brief visit to set his affairs in order, and that he would appreciate it if Major Archer would call at his convenience. Archer crumpled the note in his fist. What was concealed by its cultivated phrasing? Was Berton going to interrogate him, lie to him, break down and plead with him?

His protection of Berton had to stop, Archer knew. Berton would not kill again: he had been driven to violence by his wife's unfaithfulness. But so many had died, so many suffered, and even now it was not over. The black man who had helped Berton, whether his body servant Quintus or some other, had gone on to poison Mrs. Archer Jennings. This renegade, drawn into crime by his master, had tasted blood now, and power, and he would thirst again. Berton would know how to identify him, if not how to find him. But Berton could not hide behind his slave. Berton himself would have to confess, or be tried, so that the killings would not serve as an inspiration to other slaves.

It was almost eight o'clock at night when Archer rode up to Manakin. A silent slave took his horse, and Berton opened the door. Archer watched Berton perform the tasks usually left to servants—taking his cloak, pouring his brandy, adding a log to the fire. Were Berton, himself, and the silent man outside the only people at Manakin House?

"Where is Johnny?" Archer asked when they were seated before the fire in the library.

A shadow crossed Berton's gaunt face. "At Cantrell Hall. I'll ride over to see him tomorrow. There are some things I need to clear up—tonight, now. Dorcas died in jail. I saw her body. She was savagely beaten. And Hetty is still in jail, even though she saved Johnny's life. Clara and the child, too. They are innocent! I want them to be released. I want them to be *freed*." Berton turned and picked up a sheaf of papers from the desk behind him. "I've had the papers drawn up. I want you to see that it's done as soon as possible. They've suffered enough. The others are dead, and I will bear that guilt for the rest of my life. My mother and wife were not killed by their maids."

He's going to confess, Archer thought. He leaned forward and took the papers. Then he sat, hands on his thighs, his heart beating fast.

"I needed to be here, tonight, alone," Berton went on, turning his gaze to the fire. "Or I thought I did. I thought I could . . . accustom myself . . . to the fact that they are no longer here. My mother, and my father, and Dorothea. But I feel as if I've stepped back into that nightmare. As if I died too, and am a ghost in this house."

He wants me to know he is suffering for what he did, Archer thought. *I'm sorry, but it's not enough.*

Berton's eyes were fixed on Archer's now, as if pleading for him to understand. "When you first told me that Dorothea was with child, three months along, I thought that she . . . We had not had relations in more than four months, since before the fighting at Manassas. I had avoided her, I confess it. She was peevish about Johnny, about my parents, everything. But . . . I want to know: surely you could have been wrong? Surely the fetus could have been small, or—"

Archer shook his head. John Berton stared, eyes wide. Then he covered his face with his hands.

"John, Hetty has recovered. She has told what she saw and heard the day of the murders. She heard a black man's voice, heard Hiram talking with him. She saw a white man's hands, reaching for the old sword in your father's room." Archer paused. Berton stared at him, and then, as if he sensed something was expected of him, shook his head.

Archer felt himself getting angry, the way he felt when he had to deliver the news to a dying man. Always, the words he couldn't say. This is the way it is. There's nothing I can do. You will never know how hard I tried to save you.

"John, Dorothea's unfaithfulness was beginning to excite comment. Her behavior threatened to shame you in front of your mother and father, bring disgrace upon Johnny. You must have thought, well, that you couldn't let her live."

"You think that I killed her? That I killed my own mother, and my father?"

Archer thought carefully, then answered. "Between Hiram and Quintus, they could have handled the killings easily. But you were here; Quintus drove you here in a carriage. You handed the sword to Hiram."

"Quintus ran away months ago. I haven't seen him since. If there was a white man here, it must have been my wife's seducer."

"James Cantrell?" Archer asked.

"Cantrell?" Berton jumped to his feet. Archer got up too, ready to support or restrain him. "My cousin seduced my wife, got her with child? I'll kill him, by God I will!"

"You didn't know?" Archer asked, his hand on Berton's arm.

Berton pulled away. He held his arms out stiffly, hands fisted. "By God, Archer, if I had known Dorothea was cuckolding me with James Cantrell, with any man, I would have shot him down like a dog. But I didn't do it. Cantrell is your man, and you had better get to him before I do."

Archer picked up his cloak and hat from the hall table where Berton had left them. He stuffed into his coat the papers granting freedom to the three accused slaves. Then he went for his horse, not waiting to summon the servant. Berton was sleeping in his deep wing chair, having yielded at last to Archer's insistence that he swallow a small amount of laudanum. But Archer took Berton at his word on the matter of finding James Cantrell.

The mistake he had made, and the time he had lost as a result, drove Archer. Berton was innocent. But there was no time to feel relief, for unless Cantrell were found and charged with the murders, John Berton could yet become a murderer in truth.

RICHMOND

Brit came out of the Marshall Theater onto Broad Street. Cantrell was nowhere in sight. The only chance he had of finding Cantrell tonight was to track him to one of his usual haunts. Brit walked the three long blocks south to Main Street, then turned east. He walked fast, clasping his walking stick around the middle so that the loungers who clustered along the street, away from the gaslights, would know he was ready to defend himself. In the half-year since he had arrived in Richmond, the cutthroats and garroters had grown bolder, venturing out from the rough parts of town into the heart of the city. Now, emboldened by the drunken soldiers who made their work easy, they jostled ladies and gentlemen in the streets.

At last he caught sight of Cantrell striding to the entrance of the Star Saloon, shoulders back and head down like a man walking into a gale. Of course, there was no strong wind blowing from the Star Saloon. Rather, the force was in Cantrell, impelling him to quiet his devils, to find forgetfulness in gaming and drink.

Brit slowed his pace so as not to attract Cantrell's notice. When Brit entered the saloon, Cantrell had already disappeared through the door that led to the exclusive gambling hell above. Brit greeted some acquaintances, tossed back a glass of wine paid for with a handful of shinplasters, then made his way to the door.

Had someone spoken about him to the thick-shouldered Negro on guard? The fellow made as if to block Brit's way. Vexed at this obstruction, Brit cast about for a pretext that would get him admittance. As he did, the door at the top of the stairs swung open and Cantrell stepped out, his face dark red. He turned and started to protest, but the door closed in his face. He gave it up and trotted down the stairs, then stood for a moment, looking lost.

The Negro, confusion on his face, looked at Cantrell. "It's all right, Ike," Cantrell said dismissively, and the man backed away, his face blank.

Brit eased over to Cantrell. "Let me buy you a drink," he offered.

Cantrell followed him through the door into the saloon's public area. Brit chose a table where they could talk without being overheard, saw Cantrell seated, then brought two glasses of brandy from the bar. Cantrell drained the glass in one draft. Without comment, Brit slid his own glass over to the man, who grasped it like a lifeline but did not yet drink.

Cantrell spoke, his Virginia-gentleman drawl roughened with a kind of desperation. "You know where there's a game will take my pledge for payment?"

"Who would not take your pledge?" Brit replied. "Your name is a great one in these parts. You're one—no—two deaths away from inheriting one of the finest plantations in Virginia, and all of its treasures. All you haven't already sold to pay your gambling debts."

Anger flared up in Cantrell's eyes, then died. "Damn Lucien," he said in a tone of leaden despair. "It wasn't enough that he won those things from me, but he had to parade them in front of all Richmond at that damned tableau. And my body servant, Ike, in there. I had to give him to Lucien, and the bastard hired him out to stand guard at the Star Saloon! Just to humiliate me! Everyone knew he'd belonged to me for years." Cantrell tossed back the second brandy, coughed, and dragged his hand across his mouth.

So the tableau *had* been Lucien's scheme to push Cantrell toward a confession. Brit decided to press harder. "Lucien has you by the throat. He doesn't seem a man to forgive a debt. And how much did you spend on Dorothea Berton when she was your mistress? Or did you plan the whole thing, seduce Dorothea Berton, just to get your hands on Manakin?"

Cantrell stared, then began to shake his head. "The Bertons died because they couldn't control their niggers. As for Dorothea Berton—"

Cantrell started to laugh, his red-tinged drunkard's eyes tearing. "As to her being my lover . . . I can't get it up to go to a white woman, not even a high-priced whore I've paid for the honor!"

Cantrell seemed to come to himself at last. He looked around at the men whose stares he had attracted, then at Brit. For a moment Brit thought Cantrell was going to attack him. Then Cantrell pushed himself up from the table and walked unsteadily back toward the door to the storeroom. Brit watched him go but decided not to follow. He had pushed Cantrell far enough for the time being.

Brit walked, lost in thought, for several minutes before he realized he was heading away from the Exchange Hotel. He turned and was retracing his steps, his mind full of what Cantrell had told him, when a massive shape came sliding toward him out of the shadows, resolving into two men, bearing down on him with their heads down. Cursing his momentary lapse of attention, Brit grasped his stick with both hands and drove it into the jaw of the first man, a Negro. The man went down. Brit whirled, drew his arm back, and swung the weighted head of his stick at the other man, who was white. The blow landed with an audible crack on the man's collarbone. Got him, Brit thought with satisfaction. The man looked once before turning to stagger back toward the shadows. Brit recognized James Cantrell.

At once the other man was up again, gripping Brit's arm and squeezing it until the stick fell from his numbed fingers. Brit clawed at the man with his left hand, trying to reach his eyes. It was Ike, Cantrell's trusted body servant until Lucien had won him and set him to guard the private gambling room above the Star Saloon. Now Ike had one huge hand around Brit's throat, squeezing, and was drawing his other hand back in a fist.

Brit Wallace woke up wishing he could remember the party he had been ejected from, wondering how badly he had disgraced himself. He was lying facedown in dirt, smelling the vomit he could still taste in his mouth. He listened for the sounds of Oxford, the laughter of the other students. Then it came to him that he was in Richmond. He groaned, pushed himself up to a sitting position, and wiped his nose and mouth on his sleeve.

Brit caught sight of someone, down on his haunches a few feet away, his eyes on Brit's face. Brit was raising his arm to ward off a blow when the concerned expression, then the familiar features, came into focus—the young soldier Archer Langdon.

"Only wounded, and not dead," Langdon said lightly, slipping his hands under Brit's shoulders. "Come, see if you can walk." Langdon pulled Brit to a standing position. Brit lurched and put his hand to his head, then brought his hand down wet with blood. "I'll take you to my uncle the surgeon. He'll fix you up."

Narcissa passed through the doorway that led to the back of the Marshall Theater, holding her shawl over her nose and mouth to keep from inhaling smoke. Her heels clattered on the wooden floor; that and the crackle of the flames as they consumed the straw were the only sounds she could hear. She thought how easy it would be for her to lose her way, here in the hidden world behind the stage, with its dangling ropes and gently waving panels of hanging canvas. What was moving them? she wondered, looking around, and saw a door standing open.

There, in the bare-dirt yard behind the theater, stood the carriage that had belonged to Mrs. Archer Jennings, with four horses in harness. A black man Narcissa didn't remember having seen before was in the driver's box. And there was Lucien, at the door of the carriage. It was like a dream, Narcissa thought—or a play. Then she gathered her skirts in her hand and ran down the rough stairway.

"Where is Miss Archer?" she called out to Lucien. With another theatrical gesture, Lucien opened the door to the carriage. A woman was sitting there, concealed by a hooded cloak. As Narcissa looked, the woman pushed the hood back from her face and smiled, then held out her hands. It was Jordan.

Lucien put his hand under Narcissa's elbow and helped her mount into the carriage. Jordan gathered her in. Saying, "I will give you ladies a moment to talk in private," Lucien shut the door.

Jordan was smiling, her cheeks pink from the cold. She said nothing at first but unfolded a lap rug and tucked it around Narcissa.

"Are you ill?" Narcissa asked, unable to keep an edge of irritation out of her voice. The carriage lurched into motion. At least they would be home soon, Narcissa thought with relief.

"No, Narcissa, I am very well. I simply . . . thought better of making an appearance in public so soon after Great-aunt Caroline's death. People may think I did not grieve for her." Jordan's eyes were wide now, her mouth solemn. What an actress, Narcissa thought, admiring Jordan's ability to compose her face to an emotion she did not feel. It really is a shame no lady can go on the stage.

"Never mind," Jordan went on, her expression lightening, "we have an even greater adventure in store. We are driving up to Champs-Elysées, so that M. Lucien can cure my headaches once and for all."

"To Champs-Elysées! Who is going with you?"

Jordan was silent a moment. "You are."

"No, Jordan, I am not! Have you taken leave of your senses?"

Jordan pulled away from Narcissa and sat up straight. Her chin went up. "I am going to Champs-Elysées with M. Lucien. If you do not agree to come, very well: I will go alone."

Narcissa rejected the conventional responses that came to her mind. Jordan did not have to be told that traveling unescorted with M. Lucien would ruin her reputation, that she would never again be accepted in polite society. At last Narcissa asked, "Are you in love with M. Lucien?"

Jordan looked surprised, hesitated a moment. "No. I think he is in love with me." She smiled a little at that. "But this is not an elopement. M. Lucien's intentions are honorable. See how he arranged for you to come, so that I would have a chaperone?"

"But he did not ask me! *You* did not ask me! Mirrie will wonder what has become of me, and—" Narcissa was about to say, so will Dr. Archer, but would he? Was he aware of her at all, when she was out of his sight?

"I explained it all to Mirrie, in a letter." Jordan twisted the velvet cords of her reticule and avoided Narcissa's eyes. "What I have done is not so bad, is it, Narcissa? There is nothing I would not do, to be rid of these headaches forever."

Mate and check, Narcissa thought, sitting back and trying to compose her thoughts. She could not force Jordan to abandon this chimera and return with her to the Powerses'. Opposition, she knew, would only strengthen Jordan's resolve. Her choice was to go along, or to let Jordan bear the consequences of her foolishness.

Narcissa sighed and settled back, defeated. She would not let Jordan throw her life away, and Jordan knew it.

Surely Lucien intended to seduce Jordan. Yet if that was his intention, Narcissa wondered why he had maneuvered her into coming along as a chaperone. For he had maneuvered her, and cleverly, knowing she would follow him through the back of the theater to the carriage where Jordan had been waiting. And Jordan knew how to keep her sitting there when every instinct was telling her to get out.

When the carriage halted and Lucien climbed in, Jordan was asleep, huddled in her cloak, her head on Narcissa's shoulder. In a low voice, Lucien inquired as to whether Narcissa were comfortable. She answered him with a nod and looked away. Then Lucien pulled his hat down over his eyes and appeared to doze.

Despite her intention to keep watch, Narcissa drifted into a troubled sleep, in which remembered events took on the qualities of nightmare. A skeleton dressed in a bride's gown beckoned her up the wide staircase at Champs-Elysées. A black man with a devil's horns and tail danced before a bonfire. She struggled into wakefulness, determined not to sleep again. But she was slipping back, the thoughts and images in her mind growing wilder and more senseless, when a strangled cry from Jordan jolted her awake. Jordan had pushed away from her on the seat and was cowering against the side of the carriage. Narcissa could see that Jordan's eyes were open, but what was she seeing? Whatever it was, it terrified her so that her breath was coming in quick gasps, and she seemed poised to run, had there been anywhere *to* run.

Narcissa caught Lucien's movement out of the corner of her eye and held her hand out, keeping him back.

"Let me help her," he said in a low voice. "She must not wake too quickly."

The mere sound of Lucien's voice seemed to have a calming effect on Jordan. She turned her gaze toward him, and her breathing slowed a little.

"All right," Narcissa told him. She took Lucien's hand and let him steady her against the jolting of the carriage as she took his place in the facing seat. Then Lucien seated himself next to Jordan, leaning very close to her and speaking in a calm, steady voice, as a mother would speak to a frightened child. Narcissa could sense the movements—what Brit Wallace had called "mesmeric passes"—of his hands close to Jordan.

At last Lucien asked, "Do you sleep?"

"I sleep, and I do not sleep." Jordan's voice seemed to come from far away. Its monotone frightened Narcissa.

"Are you well?" Lucien asked.

"I am . . . well, but you must not leave me."

"What is it frightens you?" Lucien's voice was gentle.

Perhaps he can help her, Narcissa thought, surprised, and listened for Jordan's answer.

It came in a sob. "Buried."

In a moment Lucien asked, "You are afraid of something that is buried?"

"I am afraid . . . I am to be . . . buried."

"Miss Archer!" Urgency vibrated in Lucien's voice. "Who am I?"

"My friend," the answer came.

"Yes." Lucien's voice was again soothing and slow. "I am your friend. Hear only me. See only me. I tell you that you can sleep. No harm will come to you. I swear it. Sleep."

Narcissa heard Jordan draw in a deep breath and let it out in a long sigh that seemed to expel her fear with it.

Lucien turned to Narcissa. "She will sleep now."

Narcissa resumed her place next to Jordan, with Lucien opposite. It was a wonder, what Lucien had done. Jordan was sleeping like a child, her body heavy and warm, her breathing deep and regular. What a gift Lucien had, to release Jordan from whatever it was that troubled her so deeply. And yet—in making himself a wall between Jordan and her fears, he also made himself a wall between Jordan and her friends. And that, in itself, was frightening.

RICHMOND

Archer Langdon had traced Cameron Archer to the city jail and had taken Brit Wallace there. Now Langdon sat cross-legged on the floor, taking in the scene. Wallace, a bloodied white handkerchief tied around his head, sat sipping a tumblerful of brandy. Cameron Archer was addressing three old men who stood stock-straight, eyes wide open but faces sagging with tiredness.

"It is indeed unfortunate that all the provost marshal's men have been called away to combat a minor fire in a theater. Nevertheless, you men must serve." Archer paused to be sure they understood the gravity of the moment. "Mr. James Cantrell, whose name I'm sure you recognize, has been set upon in the street and injured. It was done by the same scoundrels who attacked this man here." Archer gestured to Brit, who tried not to look surprised. "The attack was made near the Star Saloon. Mr. Cantrell may be lying in some alley, bleeding and unconscious. You must find him."

"Wh—what we supposed to do with him, once we find him?" asked the tallest of the three men, every bit of seventy years old.

"Bring him back here," Archer answered quickly, "so that I can examine his injuries. On no account let him ride back to his home! He may be badly injured. If you should encounter any other ... officers of the law, give them the same instructions. Now, be off with you."

Brit watched the three jostle each other through the doorway. Then he turned to Archer and smiled. "So you've come to see we were right all along, Mrs. Powers and I, about James Cantrell being the murderer."

To judge by Archer's expression, agreement was painful. At last he said, "Yes. I thought John Berton learned of his wife's infidelity and employed his slaves Hiram and Quintus to kill her. Hiram could have gone beyond his master's instructions to kill the older Bertons. But I at last came to believe that John Berton did not know his wife was unfaithful. When I told him she was pregnant with a child that could not be his, he could not believe it. The affair, and the pregnancy, did precipitate the killings—but by Dorothea's lover, not her husband. Perhaps the older Bertons suspected the affair, and so Cantrell decided to have them killed—*What?*"

Brit had pushed himself up from his chair and was staring at Archer. "But that can't be. Cantrell is impotent with ... women of his own race. He told me so himself."

Archer thought for a moment. "He lied, to protect himself from the accusation of murder."

Brit responded tartly, "A man may tell a lie for safety's sake, but not that one! And Cantrell didn't know I suspected him as the murderer. He feared he would be accused of theft, for plundering the treasures of Manakin plantation to pay his gambling debts. No, Archer, we've got it the wrong way round. Someone else was Dorothea's lover. And someone else is the murderer. Those women servants from Manakin, the ones who survived, are here, aren't they? They may remember something. Have them brought out, ask them who was her lover!"

Clench-jawed, Archer started down the hall, his boots striking like hammer blows on the stone floor.

Archer returned with the women from Manakin, Hetty and Clara, as well as Jordan's old Auntie Lora. The little girl called Litabet he had left asleep on the straw-strewn floor of the cell. Hetty, apparently uncomfortable in the presence of the three white men, kept her eyes down and said little. But Clara was more forthcoming. Young Mrs. Berton went to parties in town, she said, and visited with friends there, sometimes for days at a time. But the blacks at Manakin, and those at Cantrell Hall, had assumed it was Mr. Cantrell who was her lover. He often called for her in his carriage, and sometimes the Cantrells' driver brought notes.

"What about Cantrell's body servant, Ike?" Archer pressed. "Did you ever hear him talk about slave rebellions? Did you ever hear him—or anyone—referred to as Gabriel?"

Both Hetty and Clara shook their heads, but Auntie Lora looked up, confusion in her face. "I knows Gabriel. But he don't work for the Bertons or the Cantrells. He come to Mrs. Archer Jennings's house one time with a message from M. Lucien."

This is it, Brit thought. He signaled Archer, by a glance and a movement of his hand, to hold up, to let him ask the next question. To Brit's surprise, Archer waited.

Brit tried frantically to sort through all the facts he could remember about Lucien. Hadn't the Frenchman expressed his unwillingness to keep a servant? But Ike had been given to Lucien by Cantrell, in partial payment of what must have been an enormous debt. Lucien had put Ike to work at the Star Saloon. And Lucien could easily have sent the slave on another errand, to the house of Mrs. Archer Jennings. But why would Ike call himself Gabriel?

Suppose it had been Ike and Lucien, not Ike and Cantrell, in league all along, as Gabriel and White Hands? Lucien, not Cantrell, who had been Dorothea's lover? And so Ike, calling himself Gabriel, had gone to spy on the household where the two men were about to strike a second bloody blow.

They were very close to solving the mystery now. Auntie Lora hadn't known Ike, who had introduced himself to her as Gabriel. But no one who had seen the huge, broad-shouldered Ike could mistake him.

Brit asked, his voice casual, "What does he look like, this Gabriel?"

Auntie Lora considered. "He a handsome man, real light-skinned, greeny brown eyes, curly hair he keep pulled back out of the way. Looked like he was growing in a beard, heavier around his mouth."

"Lucien!" Brit and Archer spoke the name together.

"Oh, no, sir," Auntie Lora corrected politely, her eyes now on Archer. "It's M. Lucien's body servant I'm speaking of."

Archer's voice was tense. "Did you ever see M. Lucien when he came to call at Mrs. Archer Jennings'?"

"No, sir," Auntie Lora replied.

"What fools we've been," Brit whispered to Archer. Langdon had come up too and the three men stood in a tight knot, speaking low so as not to be heard by the women. Brit went on, his fingers steepled under his chin, as he worked it out. "Lucien, not Cantrell, was Dorothea Berton's lover. Dorothea must have told Lucien about her pregnancy—told him she could not fool her husband into thinking the baby was his. So Lucien killed her, and the old couple, to keep the seduction a secret."

Archer took up the thread. "At Manakin that day, Lucien was both men." He paused for a moment as Wallace and Langdon frowned at him. "Yes," said Archer, "both men: White Hands, whom Hetty saw, and Gabriel, whose name Hiram spoke, whose voice Hetty heard—the voice of a black man."

Langdon broke in, his eyes bright with excitement. "We had a groom once who could make his voice sound just like my father's. He'd call out orders to the other servants when they couldn't see who it was."

Archer went on. "Lucien was white enough for his hands to convince Hetty she had seen a white man. And she had seen a carriage drive up— she *expected* to see a white man! But Lucien could speak in the voice of a colored man. And it was as a colored man that Hiram knew him . . . a colored man named Gabriel. Hiram wanted revenge on old Mr. Berton, wanted it more than anything, and Lucien found out about it. So Lucien took on the role of Gabriel and became Hiram's avenging angel. Hiram was willing to help kill the others, even poison his fellow servants, as long as he got to cut the throat of old Mr. Berton, who had probably long since forgotten he'd once sold Hiram's brother."

"And Lucien played the same part for Auntie Lora." Archer turned back to the old woman. "What did Gabriel talk to you about, that day?"

Auntie Lora looked uneasy. "It was the day after Mr. Lucien tried to cure Miss Archer of the headache and she got scared, thinking of the ghost at Champs-Elysées. Gabriel came to the house asking about Mr. Lucien's gloves that was left there. He told me he was Mr. Lucien's man. But you saying Gabriel *was* Mr. Lucien?"

Archer responded with careful patience. "Never mind that right now. Just tell us what happened, what you remember."

Auntie Lora nodded and went on. "It was only Tildie, the cook, and me around when he come, and we didn't know about no gloves. But Gabriel was real sociable. He asked me about the ghost story—said he heard about it from his master—and I told him. Then he asked if he could try the animal magnetism on me: my joints was acting up. But I told him no, I had a tonic from the doctoress Judah Daniel. I showed him the bottle."

"He must have come back later and put the poison in it!" Brit could keep silent no longer. "That way, when it came out after the murder that the poison was in the tonic bottle, the cry would go up against Judah Daniel. Damned clever of him to seize the opportunity! To have Judah Daniel under suspicion would work to his benefit, since she had questioned Hetty and the rest of you, and he had no way of knowing how close she was to the truth. More importantly, by killing Mrs. Archer Jennings and poisoning you, Auntie Lora, Lucien removed the two strongest barriers between him and Miss Archer. He had found out just enough about the treasure at Champs-Elysées to whet his appetite. Now, with Miss Archer relatively unprotected, he could mesmerize her again and again, rummaging around in her mind as if it were his personal library."

Auntie Lora looked troubled. "Did I do wrong?"

"No, Auntie Lora," Brit said quickly, crossing to her and putting his hands on her hunched shoulders. "And thank God you were here tonight to tell us what happened. It's true, God works in mysterious ways."

Archer snatched up his cape and hat. "Wallace, are you well enough to ride? You, too, Langdon. We must find Lucien—and Cantrell. Berton thinks Cantrell seduced his wife, and he's angry enough to call him out, if not shoot him down in the street.

"Auntie Lora, I will be sending someone for you. Jordan will need you with her. Clara, Hetty," Archer went on, "I must take you back to your cell. But be comforted—it is only for a little while. John Berton has freed you, and Litabet."

Archer said the words almost as an afterthought, but for Hetty and Clara, the world had suddenly changed. For a moment, neither of them spoke. Hetty stood still, as if afraid to wake from a dream. But Clara brought her hands to her face, where tears were running. "Praise God!" she said. "Mysterious ways, indeed!"

———◦◦◦———

Cameron Archer, Brit Wallace, and Archer Langdon were hastening from the jail when a hired carriage pulled up. A man seated on the driver's box hailed them—it was one of the three old men sent to look for Cantrell. "We've got him, sir! Mr. Cantrell. He done passed out from the pain."

Archer took command. "Wallace, it's just as well at this point if Cantrell doesn't see you. You and Langdon go along to the Spotswood Hotel and find out if Lucien is there. If he's not there, wait for him. Don't let him know we're onto him, and for God's sake don't try to take him yourselves. I will join you when I've done with Cantrell."

Brit hesitated as if wanting to argue but as last picked up his silver-headed cane and headed off.

Then Archer turned to the decrepit guards. "Go all over this town and look for the Frenchman Gerard Lucien. There must be someone who's seen or heard something of him."

"Wha—what if there ain't?" asked the boldest of the three.

"Then go and find him yourselves," was Archer's terse response.

The old men shook their heads and started off at an unenthusiastic pace. "Go, or I'll set a fire to your tails!" Archer roared at them. Then he mounted into the carriage beside Cantrell and closed the door behind him.

"Where is the wound?"

Cantrell did not answer, or even open his eyes. Archer took hold of his right arm to pull it free of the sleeve.

Cantrell shifted then, opened first one bloodshot eye and then the other, and said thickly, "God damn you." But he sat up and allowed Archer to pull his coat away, loosen his shirt, and feel along his shoulders until he cried out with pain.

"The left clavicle is fractured," Archer said at last. "That British fellow acquitted himself rather well against two of you."

Cantrell glared. "Had to bully Ike into helping me. Not much loyalty left for the 'old massa.' He must have taken off running when he saw me go down."

Archer knew Ike had shown more loyalty than Cantrell realized. But he said simply, "Easy enough to bind up; I'll have one of the boys do it. But I'll do it myself—and, I swear, I won't be gentle—unless you tell me the truth about Dorothea Berton."

Cantrell's eyes narrowed, and his mouth puckered as if he would spit. "That damned British fellow has some fool notion . . . She wasn't my mistress. It was Lucien. He let me off some of my gambling debts in exchange for arranging meetings with her. Dorothea was always mad for a party, for admiration. Whether he coaxed her into a liaison . . . if he did, she deserved what happened to her."

Archer was glowering at the dissolute man before him. "Has gambling and drunkenness brought you to this, that you care nothing for your honor?"

Cantrell made as if to turn away. Archer grabbed his arm. Cantrell gave a low sob and faced Archer, speaking through jaws tight with pain.

"Honor?" Cantrell repeated the word. "I did it to *save* my honor. Lucien would have disgraced me. The more I helped him, the more he seemed to enjoy my debasement. He told me things, awful things, that he knew I would never tell, because of the shame to me and my family." Cantrell gave a flat, joyless laugh. "That claim to be a French aristocrat? After he made me his go-between, he told me the truth: his grandfather was a French aristocrat, but his grandmother was a slave! Lucien liked to talk about the killings in Santo Domingo in 1791. He talked about it as if he'd been there. The blacks streamed through the cane, running just ahead of the fires they had set, waving machetes. They fell on the plantation, raped and tortured the women, stuck babies on pikes and carried them off—"

Cantrell licked his lips. Lucien had had an appreciative audience, Archer thought, sickened.

"The white baby was killed, slung against a wall and its brains knocked out, but a house servant saved her mulatto son, pretended he was the heir. That was Lucien's father. Many years later, the old servant told her young master the truth: that he was her son. He stuck his sword through her— better to be known as a servant's murderer, than as her son!—then fled to America, to commence upon a life of debauchery. He seduced a girl from a good family, then abandoned her. No one knows what became of him after that. The girl gave birth to a son, then went on the stage to support herself and him. That son was Lucien. From the time he was big enough to take a bow, he was an actor himself. Now, he likes to say, he's playing the part of his life. When the war broke out, he decided to come south and try his luck. Always fancied himself a planter, he said. If only I could tell the truth about him, he'd be picking cotton, not planting it!"

A bitter laugh rose in Archer's throat. How cleverly Lucien had used

Cantrell's racial fears and lusts to torment and excite him. Any European born in the West Indies was tarred with the suspicion of black blood—the rumor had driven the eminent doctor Brown-Sequard from Richmond years back. Lucien must have known it would drive Cantrell wild to think he was in debt to—was, in some sense, *owned by*—a man descended from slaves, and that a descendant of slaves could enjoy a white woman whom Cantrell himself might desire but could never possess.

"Did you help Lucien to kill the Bertons?"

"The house servants killed them," Cantrell replied without hesitation. "For God's sake, man, they were found with knives, bloody! Why would Lucien kill them? Through Dorothea . . . and through me, Manakin was Lucien's goose for the plucking."

"Did you know Dorothea was pregnant?" Archer asked.

"No. By God!" Cantrell broke into an ugly laugh. "That would cook *her* goose well enough, to give birth to a mulatto baby! I suppose he did kill her, then, so as not to reveal his secret. He knew I would never tell. And neither will you, Archer. After all, you're one of us."

Cantrell raised his head and looked Archer square in the face. Archer turned away in disgust. The blue blood that flowed in Cantrell's veins was polluted; it stank like his drunkard's breath. But much as he wanted to deny Cantrell's words—*you're one of us*—he could not. After all, when he had thought John Berton did the murders, he had worked to keep that a secret. Was this what their gracious, aristocratic breeding had engendered? Even now, would he tell the truth, given the harm that would be done to John Berton?

And Lucien had gotten close to Jordan. How close? Had Lucien confided to Cantrell his intentions to gain Jordan's confidence, to mesmerize her, perhaps to seduce her? Had the two men shared a laugh over Lucien's plans for his latest victim? Archer felt his hands ball into fists. Angry as he was—angry enough to kill Cantrell, then set off after Lucien and shoot him down in the street—he had to phrase his question carefully.

"Did you know that Lucien visited Mrs. Archer Jennings?"

Cantrell's red eyes viewed him with suspicion, then amusement. "What, your aunt or something, wasn't she? She was rich enough. But I would think there were enough rich young girls around that Lucien wouldn't have to dine on cold mutton."

Archer felt almost weak with relief. *So Lucien didn't tell him about Jordan.* If Cantrell did not know about Lucien's attentions to Jordan, there was a chance that, as yet, they had not progressed too far.

Archer paid the hack's driver to take Cantrell to a doctor and was mounting his horse to ride over to the Spotswood Hotel when he heard hoofbeats pounding in the dirt of the street. Brit Wallace and Archer Langdon reined in their mounts, and Brit called out, "Lucien's not in his rooms."

"We must search the entire city," Archer called out as he swung himself into the saddle. "Every gambling den and whorehouse. Hell, the churches, too. Lucien's a cunning villain. If he finds out we're looking for him, it's ten to one he'll never be found."

It was nearing midnight when Archer, Brit Wallace, and young Langdon repaired to Archer's house on Marshall Street for a restorative meal of eggs, ham, biscuits, and coffee. As they entered the house, Archers' manservant greeted his master with words that jolted them alert.

"Miss Powers been waiting to see you, sir, waiting long about two hours."

Archer rushed into the front parlor, followed by Brit and Langdon. Mirrie was standing, holding a piece of paper. "I found this letter. It's from Jordan." She handed it to Archer. "I came in very late last night, and only found it this morning. I fear valuable time has been lost."

Archer opened the paper and read,

Dearest Mirrie,

Forgive me for keeping this secret from you. I was afraid you would tell my cousin Cameron Archer, and that he would prevent me. Narcissa and I are going up to Champs-Elysées with M. Lucien. He feels that he may be able to rid me of my headaches, if he can mesmerize me there. Perhaps, by the time you read this, I will be cured. Have patience with,

Your friend,
Jordan Archer

Archer handed the letter to Brit without a word. As Brit and young Langdon read, Mirrie talked nervously. "I know what is the cause of her headaches. I saw it when she was trying to read the books I brought her. It is her eyes, she cannot focus on the page. If she would wear spectacles . . . but I did not speak of it to her, I thought she would resist me—"

"You did right to bring this to me at once," Archer said, as gently as he could. He felt as if his heart would burst with anger at Lucien, at the weak and depraved Cantrell, at himself. *First, do no harm:* he had sworn that oath as a doctor, but harm had come, and swept through Richmond like a fever, and he had done nothing. "We will go after them."

Chapter Nine

CHICKAHOMINY SWAMP
OCTOBER 24

Judah Daniel woke startled, with smoke in her mouth, in her eyes. The house was burning, but this time she was in it, trapped. She struggled to push the heavy covers away, to sit up. The feel of the soft tanned hides brought back memory. She was in Scratch Hall, King's log house in the Chickahominy Swamp. The fire burned day and night in the center of the house, and the smoke that did not find its way through the opening in the ceiling hung in the air.

She lay back, realizing something else had wakened her. She clutched the hilt of the knife that she kept by her side. Not many women came here alone, she figured, and King had likely been without a woman for a long time. She was grateful to him, even dependent on him, but she did not belong to him. If he tried to force himself on her, she would make sure he didn't succeed.

Then she heard it, very close: the hooting of a barred owl, eight notes, the last one drawn out. *Who cooks for you, who cooks for you-all . . .*

She looked across the room to see King slip as silently as a cat out through the door and into the night. She sat up, waiting, gathering her thoughts. In a few moments King returned. He crept to where she sat and muttered, "They's come for you."

Quickly Judah Daniel gathered the few things she had with her. Then she was through the door and down the ladder. A silent rain was falling. The two men who waited there were only shapes in the dark, but it seemed to her they were the men who had brought the wounded Tyler home from

Champs-Elysées: men of the Loyal Brethren. They set off through the swamp, following some secret path. She struggled to keep up, wondering what would happen if she fell into sucking mud, or hurt herself so that she could not walk. This is how it feels to be a runaway, she thought.

At last the path grew clearer, the ground firmer underfoot. They must be close to the edge of the swamp. Then the curtain of rain lifted for a moment, revealing a sight that made her skin prickle. They had come upon a funeral carriage drawn up in the road, a carriage such as would carry a wealthy person to his final rest. The body of the carriage reached several feet above her own height, and its boxlike wooden form was carved into ponderous decoration: columns, rosettes, and draperies, all painted black with touches of gilt. Four black horses stood stamping and blowing. Judah Daniel stood very still, afraid the driver would see them there, but her two rescuers stepped up to the driver's box, and she followed. A deep overhanging roof and windowed sides protected the driver. She peered up at him and saw that it was Tyler. He grinned at her. In another moment, Judah Daniel was inside the carriage, lying in a coffin—running away.

FREDERICKSBURG

The sun was well up when Narcissa heard Lucien rap on the carriage wall. The carriage pulled up, and Lucien got out. To her surprise, Narcissa saw they had come to a bustling town—Fredericksburg, she calculated, about halfway between Richmond and Leesburg. Jordan was quiet, but cheerful enough, and said that her headache was gone. After breakfasting at a hotel, they returned to the carriage, which now had fresh horses.

"Where is the driver?" Narcissa said to Lucien.

"No need for a driver. Now I have rested, I will drive the carriage from here."

As the women settled themselves back in the carriage, Narcissa had Jordan lie down, knees tucked up, on the seat across from her. As they set off, Narcissa found herself regretting the loss of the driver. It seemed Lucien was cutting them off from the world. So many times it seemed fate had conspired to separate Jordan from those who would care for her, beginning with her mother's early death. Her father, absent for much of her childhood, now seemed to have cut himself off from her by siding with the Union. The rumors about him, and her defensiveness on his behalf, had made Jordan reluctant to go to those relatives who wanted to take her in.

Fate had not been kind to Jordan; but with the death of Mrs. Archer Jennings and the jailing of Auntie Lora, a human agent had entered the picture. From her current perspective, Narcissa could believe the old lady had been killed, and the old servant poisoned, just to make Jordan more vulnerable. She thought again of Lucien, how completely at his mercy both Jordan and she herself now were. Yet on the day of Mrs. Archer Jennings's murder, Jordan had said she was with Lucien at the house of some friends.

With this thought, Narcissa relaxed a little. She looked over at Jordan, face softened in sleep. Lucien's ministrations really seemed to have eased the girl's pain. Perhaps it was time for Narcissa to put aside her suspicions of him.

CHAMPS-ELYSÉES

In the kitchen of Champs-Elysées, Narcissa poked and blew on the fire, hoping the pot would boil soon. It was high time Jordan tired of this diversion. A supper of stringy boiled chicken and tough greens should dim the romantic allure of running away to her old plantation home. Even to Narcissa, raised on a farm and sharing in the work there, it was dauntingly difficult to provide for even the simplest needs without servants. Had Jordan purposely packed Narcissa's oldest and dowdiest skirts and blouses, the better to fit her into the servant's role? Jordan was flitting around who knew where, exulting in her return to her beloved home. Lucien had ridden out in the rain to procure the chicken that Narcissa was trying to cook. He had also brought the wood and the water. She realized she was beginning to think of him as a fellow servant, a fellow victim of Jordan's caprices.

After a supper that did more to stifle appetite than to satisfy it, Lucien made ready to mesmerize Jordan once more. He arranged a low seat for her at the center of the great hall, facing the stairs where, according to the ghost story, Eulalie had stood dressed as a bride. The hall was chilly, and Lucien brought a glass of brandy to Narcissa, who was sitting eight or ten feet away on a plank bench drawn up to the trestle table at which they had had supper. She sipped it gratefully.

Lucien performed the now-familiar mesmeric passes. Soon it seemed that Jordan had fallen into a deep sleep that left her nevertheless alert to every movement, every suggestion on the part of Lucien. Lucien was asking questions, taking Jordan back to the scene she had described when he had first mesmerized her at Mrs. Archer Jennings's. Narcissa heard the words "treasure," and "bride"—or was it "buried"? As Narcissa watched, she felt her own eyes grow heavy. As their weight became irresistible, she wondered: Has he mesmerized me?

After midnight

When Narcissa awoke, all was in darkness. She sat up and stretched, feeling the pain in her neck and back from the uncomfortable position— half-turned and resting her upper body on the trestle table—in which she had slept. She had a pounding headache and a sour taste in her mouth. Slowly, carefully, she got up from the table and walked outside.

The rain had stopped, and a wind high in the sky drove ragged clouds across the watery moon. Narcissa pulled her shawl around her and set out at a brisk pace. Ten minutes later, the cold had turned from invigorating to wracking, and she made her way back to the house along the moss-covered brick walk that passed between a rose garden and the high brick wall of the family cemetery. Walking quickly, she stumbled. Something had caught her skirt—a rosebush, she saw, had snagged it with a single long thorn. She bent down, grabbed the stem, and worked the sharp spur loose. In the moonlight the rose's few remaining leaves were pale, mottled with mildew that spread like ink on wet paper.

The walk had cleared her mind. It was time to tell Jordan that the game was over, to insist that Lucien take them back to Richmond. If his mesmeric treatments were easing Jordan's headaches, they could be continued there. She wondered about the message Jordan said she had left for Mirrie. Would Mirrie's patience be wearing thin on Narcissa's behalf? Perhaps, even now, she was on her way to bring them back. Should they wait for her? As Narcissa posed the question, she found she knew the answer. They had to get away, as soon as daylight broke.

As she walked, lost in thought, she heard the scratching. A rough, raking sound—the ghost of Eulalie's lover trapped in the tunnel, trying to claw his way out?

The sound came again. It was very close—just over the wall, she thought. Slowly, silently, she walked across the grass strip that separated the cemetery wall from the walk and peered over. The monuments at Champs-Elysées were elaborate as the house itself, and they cast fantastic shadows in the moonlight. When she heard the sound again, she knew what it was: a shovel rasping into the dirt. And she saw the movement, strained her eyes to make it out . . . dark hair, white hands . . .

It was Lucien. What was he doing here, in the middle of the night— digging in the family graveyard of the Archers at Champs-Elysée? *He plans to bury us.* Then, *bury . . . treasure . . .* The words spoken by Jordan earlier that night, under Lucien's mesmeric spell, came into her mind. And before, the first time Lucien has mesmerized her, Jordan had spoken of jewels so bright they hurt her eyes. The buried treasure, the buried bride . . . Lucien was trying to locate that treasure, here where Eulalie was buried among the dead of Champs-Elysées, her space of earth marked by an elaborate angel, wings unfurled as if ready for flight. He was digging in secret, in the dead of night. It seemed he did not intend to share what he found with Jordan herself. Perhaps, after all, he *was* digging their graves.

Lucien seemed to feel her eyes on him, looked around. She ducked, fearing he had seen her, but in a moment the digging resumed.

Quietly, with the sound of digging to reassure her, Narcissa made her way back to the house. She found Jordan upstairs, asleep in the huge bed that had been left in the house. Narcissa loosened and slipped off her hoops and petticoats, then climbed up on the bed. "Jordan," Narcissa whispered as she took hold of the girl's shoulder. "Jordan, wake up!"

"Jordan!" It came from the doorway, a deeper, more commanding voice than Narcissa's own. "I tell you to sleep, and not to wake."

Jordan's breathing had changed, was quick and shallow. Was she awake? Narcissa drew her hand from Jordan's shoulder. Lucien was standing over the bed now. "Come, Mrs. Powers. I am sure you wish to be away from here. But it is better for Miss Archer that she remain until I have finished what I came to do."

"Jordan!" Narcissa called out one last time as Lucien's gloved hand, caked with stale-smelling earth, closed over her mouth.

Lucien walked her before him down the stairs. His hand was away from her mouth, but he persuaded her to silence with the knife he held at her throat. When they came to the trestle table in the great hall, Lucien poured a glass of wine. He held it up to the light from the oil lamp that stood on the table and said, "Corked. What a pity. Drink it anyway, Mrs. Powers.

You will need the warmth of it, where you're going." His fingers cruelly gripped her jaw, and she could taste dirt as he held her mouth open and poured the wine down her throat. Against her will, she swallowed most of it.

Then Lucien picked up the lamp, took her by the arm, and drew her with him to the wall under the stairs. One of the panels stood open like a door. This was the trick panel, Narcissa remembered, the one Jordan had used to entertain the young soldiers. Lucien pushed her through it, then followed her in, alternately pushing her and halting as she stumbled, down a narrow staircase. In a few moments she could see in the light that came over her shoulder a brick floor, above that a honeycomb of little squares that stretched to the low ceiling. Wine racks. They were in the wine cellar below the house.

"You remember the tunnel, I'm sure, Mrs. Powers, that collapsed on Eulalie's unfortunate lover? Only the entrance remains open, here." Lucien held the lamp into a narrow space between two of the racks. "Not the most pleasant place to spend the night, but take heart: this will not be your tomb, unless something prevents my return. After I am safely away with the treasure, you and Miss Archer will be found together: rivals, enemies in life—united in death. You cut her throat, then took poison. So you see, it suits my purpose for you to stay alive a little longer."

Lucien pushed her ahead of him through the opening. He stood in the doorway and held the lamp aloft. What had once been the entrance to the tunnel was an irregular chamber, walled on all sides with brick.

Narcissa turned back to look at Lucien. His face seemed to be growing dimmer, darker, as if he, not she, were disappearing into a tunnel. She realized he had set down the lamp and picked up a thick wooden bar that would brace the door closed. The lamp was glowing brighter now; it hurt her eyes.

"Permit yourself to scream, or scratch, or claw," she heard him say. "Even if you can be heard, which I doubt, such ghostly touches . . ." She saw his lips were moving, and she strained to hear, to understand. ". . . in that romantic nonsense, is the location of the treasure. And I will have it. Farewell, Mrs. Powers, until I have need of you."

Lucien receded farther, then vanished. She heard the bolt fall into place. In the darkness, black as pitch, dark as the tomb, tiny forms were dancing before her eyes. Their twisting movements frightened her. She tried to brush them away.

Narcissa struggled to take command of her thoughts. The dancing shards of light that she could not brush away, the pain in her stomach, meant something. *Poison.* She bent over and stuck her finger as far as she could down her throat. The contents of her stomach rushed into her mouth. She coughed it out. Suppose some was left? Again and again she forced herself to vomit, until her heaving stomach brought nothing up. She knelt, clutching her stomach. Gradually she felt her stomach settle, and with it, her mind.

At last Narcissa wiped her mouth on the hem of her dress, then crept backward on her hands and knees as far as she could from the stinking mess. At last her back pressed against the brick wall. She thought it was the wall opposite the door, but she did not care very much. Perhaps someone would come for her. Perhaps not. There was nothing she could do.

All at once she felt the wall she was leaning on give just a little. She sat up quickly, then almost laughed. Facing death by suffocation or starvation, what instinct told her not to let herself be buried beneath falling bricks? But no bricks fell. She put out her hand, pushed against the wall. The bricks did seem loose. She pushed at one with the heel of her hand. She felt it yield, heard it fall, then another, and another. Through the opening she felt air flow into the room. Mad with hope, she shoved again and again. Some bricks yielded, others did not. When she finished, her bloodied, dirt-caked hands traced an opening about three feet across, low to the ground. Something braced the upper bricks, keeping them from falling in. This must be the tunnel, she thought. Perhaps it is fallen in farther along its length. Perhaps her hand would meet the skeletal hand of Eulalie's lover. But perhaps, just perhaps, the tunnel led to freedom.

Narcissa felt along the brick walls of the tunnel, which curved to meet in an arch just over her head. Then she began to walk, slowly, carefully, the fingers of her right hand never leaving the tunnel wall. A few steps in, there was a break in the wall, a space of three or four feet, but she kept walking straight ahead, reassured by the solid feel of the bricks. She thought she had come a quarter of a mile, at a slight downward angle—of course, toward the river. Then she felt the tunnel narrow, and groped to feel it end in a big wooden door. *Please God, don't let it be bolted.* She put her hands on it and pulled. The door swung open. She stepped out into the night, fresh and cold, the rustle of dry-leaved trees, the murmur of the river. The faintest hint of dawn lightened the sky. Narcissa sank down on her knees, thanking God for deliverance. Then she heard a voice.

"Tyler! Was you expecting some of the Brethren to meet us?"

Could it be . . . ? "Judah Daniel?" Narcissa called out.

"Mrs. Powers?"

At the sound of Judah Daniel calling her name, Narcissa struggled to her feet and began to run.

Judah Daniel reached out and caught the sobbing woman, then beckoned to Tyler, who helped her ease Narcissa onto the ground, propping her back against the lichen-covered rock that shielded the entrance to the tunnel. Then she picked up a dark lantern and adjusted it so that it cast a sliver of light.

Tyler stared at Narcissa, his expression perplexed. "The Brethren ain't told me about any more runaways to be meeting. Don't know why this one didn't just ride the train up north. Her skin's light enough to pass for white."

"She *is* white, Tyler," Judah Daniel replied in a wry voice. "That there's Mrs. Narcissa Powers."

Narcissa could not believe her ears, or her eyes. How could she be mistaken for a colored woman? She looked at her dirt-stained hands, her bedraggled skirts—yes, she supposed she could "pass" for a runaway slave! And who else would be here, hiding in the brush near the river that separated North from South, Union from Confederacy? This black man saw what he expected to see.

A dark-haired woman in ragged clothes, found where no lady would be, is taken for a runaway slave. Her mind seemed to snag on something. She thought of Brit Wallace's story from Ball's Bluff: an officer who orders Federal soldiers to charge is taken for a Federal officer. And a dark-haired, light-skinned man with an actor's control of his voice and body, an actor's flair for costume and staging, could make people see in him exactly what they expected to see. What he had made them expect to see . . .

"Judah Daniel, Lucien is Gabriel—*and* White Hands! I've got to go back." Narcissa struggled to her feet, wiped her eyes and nose on her sleeve. "Don't you see? He's a . . . a chameleon. He sets the scene, prepares us for what to expect, and then he *becomes* what we expect. He mesmerized Jordan so that he could find out where the treasure is hidden. She trusts him, but if she asks where I have gone, if she gets suspicious, she is at his mercy! And once he finds the treasure—"

Judah Daniel was silent for a moment. When she spoke, her voice was heavy with irony. "He be one disappointed man. There ain't no treasure at Champs-Elysées."

"But Jordan—" Narcissa started to protest.

"Tyler and I got to talking on the ride up, soon as I got outside of Richmond and got out of that coffin and up in the driver's box."

Coffin? Narcissa wondered, but she did not dare interrupt. Every moment was critical to Jordan.

Judah Daniel was still talking. "There's some folks helping slaves escape to the North. They opened the tunnel, and they found—wait. Where is Lucien right now?"

Narcissa pressed her hand against her temple. "He may have gone back to the cemetery. He's digging up Eulalie's coffin, I think."

"Tyler," Judah Daniel said in a voice of command, "go around to the cemetery. If Lucien's busy digging, you sneak into the house and open up the tunnel from the inside. Then go back and keep Lucien talking. Don't let him go back to the house. But don't tangle with him if you can help it—he's a dangerous man."

Tyler nodded and took off.

"I can show you the treasure of Champs-Elysées—and the truth of the ghost story," Judah Daniel said grimly. "But you got to go back into the tunnel."

Narcissa hesitated. Then she thought, she should trust Judah Daniel if she should trust anyone. The tunnel had been opened to aid fleeing slaves. In some more innocent time, now long past, Narcissa might have found the revelation frightening. Now she was only grateful. If the tunnel had not been opened, Lucien's trap would have held her fast. And, in telling this secret, Judah Daniel had shown her trust in Narcissa.

Narcissa nodded. Judah Daniel picked up the dark lantern and started in, Narcissa following.

Going back into the tunnel with Judah Daniel holding a lantern was nothing like coming through it alone, in the dark, unsure of where it would lead. Soon she saw what must have been the opening she had felt, branching off to the left. As they came closer, she saw that, for a space about four feet across, the bricks had been torn down. Judah Daniel held up the lantern and peered in, then stood aside, holding the lantern, for

Narcissa to look into an earth-walled chamber. A burial chamber, it was, about five feet deep and six or eight feet long. It held two bodies. One was a black-haired and bearded skeleton dressed in a faded green velvet coat with gold buttons.

"Mr. Jennings," Narcissa said aloud, remembering the portrait that hung above the fireplace in Caroline Archer Jennings's mansion.

Judah Daniel glanced her way, smiled a little. "Is it? Well, now, I reckon I can understand some things better knowing that."

The other was a collection of bones in a once-white dress, its bodice embroidered in seed pearls and still-bright paillettes. The gold of the buttons, the sparkle of the paillettes, seemed so bright in the lamp's flickering light that Narcissa blinked. *Eulalie,* she thought. The long-vanished Mr. Jennings had worn his finest coat to run away with his wife's sister, who, romantic to the end, had dressed the part of fairy-tale bride.

Judah Daniel was watching Narcissa's face. "That's the treasure. Gold buttons and the frippery on a woman's dress. Jordan was so little when she came on this, it was treasure to her."

Despite the disarrangement of the bones, it was clear the bodies had been laid out. Narcissa wondered if Mr. Jennings's death had been an accident, like Eulalie's. At least they were dead when they were buried, she thought. Which, if Lucien had had his way, would not have been true of me.

Narcissa turned away from the pathetic tableau and said to Judah Daniel, "It won't be treasure to Lucien, if he finds it. And once he knows the treasure doesn't exist, he has no reason to keep Jordan alive."

The truth would be a shock to Lucien, but it would be another kind of shock to Jordan, she realized. The romantic story of the ghosts at Champs-Elysées had dwindled to a sordid tale of lust and betrayal. And Jordan's own romance, her awakening sense of her womanhood in response to Gerard Lucien, had turned to a cup full of poison.

After what seemed to Narcissa like an eternity, a scraping sound at the wooden door separating the tunnel entrance from the wine cellar told them Tyler had made it into the house.

"He still digging," Tyler told them, amusement in his voice. "Digging, and cussing."

Judah Daniel put her hand on Tyler's arm. "Try to hold him there—

long as you can. Then get out. Don't risk getting caught up here doing the work of the Brethren." Tyler nodded.

In a moment the three of them were standing on the marble floor of Champs-Elysées' grand hall. Then Tyler was gone, and Narcissa was heading up the stairs to wake Jordan.

She found Jordan fully dressed, standing by the window. Narcissa called her name, and Jordan ran to her.

"Narcissa! I had the most awful nightmare. I dreamed an undertaker's carriage was coming for me. It was huge, black and gold, and four black horses pulled it."

Narcissa put her arms on Jordan's shoulders and looked her in the face. Be careful, she told herself. "Jordan, did you know that M. Lucien is looking for the treasure?"

Jordan stared at her.

"Well," Narcissa went on, "I know where it is. Judah Daniel learned the secret from Auntie Lora. I can show you."

Jordan shuddered and made as if to pull away.

"M. Lucien will be so pleased when you show it to him," Narcissa cajoled. God, make her come, she prayed frantically. If Lucien takes it into his head that something is wrong—

"I . . . will come," Jordan said at last. "I thought you were angry with him. I thought you had come to take me away."

"The treasure is here, in the house." Narcissa spoke in Lucien's mesmerizing intonation. God forgive me, she thought: I hope she can bear the shock of what we are going to show her.

At last, Jordan responded. "I will come."

Narcissa took Jordan's hand, and the two women hurried down the staircase to where Judah Daniel was waiting with the lantern.

"It's this way," Judah Daniel said, and stepped through the open panel.

"Here!" Jordan's eyes grew wide. "But I have played here all my life. I never—" As they came down the stairs into the wine cellar, following Judah Daniel's swift, sure pace, Jordan fell silent. When Judah Daniel stepped through the narrow doorway into the tunnel, Jordan followed, with Narcissa after. The stench of vomit was strong where Narcissa had rid herself of the poisoned wine.

"What is that horrid smell?" Jordan cried.

"Never mind," Narcissa said in the soothing voice. "It is not far now to the treasure."

When they came to the narrow opening made by the fallen bricks, Narcissa said lightly, "The tunnel did not collapse, after all. It was merely sealed off with a thin layer of bricks." No need to mention the role of the Loyal Brethren, whose illegal and dangerous work had saved her life.

Judah Daniel set the lantern down on the other side of the opening and crawled through. Jordan followed, then Narcissa. Judah Daniel handed the lantern to Narcissa as if passing the leader's role to her. Narcissa held the lantern so that it illuminated her own face. It was time to prepare Jordan for what she was going to see.

"Jordan, do you remember the first time M. Lucien mesmerized you, at your great-aunt's? I was there. You talked about a treasure, here at Champs-Elysées. When he mesmerized you again last night, you talked about it again. What you have said has led M. Lucien to believe there is a treasure, gold and jewels, buried here at Champs-Elysées . . . buried with the body of Eulalie. M. Lucien wants that treasure very badly—so badly that he has been digging up Eulalie's grave in your family graveyard. So badly that he gave me poison and locked me in here."

"No! I won't listen!" Jordan turned away, her hands over her face, but Narcissa went on.

"He will soon find, if he hasn't already, that Eulalie's grave is empty. And then his mind may turn to the other part of the ghost story, the lover who was buried here, in the tunnel. He may come here to search, and when he does, he will learn—"

Jordan was listening now. "What? Tell me!"

Narcissa pulled Jordan to her and spoke as gently as she could. "There never was any treasure, Jordan. As a young child, you saw something, here in the tunnel. You did not know what it meant, but the image of it has haunted you ever since. Eulalie is *here*, buried; and her lover with her." No need to mention that the lover was Mr. Jennings. The truth was cruel enough without that. "You saw the sparkling paillettes on her dress, the shiny gold buttons on his coat. You thought they were treasure."

Jordan's chin spoke defiance, but her eyes probed Narcissa's face, seeking assurance. "Show me," she whispered.

"Jordan . . . they are skeletons. That is why the memory of it has frightened you so much, all these years. Are you ready to see the truth, not with a child's eyes, but with a woman's?"

"Show me!" Jordan's voice was insistent this time.

"Come, then," Narcissa said, turning toward the windowlike hole in the wall. Keeping one hand on Jordan and holding the lantern with the other, she moved toward it. The three of them stood looking down at the dead.

At last Jordan spoke, in the quiet, flat voice she had used when mesmerized by Lucien. "We were playing, my cousins and I. I came down here to hide. A brick was loose, and I pushed it, and more bricks fell. I crawled through. I had a lantern with me. I saw them. I started screaming. Somehow I got back out, I ran upstairs, shrieking, trying to tell what I had seen. Great-aunt Caroline grabbed me. She said she was going to whip me. No one saw; no one stopped her. But she did not whip me. She asked me what I had seen, and I told her. I was crying for my father. It made her angry, and she said things about him, terrible things—that he didn't care about me, he wouldn't have me with him. Then she said, 'If you ever tell what you have seen, I will put you down there in the tunnel, with *them,* and the rats will eat you, too!'"

"How could she say such a thing, to a child?" Jordan looked at Narcissa, tears in her eyes. "Just because I disobeyed?"

"Not because you disobeyed." Judah Daniel's voice rang out in the little space. "You found out she killed her husband, and let her sister die."

Jordan stood transfixed. Narcissa, too, was chilled into silence. It's true, Narcissa thought, and the truth of it was reaching the girl in a way no soothing words ever could.

Judah Daniel went on. "Auntie Lora knowed what happened, part of it, anyway. Eulalie was planning to run off with Caroline's husband. Eulalie was expecting a baby. She fell down the stairs—or Caroline pushed her, maybe. The fall caused her to lose the baby. Sometimes, when that happens, the woman bleed to death. Maybe the midwife could have saved her. But Caroline turned the midwife out and let Eulalie die. The man—Mr. Jennings"—Judah Daniel directed the lantern's beam at the skeleton's head—"look like he got his skull bashed in."

Narcissa, looking, saw where the bone was splintered on the left side, above the temple.

"Narcissa," Jordan said at last, "I want to go home—to Richmond."

"We'll go through the tunnel to the river road, then follow it to the camp," Narcissa said.

Tyler came up the road whistling, hands in his pockets. It was best Lucien have plenty of warning he was fixing to have a visitor. From what Judah

Daniel said, the killer of the Bertons and old Mrs. Archer Jennings was handy with a knife.

As he entered the graveyard at the far end, Tyler could see Lucien watching him, leaning on his shovel, one hand on his hip. The man was light-skinned, right enough, thought Tyler as he came closer. So what was he, really?

Lucien's first words seemed to answer the question. There was no fancy foreign accent, only a husky drawl spiced with the sass of one servant calling to another, out of the master's earshot. "Well, brother, come to give me a hand with this here shoveling?"

"Nah," Tyler answered. He stopped about six feet away from Lucien and stood behind a low gravestone, leaning his arms on its arching top. His stance, though it looked casual, was chosen with care. If Lucien pulled a knife and went for him, the thick stone slab would be between them, giving Tyler a chance to judge the man as a fighter and to draw his own knife, or to run.

Lucien gave him a sharp look. At last he asked another question. "You been fishing in the river? Fishing for those Yankees who went down with gold coins and watches in their pockets?"

"Nah," Tyler answered again.

"Well," Lucien said then, dropping the shovel and wiping his brow with a dirty handkerchief, "since you don't do nothing, must be you a slave on one of these here places. This here's the Archer place. You one of their niggers?"

"Ain't no man's. The Loyal Brethren take runaways through here, up north to freedom. I'm one of them." Well, he got a rise out of me, Tyler thought. Let's see what he can do with it.

Lucien looked pleased. "I like that answer, brother. I could use a man like you."

"Yeah?" Tyler put just a little interest in his voice.

Lucien came a step closer. "The Loyal Brethren, I got no quarrel with them, but stand to reason they ain't never going to smuggle all the slaves out of Virginia. I got it in mind to raise up those of African blood in a rebellion. With all the white men away playing games, what stopping us from claiming *our* liberty?"

"Well, they got the guns," Tyler answered.

"Yeah, but we can get guns. Don't you know the Yankees would give us guns to raise up an insurrection behind the lines? What we need is money—to pay the sorry white trash they got stopping people on the roads to keep their mouths shut."

Tyler kept quiet for a moment, then said, "You sure that's what you want money for? What about them two white women you got over to the house?"

Tyler could see Lucien tense with anger, then relax, smile. "I ain't spending money *on* them. I'm getting it *from* them. One of them knows where a treasure buried, here on these grounds. Once I get it out of her where the treasure is, I'm going to slit her throat, and leave it looking like the other one done it."

"Ain't nobody going to believe your word against a white woman," Tyler objected.

"Oh, she'll be dead too, and I'll be long gone. Once I get the treasure, I'm going back to Richmond, raise up a army to fight for our freedom."

"Ain't no slaves around Richmond going to rise up." Tyler saw the gleam in Lucien's eye in response to his words.

"You reckon? Ain't you heard of the uprising down in Goochland? Killed the old master and mistress, the young mistress too. That was just my dress rehearsal."

"And just what is it you want?"

"I told you." Lucien's voice was impatient. "Just like Prosser's Gabriel. Throw down the whites, get our share of what we done earned. Get our liberty."

Tyler's lip curled. "You ain't the man to speak of Prosser's Gabriel. I heard about that uprising in Goochland. As many slaves died as whites. And more slaves still in jail."

Lucien's smile faded. "A mistake; I regret it. Still, I proved what I can do. With just a few likely men giving out guns, up and down Virginia, I could light the powder keg that would blow the South into disarray. By the time the Yankees ride in, President Abraham Lincoln will have to deal with *me*. And you," he added, "if you're interested in throwing in with me."

Tyler stood there, wondering. The man was persuasive. If he could do the things he talked about . . . if he even tried to do them . . . Then Tyler thought of his wife, and his son, and the baby that was coming.

"Nah," Tyler said at last, "I got things I got to see to. But if you want to raise some men against Richmond, go see King in the Chickahominy Swamp. And now, you best make tracks. There ain't no treasure. That woman done played you for a fool. And now she heading to the army camp, and she ain't alone no more."

With a roar of rage, Lucien started forward, a long knife in his hand. Tyler pulled his knife and stood his ground. Lucien stopped. His eyes moved over Tyler as if judging whether he could take him.

Then Lucien smiled, put his knife away. "I suppose I'd best not take the time to ask how you came by this information. I am much obliged to you, sir. I hope you may be proud to remember you came to my aid with your timely warning." Lucien gave a deep bow, then turned and walked swiftly away.

Tyler stood looking after him for a few moments, marveling at the man's ability to transform himself from servant to gentleman. "I hope I ain't got cause to regret it." Then he, too, hurried away.

NORTHERN VIRGINIA
THAT EVENING

"Hold up, boys," Cameron Archer called out, reining in his horse. Brit Wallace and Archer Langdon drew up beside him in the road. Coming toward them, on foot, dusty and ragged, was a little band of refugees, two white women and their servant—or was it—was that—?

"Good God," Archer said aloud. "It's Narcissa, and Jordan, and Judah Daniel!"

There might have been a foot race between Archer and Wallace to be first to reach Narcissa Powers, but Narcissa would never know. Just as the men were closing to within a few yards, Jordan Archer fainted.

$\mathcal{E}pilogue$

RICHMOND

THE END OF OCTOBER

The three women who had bluffed Gerard Lucien at Champs-Elysées came south on the train. Their arrival was unheralded, though all Richmond was afire with the news that the fraudulent aristocrat had killed whites, and blacks, as part of some insane plot to steal from the plantations. A few called for a massive manhunt to capture Lucien and bring him back for trial, but most believed he had fled north across the Potomac.

Since the others involved, especially Cameron Archer, seemed reticent to talk about Lucien, Brit found himself being interviewed by other reporters—after his own dispatch was completed and on its way. Once his account made it through the blockade and was published in the *Argus,* his career would be made. Of course, his dispatch made no mention of Jordan Archer or Narcissa Powers; of Dorothea Berton; or of Judah Daniel, whose story of walking alone from Richmond to Champs-Elysées Brit had never quite believed. Even a journalist knew that, in times like these, some questions were better not asked.

Once it was clear to all that the man who had called himself Gerard Lucien was no French aristocrat, Richmonders vied with each other to disclose their suspicions, based on this or that in his appearance or behavior. Some claimed they had seen the brand of a runaway slave on his back, or scars from a beating. Why they had never seen fit to mention this "evidence" before, they did not say.

Judah Daniel had found the question rising in her mind again and again: What should Tyler have done? She was relieved Tyler had not tried to overpower Lucien, who was at least his equal in strength and cunning. But why not send Lucien up north, where the strife between the races was less acute, where Lucien might not find it so easy to pour his venom into ears ready to hear, and to kill? Why had Tyler sent Lucien back to Richmond— to King? Lucien, who had killed Hiram, Dorcas, and Zemora, as surely as he had killed the Bertons and Mrs. Archer Jennings?

Deep down, she knew the answer: Tyler wants a savior for our people— a savior who brings a sword. Pray God the whites never found out: they would be all over the Chickahominy Swamp looking for Lucien, armed men and dogs, enough that for every one that went down, two more would take his place.

She resolved to go in alone. She had no doubt that King would find her, as he had before. But long before she came in sight of the sycamore tree, she saw the buzzards circling. She kept on, slowly getting closer, until she saw the man hanging there, dark-haired, dressed in tattered black rags. She had been fairly sure, had gone closer than she wanted just to be certain. It was Lucien, his face, hands, and feet shredded to reveal the bones beneath.

They were gathered in the Powerses' back parlor. Nat Cohen sat close to Mirrie, who for once accepted his solicitude. Jordan, with Friday asleep in her lap, was sitting between her young cousin Archer Langdon and her old servant, Auntie Lora. Langdon seemed to view all that had happened to her as a rather enviable adventure, and Jordan's rising spirits indicated she might soon see it that way herself. Brit Wallace and Cameron Archer, always uneasy allies, sat facing each other, arms crossed on their chests, like mirror images.

"I gone down to the swamp looking for plants to use in my doctoring," Judah Daniel was saying. "When I saw him hanging there, I thought he might be a runaway slave strung up by his master as a warning. But I could see his clothes was fine, and saw his long hair and beard, like a white man's. I knowed it was Lucien."

"So he hanged himself?" Mirrie asked. "Why ride so far, only to give up at the end?"

Brit spoke up. "I had a friend in the telegraph office send around to cities visited by acting troupes. Some had heard of Gerard Lucien, or knew of some actor who fit his description. But no one knows anything about his birth. That story he told Cantrell about his ancestry"—Brit nodded toward Archer—"it could have been pure moonshine. Lucien was clever as the deuce at concocting stories—and at getting people to believe them. But his conceit got the better of him at last. The very idea that Mrs. Powers could have hurt Miss Archer, out of some kind of jealousy—"

Cameron Archer joined in. "Seems to me he may have tried one trick too many, on someone who was less easy to manipulate than James Cantrell. And whoever it was 'called his bluff,' as it were, for the last time."

Brit nodded eagerly. "To hang him that way may have been a kind of verdict, a judgment. But whose?"

Let judgment run down as waters, and righteousness as a mighty stream. Judah Daniel thought of King, who, it was said, would kill a white man as free as eat. Had King thought Lucien was a white man, strung him up without giving him a chance to make up a tale? Or Zed Truesdale, who all those years ago had followed the real Gabriel: had Truesdale presided when Lucien was weighed in the balance and found wanting? Lucien's attacks had killed four whites, and resulted in the deaths of three blacks.

Strange: though Lucien himself could not have guessed it, his evil had done some good. Clara and Litabet had been freed, and were on their way north to where Berton's runaway servant Quintus waited. "Her name Elizabeth now," Clara had said, hugging her granddaughter, her eyes full of pride.

"That black devil you saw, in front of the fire?" Judah Daniel had asked, and had seen fear creep into Clara's face. "It was that fellow Lucien. Soon as I knowed it was him, I figured it out: if he was standing in front of a big fire, and you with your eyes all hurting from the poison, any man would look black."

And Hetty—who but God himself could understand that Hetty, though freed, had chosen to remain in Berton's employ, to be close to the child she loved, and who loved her—Johnny Berton?

Jordan Archer was talking. "You are all too kind to say it, but I want you to know I am well aware of my own foolishness. There is one thing in particular I must apologize for." Jordan's face was pink, but her eyes were steady as they gazed at each listener in turn, finally resting on Narcissa. "On the day of my great-aunt's murder, I told you I had hoped to meet with Lucien. You asked me if I had seen him, and I told you that I had. It was a lie. I was—daring you to say something, to chide me, so that I would know that you were against me, too, just like my great-aunt and my cousin Cameron." Jordan's glance at Archer expressed contrition. "It made me angry to think everyone suspected I was in love, that I was being indiscreet, when I knew that I was not! It hurt to feel that no one understood, that I was alone—and yet it was a pain I sought." She frowned for a moment; then her expression lightened. "And after all, Narcissa, it was vexatious to always be confronted with your beautiful face, your gentle manners, your *admirers*"—Jordan looked at Brit and Archer in turn, then laughed—"though I would not choose such a bunch of stragglers to wear *my* colors. How I enjoyed it, when I was able to pique you into losing your temper! Do you remember, at the hospital, when you said my frown made me look like my great-aunt?"

Narcissa felt herself blush, then remembered something she had wanted to ask Jordan. "Why did you leave the hospital that day, when you had offered your help and been accepted?"

Jordan looked down, then back up at Narcissa. "It was because you wanted me to read to the soldiers, and write letters for them. I am ashamed to say that I can scarcely do either, despite my years of schooling. They used to try to force me, but the letters just swam on the page. They gave up on me at last, told me I was stupid."

Mirrie sat up straight. "Jordan, you are not stupid! It may be that your eyesight is the problem. Let us help you—Father and me."

Jordan looked pleased. "Perhaps . . . if you think so, Mirrie."

After the others left, and she and Mirrie were alone, Narcissa wondered if Archer himself had caught up with Lucien and performed a summary execution. Given Archer's sense of justice, and his family pride, the idea seemed possible. She did not have the right to ask him, since there were so many things she would not tell him—about Tyler and the men who helped him, about the use of Champs-Elysées as a hiding place for runaway slaves.

If only they could be open with each other, she and Archer. She was drawn to him, she had to admit it. She could still feel the scratchy wool of his surgeon's tunic as he placed it around her shoulders, there on the road from Champs-Elysées. That was the effect he always seemed to have on her—warm, but prickly. But she could not relax into that warmth as long as there was this constraint between them. He, a man, put on the uniform and gave his loyalty to its cause. She, a woman, was knitting together a complicated pattern of loyalties that sometimes crossed over one another. Then there was Brit Wallace. It surprised and flattered her that, after all these months with no encouragement from her, he still seemed to prefer her company to that of any other woman. He had chosen a journalist's impartiality as his uniform. Well, why not? This was not his country. But it was hers.

What would happen with Mirrie and Nat Cohen? He was preparing to run the blockade to France. Although they had not announced an engagement, it no longer seemed out of the question that they might do so. Could Mirrie's loyalty to him survive against the conflicting strands that ran so strong in her—particularly her commitment to abolitionism?

"I feel guilty for not telling the entire truth," Narcissa said to Mirrie at last.

"You think you know the entire truth?"

Narcissa looked, startled, into Mirrie's smiling face and sad eyes.

"If anyone does know," Mirrie went on, "it is not one of us at the top of society—well, relatively so, anyway. It is someone at the bottom, a slave, or someone who knows their secrets. Their world is hidden from us, while ours lies open to them."

Narcissa nodded, thoughtful. Judah Daniel may know. And again, she, Narcissa, could not ask.

A message came to Judah Daniel from King, this time in the shape of a tall, big-shouldered black man named Ike. It seemed a man calling himself Gabriel had turned up in the swamp, asking for help. King called the swamp's runaways to gather at Scratch Hall, and Gabriel talked, piling up phrases like cloud-cities, hurling words like thunderbolts. When Gabriel ran out of words, Ike told what he knew about the killings at Manakin and their aftermath. King spoke last: "Just 'cause the dog bite the master's hand, don't make it no wolf."

Gabriel could not believe the outcasts in the swamp would not follow him. He frowned, argued, pleaded. At last he tried to run. King told them to string up Gabriel where the white folks could see him, so they would not need to come looking for him in the swamp.

An ugly ending. Judah Daniel shuddered at the image of Lucien hanging as buzzards tore his flesh. She would see if she could get something that had been his to perform the rites that would give his soul peace.

She was tempted to tell Narcissa Powers that Tyler had done the right thing. He had sent Lucien to stand before the judge and jury that had the most right to try him on the charge of being a false prophet. But Judah Daniel could not risk her betraying King. King had a power that she had to acknowledge, though he was hardly a man at all, more a force of nature, standing outside all that she had ever known. It amused her a little that she prayed to God to keep him safe, but she told herself: If God made Leviathan without fear, surely he created King.